Emma With Something Extra

by

Pamela Woods-Jackson

Emma With Something Extra

Cover Art by *Debbie Taylor*

The Wild Rose Press, Inc.
PO Box 708
Adams Basin, NY 14410-0708
Visit us at www.thewildrosepress.com

Publishing History
First Edition, 2023
Trade Paperback ISBN 978-1-5092-5353-1
Digital ISBN 978-1-5092-5354-8

Previously Published July 2018 Evernight Teen
Published in the United States of America

"Girlfriend, who was that?" Flip demanded as he craned his neck to get a better look.

"Said his name's Nick." I took a few gulps of air, hoping to control my rapid heartbeat. "And I'm pretty sure he's not playing on your team."

"That means he's playing on mine," Hattie exclaimed, with a fist pump to the air. "Did he say anything about a girlfriend? Think anything?"

I shook my head. "Just said he was a new transfer from Colson Academy up near Chicago. I must have been too flustered to listen to his thoughts."

"But you'll find out, right?" Hattie stood up, scouted out the cafeteria, and spotted Nick as he sauntered to a table with some giggly eleventh grade girls. She scowled when he sat down next to a cute one.

I had to admit Nick was intriguing. Then it hit me. Maybe the reason I couldn't hear his thoughts was because they were about me. Since I've never heard any guy's romantic thoughts about me…

Dedication

To Faith, who always reads my books, and for allowing
me to borrow her name for a character.

Chapter 1

My eyes darted left and right as I hurried down the hallway, hoping to blend in with the early-morning crowd. I opened my locker in the middle of the senior hallway, stuck my head in like an ostrich, and checked the text message one more time. I groaned, frowned, and shoved the phone back in my pocket.

"Hey, bestie. What's up?"

Startled, I pulled my head out of the locker, only to bang it on the door's sharp edge. I rubbed the sore spot and hoped it wouldn't leave a bump. "Trying to avoid Sara Davis. She's been hounding me to do that interview, chasing me all over school, sending texts."

Hattie shrugged. "Maybe you shouldn't have told her you'd do it."

"Ya think?" I was pretty angry with myself for letting Sara talk me into this.

"Sara's been suspicious of you since the first day of ninth grade. Ever since you…"

"I know what I did," I said.

"And now you're trusting her to write a newspaper story about you?"

"I thought it would shut her up," I said. "I didn't think Mr. West would actually let her publish a piece of fluff like that."

Hattie leaned an elbow on my locker and frowned. "Too late now."

I dug around in my locker for my Family Relations textbook. "Maybe I could suggest she interview…" I tilted my head in her direction, "…Hattie Smythe, star of our Lady Eagles basketball team."

Hattie waved that away like a buzzing fly. "I'm old news. Sara wants a unique story that will get her noticed by the college rags. That's why she's fixated on you." She gave my arm a playful jab. "Mel High's famous date wrangler."

I thought about some of my past successes, like my handsome African American friend Flip and the love of his life James, but then shrugged off the whole idea. "I wouldn't exactly say I'm famous, just spot on. But you know I can't talk about it. That would be the end of my life as I know it."

"It would not." Hattie slid her backpack off her shoulder where it landed on the floor with a thud as she spun the lock on her own locker.

"Uh-oh, there she is." I ducked my head back into my open locker in a futile attempt at invisibility.

Sara spotted me anyway. She walked up, and despite her petite stature, planted herself in front of me to block my exit. "So how do you do it? Find the perfect guy for the perfect girl? My readers want to know." She shoved her official-looking recorder in my face.

I tried to appear casual as I backed out of the locker, this time without bumping my head. "Oh, hi, Sara. I didn't see you there."

"Ha ha," she said with a snort. "You agreed to do this newspaper interview weeks ago and you've been dodging me ever since. I'm on deadline, so start talking." For emphasis, she pushed the recorder at me again.

Most of the kids she's written about in the Senior

Feature section have made some kind of important contribution to the school, like Hattie on the basketball team, or my close friend Hank Zimmerman, who led the debate team to victory. All I've done is arrange a few dates. Okay more than a few, but no one has ever complained about being fixed up with their crush, regardless of how I figured that out. But Sara Davis has suspected the truth for years and now she wanted to print it in the school newspaper.

"Well, I've been really busy lately…" I hedged.

Sara rolled her eyes. "Emma, for heaven's sake. Just tell me what made you start this fixing-up-people thing so I can wrap up this story."

I struggled to come up with a plausible answer. "Uh, I guess with a name like Emma Austin, it was sort of a given."

"Huh?"

"You know, Jane Austen's *Emma*. Matchmaker extraordinaire?"

Sara took a step back, which gave me some welcome breathing room, and cocked an eyebrow at me. "Yeah, okay, but just exactly how do you do it?"

Hattie wedged herself between me and Sara, and at six feet tall, she was an imposing figure. "Emma's just got good instincts."

"Answer the question," Sara said, skirting around Hattie.

The fact that I arranged dates wasn't a secret, since a lot of kids have availed themselves of my services. But the "how" question? Well, it was definitely something most people either wouldn't believe, or would blow all out of proportion.

"I just pay attention, you know, to what kids say, to

their body language."

But Sara wasn't buying it. "If that's all there is to it, why can't anybody do it?"

"Maybe no one else wants to?" I said.

A really cute guy with his nose glued to his phone walked past us in the crowded corridor, and bumped right into Sara. "Hey, watch..." She stopped when she saw what a hottie he was, batted her eyelashes and adjusted the headband that kept her frizzy red hair from falling into her face. *Wow! Did he just do that on purpose? He must have. He's cute!*

Not bad was what he was thinking as he looked down at Sara. "Sorry," he said with a grin before hurrying on his way.

I cleared my throat. "He's a junior, but if you're interested, I can see if he's available."

Sara crashed back down to Earth. "How did you know I...?"

"Body language. And here I'd already started working on Jeff Atwell, like you asked me."

Sara's jaw dropped. "When did I...?"

Okay, maybe she didn't really ask me, but I've heard her thinking about him for weeks now. At least I'd thrown her off track for the moment. I grinned. "Like I said, just paying attention."

The warning bell rang to signal the start of the school day and I took advantage of Sara's confusion. "Are we done here?" I slammed my locker shut and hoisted my book bag over one shoulder.

Hattie elbowed Sara out of her way, picked up her backpack and gave me a subtle two thumbs up as we headed to class.

"You'll be sorry, Emma," Sara shouted after me.

I winced, but kept walking. I didn't doubt for a minute that Sara could make my life miserable. "Thanks, Hattie. For having my back."

"So for payback, how 'bout you help me study for the upcoming Family Relations midterm exam?"

"Between your practice schedule and my after-school job, I don't know when we we're gonna fit in a cram session."

"Look, you talked me into taking that boring class," Hattie said.

I shook my head. "No, your counselor did. She said you wouldn't graduate without another senior elective, and since you have to keep last period free for basketball conditioning, it was either Family Relations or something online. I just agreed."

We settled into our seats in first period class, on the back row with about thirty other kids in front of us.

"I'm starved," I whispered to Hattie as I glanced up at the clock. My alarm didn't go off this morning, so I was running late. On top of that, I didn't do laundry last night so I was forced to find something to wear in my sister Isabelle's closet, and as a result breakfast didn't happen. Now I was sorry because my stomach was rumbling up a storm, and lunch was hours away. "What's the cafeteria's special today?" I said that a little too loudly and it got me a few dirty looks from other students.

"I didn't check the menu," Hattie whispered with a furtive glance at the teacher, who was hurrying to finish her lesson before the dismissal bell. Hattie stifled a yawn. "I hope I don't fall asleep before Miss Taylor gives us the homework assignment."

"Homework is to read pages one-hundred fifteen

through one-thirty and answer the questions at the end," I whispered. Hattie groaned and tossed me that look I was so familiar with. "Miss Taylor just reminded herself to write it on the board."

I always knew there was something weird about me. Early on, I'd just chalked it up to having a kid's vivid imagination when I'd "hear" things that hadn't been spoken. Sometimes I wasn't even sure that they hadn't been said out loud. My grandmother was the first to figure out what was going on with me.

"Emma," she told me, "you have a special gift. One that's been passed down through the women in our family."

I was probably about six at the time and "special gift" didn't register. After all, it wasn't Christmas or my birthday.

But my thirteen year old sister Isabelle demanded answers. "Why does she get it and I don't?"

Good question, one Grandma Austin didn't have an answer for, or if she did, she didn't share it with either of us. "Keep in mind, Emma, people may not understand, so it must be kept a secret within the family."

My grandmother was right that people wouldn't understand. And in this day of social media, my secret could spread like wildfire. If that happened, any hopes I ever had of a normal life would be gone.

****

"Hey, Emma!" Flip stopped to talk to me at my locker after first period class. "That little parlor trick you do? It's about to backfire on you."

"Parlor trick?" I lifted an eyebrow at him.

He waved my objection away. "Whatever you call it. The rumor mill's running wild about that story Sara

Davis is writing about you."

I blinked. "But she only did the…" I put my fingers up in air quotes…"'interview' two hours ago. What rumors?" I tossed my Family Relations textbook into my locker, pulled out my math book and slammed the locker shut.

"Girlfriend, brace yourself, because everyone's saying Sara's mad at you for not cooperating, so she's writing all kinds of crazy stuff." He winked at me. "Of course, we know it's not so crazy."

"What?" Panic was rising up into my throat. "How?" I felt like I was choking.

"Reporter's instincts, I guess." Flip shrugged. "What's the worst that could happen if she gets it right?"

I think my jaw dropped, at least metaphorically. "Flip, think about it. Remember when I broke down and confided in you and Hattie back in middle school? How did you react?"

He thought for a moment. "I was mad at you for weeks. I thought you'd been spying on me. It creeped me out."

"Exactly," I said. "I thought I'd lost your friendship for good."

He grinned, causing his big brown eyes to twinkle. "But then I got the idea to have you listen in on James's thoughts, to see if he was interested."

Which he was. And that was the start of my matchmaking career.

Flip scrutinized me. "What about Hank? You never told him, right?"

I shook my head "no" and exhaled. "What if he freaked out? Wanted nothing more to do with me?"

Flip patted me on the back in mock sympathy. "Poor

7

Emma."

"And what about every other kid in this school? Twelve-hundred some-odd angry thoughts all directed at me for spying on them all these years, followed by social isolation, followed by slams on social media…" I was picturing the posts calling me "witch," or "fraud," or just accusing me of manipulating people by digging around in their heads. "Forget going to a big state college. I'd have to slink off to some out-of-the-way place where no one knew me."

And they call me *a drama queen.* Flip rolled his eyes.

"Yeah, okay," I responded to his unspoken thoughts.

Flip glanced at the clock. "I gotta go, but Emma, since you and Hank are dating, you should at least trust him enough to tell him the truth. Before he reads it in the Herald." Flip waved at someone over my head before hurrying off.

"We aren't dating," I muttered to myself.

Hank Zimmerman and I have known each other since seventh grade when he moved up to Melville from Indianapolis. And I've been crushing on him since that exact moment. Yet in the five years I'd been date-wrangling for other people, I'd never once heard Hank, or any other guy for that matter, think anything the least bit romantic about me.

I was about to head to class when I saw Hank heading towards me in the locker bay. He always brought a smile to my face, a close friend that I couldn't help wishing was more. Other than seventh grade speech class, we've never had classes together. Hank was in all honors and Advanced Placement while I toiled away in regular classes. But I saw him a lot between classes, and we almost always ate lunch together.

"Hey Emma." He gave me a cute grin as he reached around me to spin his lock. "Um, do you mind?" He hesitated for a couple of seconds, polite as always, until I stepped out of his way. *I can't be late to AP Calc.*

Nope, no romance, just all business. I watched while Hank threw one book into his locker and retrieved another. I leaned on the wall. "Got plans for lunch today?"

Hank shrugged and shut the locker. "Cafeteria, as usual."

"I'll save you a place. See you then." I waved as I walked off.

Maybe I've been chicken not telling Hank the truth about my special abilities, but why haven't I ever told Hank I've been crushing on him all these years? Scared I guess. I just kept hoping I'd "hear" what he thought about me and save myself the heartache if he didn't reciprocate. I'd love it if smart, handsome, well-dressed Hank and I were dating for real instead of being each other's "go-to" dates. But it was possible he was more into Rachel Bomburg, a girl I knew he was seeing weekly at Synagogue and talked about a lot. I met her at his bar mitzvah back in seventh grade when she was chubby and awkward. Now she was a stunner.

Okay, I social media-stalked her.

****

"It's tacos again," Hattie said with a curl of her lip as we walked into the lunchroom.

Someone tapped me on the shoulder. "I'm surprised you didn't already know that."

I turned around. "Sara." I was determined not to let her snarkiness get to me. "I didn't check the online menu, so how would I know?"

"Aren't you some kind of psychic?" She put her hand on her hip and cocked her head to the side.

"You have an active fantasy life." Okay, so I didn't want to lie outright.

"Be sure to read my story about you when it comes out tomorrow."

"Wouldn't miss it," I mumbled.

"I'm going to the salad bar." With a sneer at Sara, Hattie turned on her heel.

The school cafeteria's tacos were a little too bland for some kids, but I didn't much like Mexican anyway, so they were fine for me. They were served in generous portions, huge shells with lots of ground meat, and all the cheese, lettuce, tomatoes and sour cream a person could want. "I'll meet you at our table," I called after her.

The seniors had an unofficial section at the back of the lunchroom, and Hattie, Flip, Hank and I always sat together. I got my tray of tacos, stopped for a bottled water, and then plopped down in a chair next to Flip. He'd already been to the salad bar and was tucking into his food with gusto.

I scouted out the lunchroom. "Anybody seen Hank?"

"Stuck in the hot lunch line." Hattie pointed her fork in the direction of the lengthening line, where Hank was staring at his phone, inching along slowly with the queue.

Yuk, mystery meat on a stale shell, Flip thought as he made a face at my food.

"I happen to like the tacos," I sniffed.

Flip paused mid-fork and glared at me. "Girlfriend, I've asked you…"

"Okay, sorry." I took a bite of taco, but it dripped all over my fingers and I realized I'd forgotten napkins, so I got up and headed to the utensils table. I reached for the napkin dispenser and as I did, another kid reached out at the same time and our elbows collided.

"Excuse me, I just need…" I reached for the napkins again, but then I looked up at the kid, and honestly my mouth dropped open. I'd never seen him before, which was weird since Melville, Indiana, was a small town, and most of us have gone to school together since kindergarten (except Hank). We all knew each other really well, too well actually, and now that it was senior year we were pretty tired of each other. So a new guy who looked as good as this one was going to get a lot of attention. He was taller than me (and at five feet nine inches I wasn't short) with blond hair, fair skin, and the most piercing blue eyes I'd ever seen. He was dressed like most of the other guys around here, in jeans and a hoodie sweatshirt, but somehow he looked more mature than the other senior boys. There was a tattoo peeking out from under his right sleeve but I couldn't quite make it out.

The guy handed me some napkins while I stood gawking at him, and then the most gorgeous smile lit up his face. I knew it was a cliché to be smitten at first sight, but something about this guy…

"Hi. Name's Nick," he said.

"Uh…" I dropped the napkins he just handed me and awkwardly reached down to pick them up. I stood back up, dignity somewhat shaken, and smiled back at him. "Emma Austin. Senior. You?"

He grinned. "Senior also, just transferred in from Colson Academy up in South Bend."

I waited for his thoughts to tell me why he'd transferred out of a private all-boys prep school in October of his senior year, but I didn't "hear" anything. Maybe I just couldn't concentrate with him looking at me with that twinkle in his eye. I shrugged it off and pointed at the table where Flip and Hattie were waiting for me, as well as my now-cold tacos. "Wanna join us?"

"Another time. I've already staked out a spot." Nick tossed his napkins and eating utensils onto his food tray.

Bummer. But it didn't surprise me that someone else had already snagged the new guy. "Okay, well maybe I'll see you around."

"Hope so, Emma," he replied with a cute grin.

I tried to figure out where Nick might be heading. Jocks table? Artsy kids? Underclassmen? I spotted Sara Davis on the other side of the room with her crew Katherine Howard and Faith Barlow. Sara and Katherine had their heads together giggling, and Faith occasionally smiled, but she couldn't have been paying much attention because she had on her headphones and was busy writing in her notebook. I just hoped that Nick wasn't headed over there. No telling what Sara might tell him about me.

Despite my unrequited love for Hank, I was still feeling gooey from Nick's adorable grin. I took a deep breath and, with one quick glance over my shoulder, hurried back across the room and sat down between my two friends. I took a bite of taco, but I'd suddenly lost all interest in food.

"Girlfriend, who was that?" Flip demanded as he craned his neck to get a better look.

"Said his name's Nick." I took a few gulps of air, hoping to control my rapid heartbeat. "And I'm pretty sure he's not playing on your team."

"That means he's playing on mine," Hattie exclaimed, with a fist pump to the air. "Did he say anything about a girlfriend? Think anything?"

I shook my head. "Just said he was a new transfer from Colson Academy up near Chicago. I must have been too flustered to listen to his thoughts."

"But you'll find out, right?" Hattie stood up, scouted out the cafeteria, and spotted Nick as he sauntered to a table with some giggly eleventh grade girls. She scowled when he sat down next to a cute one.

I had to admit Nick was intriguing. Then it hit me. Maybe the reason I couldn't hear his thoughts was because they were about me. Since I've never heard any guy's romantic thoughts about me…

Hattie was tugging on my arm. "Emma, you've got to introduce me."

"Um…" My best friend wanted to go out with Nick and I realized I wanted a chance with him myself. Since there was never anything official between Hank and me, and all he ever talked about was school or Rachel, maybe I was wasting my time hoping for more.

Then I heard a loud screech – okay, only in my head – but I recognized it and instinctively covered my ears to block out the internal noise.

Flip scrutinized me and lifted an eyebrow. "Kendall?"

I nodded as I located her in the crowded lunchroom as she made a beeline to the new guy. Kendall Manheim had radar when it came to hot guys. She'd already pulled up a chair next to Nick and was stroking his arm and batting her eyes. Vintage Kendall.

Hattie groaned. "Kendall?" She looked me in the

eye, all serious. "I still don't have a date for Homecoming and you know how tongue-tied I get around boys."

Flip loudly cleared his throat.

"I don't mean you, okay?" She turned back to me. "Can you please ask Nick if he'll take me to the dance? Before Kendall gets her claws in, because then I'll never have a chance."

Hattie wasn't the kind of girl guys were instantly attracted to. In fact, unless she was on the basketball court, they rarely noticed her at all. I scrutinized her look - no makeup, hair pulled back in a ponytail stuffed into a bun, and dressed in her usual athletic pants and matching jacket. I loved her, really, but she was so not Nick's type. Kendall, however, might be. I shuddered involuntarily.

"I'll see what I can do." If my best friend wanted to go out with this guy, maybe I could make it happen, despite my own agenda. But if Kendall got her hooks in, Hattie and I were both out of luck.

And I didn't even find out his last name.

Chapter 2

The next day after Sara Davis "interviewed" me, her feature article came out in the *Melville High Weekly Herald*. Copies of the paper were available before school in both the library and journalism room, and if I could've gotten my hands on all the printed copies and tossed them in the recycle bin, I would have. Of course they were online, too, so there was no getting rid of them. Ever. I sat down at a table in the school library and cringed at my unflattering sophomore yearbook picture next to the article. The story sent chills down my spine, and not in a good way.

SENIOR FEATURE

Emma Austin: Miss Match

By Sara Davis

Readers, nothing is more maddening to this journalist than a classmate who agrees to be the Senior Feature and then reneges. For four years I've been eager to learn how Mel High's version of Clueless *Cher does what she does, so I was psyched to get this assignment. But since Emma Austin wouldn't give me the 4-1-1 on how she makes her matches, I was forced to use my investigative skills to get the inside scoop.*

I have personally witnessed Emma making some uncannily accurate matches, and was even the subject (victim?) of an intended arranged date. Deductive reasoning leads me to believe that she can read kids' minds, but in order to be objective, I decided to interview some of her known successes: seniors James Harrison and Flip Richardson, and Beth Holiday and Barry Curtis, plus alumni power couple Tyler Paulson and Lucy McKinney.

First I asked Flip how Emma came to fix him up with James. "I asked her to. I had a crush."

So no mystery there.

Next I interviewed Beth and Barry. These are the two you probably see eating lunch together every day, or with their heads together in the library, or holding hands in the hallways, or cuddling under a blanket at football games.

"What made you ask Emma for a fixup?"

They exchanged cute glances and shy smiles, and Beth said, "I didn't ask her. Did you?" Barry shook his head. "Barry and I had U.S. History together last year, and although I had a crush, I never told anybody. Emma was in that class, too, and one day she asked me if I'd like to go out with Barry. It was like she could hear what I was thinking. Anyway, I said I didn't know if he even liked me, but Emma was just sure he did. Our first date was after school at The Mellow Coffee Bean." And they've been together ever since.

See that's what I find so weird, the part about Emma just knowing *Beth and Barry were attracted to each other, without either of them confiding in her. Is Beth right? Can Emma Austin read minds?*

It got even weirder when I rang up Lucy McKinney, now a college freshman, to get her take on Emma's matchmaking skills.

"Emma's got a sort of sixth sense about these things," Lucy told me. "As you know, Tyler and I were

an item from middle school on. But senior year, right before the holidays, we had a big blowup when I caught him flirting with Kendall Manheim. Emma came to me and told me she just knew Tyler wanted to ask me out for New Year's Eve, but he wasn't sure if I'd forgive him. Eventually Tyler and I patched things up, and when I asked him why he'd confided in Emma, he said he hadn't. He told me that one day at lunch he'd been thinking about how he'd messed things up between us, when Emma stopped by his table and said she could help us get back together. Well, as you know, we did."

So there you have it, Readers. Whatever her secret is, she does have a knack for getting the right two people together. Emma herself says she just pays attention to kids' body language, but that seems a little too convenient.

So whether she's a mind reader or just a reader of body language, I suggest you try this experiment: go ask Miss Match to find you Mr. or Ms. Right. It may be your lucky day. But to be on the safe side, keep your thoughts pure.

I broke out in a sweat and my head throbbed as I read and re-read the article, visualizing my whole world crashing down around me. Sara Davis actually told the world, okay everyone at Mel High, that I was a mind-reader and that I'd been spying on all my friends. They were probably picturing me lurking in shadows and sneaking up behind them, just to catch their inner-most thoughts.

The rest of high school suddenly seemed bleak, with me alone, friendless, and mistrusted. I could just picture my social life falling apart, being abandoned by all my friends, my attempts to help out classmates by arranging dates now suspect. College prospects weren't looking too great, either. So I guess in order to escape my notoriety, I might be forced to go to one of the other schools that would accept my scholarship, like tiny Community College instead of Ball State University. As I was wallowing in self-pity and imagining worse-case scenarios, Hattie tapped me on the shoulder.

"You okay?" She gave me the sympathetic head tilt.

"Hattie," I choked out, "it's like Sara *knew*. What if people believe her?"

Hattie gave my shoulder a squeeze as she folded up her copy of the school newspaper and stuffed it in her book bag. "It's just a stunt. No one's gonna believe you can eavesdrop on people's thoughts."

I glanced around to be sure we were alone. "But I *can*," I whispered. "I mean, you and Flip were weirded out at first. What do I do if Hank asks me if it's true? And what about that new kid, Nick? What's he gonna think?"

Hattie smirked. "Hank probably can't be bothered reading Sara's drivel, and Nick barely knows you." *And you're supposed to be fixing him up with* me.

"I haven't forgotten." I held up my hand to stop her inevitable objection.

Seemed like everybody in school had read Sara's article, because everywhere I went I got dirty looks and mean thoughts about the way I made matches. I was even tempted to do a few bad ones, just to prove Sara wrong, but then I realized that wouldn't be fair to kids who sincerely wanted my help.

When I got to Family Relations class hoping to go unnoticed, the teacher Miss Taylor commented on my sudden notoriety.

Holier-than-thou Katherine Howard, Sara Davis's

bestie, glared at me from across the classroom. "Psychics are strictly forbidden in the Bible. You're going to hell."

I glared back. "I'm not psychic." Which is technically true. All I could do was hear people's thoughts. I had no idea what the future held for anyone.

"I believe Sara's article was an exercise in creative writing, Katherine." Miss Taylor looked sternly at her and gave me a smile. She was a fan of our school newspaper. In fact, all the faculty raved about how Mr. West had turned a four page photo-shopped gossip rag into a real newspaper that rivaled the ones put out by the state's biggest five-star high schools. Small wonder Sara was using the *Melville High Herald's* rise in stature to further her journalism career.

I spent most of Family Relations class with my head buried in the textbook, afraid to make eye contact with anyone, even Hattie.

It had been a really long day and I was ready to be out of the pressure cooker. I was standing in front of my locker trying to remember what homework I had, when Katherine Howard approached me. *I'm gonna see if Sara was right about you.* I pretended to be concentrating on my locker combination so I wouldn't react to her thoughts.

"Hey, Emma," Katherine said.

"Sorry, no time to chat. I'm gonna be late for work." I slammed the locker and hurried off down the hall.

"Rude, Emma!" Katherine called after me.

I was mad at Sara Davis for igniting this firestorm, but also pretty upset with myself for agreeing to that feature article in the first place.

****

I've worked at Miss Margaret's Playtime Daycare

since last January, mid-junior year, when I saw an ad in the town's newspaper for an afternoon helper. My job was to give the kids their afternoon snacks, read them a story or start them on a game, assist some of the older ones with homework, and then help them gather their belongings when it was time to go home at six p.m. The daycare was an easy walk from school, and Isabelle picked me up on her way home from the real estate office where she worked.

I've socked away most of my earnings in a 529 college savings account that my brother-in-law Jonathan Calloway set up for me. I got a scholarship set up for kids who lost a parent to cancer, but it will just barely cover tuition and books at a few select in-state schools. I planned on using the savings account for room and board, and will probably have to get a part time job, too.

Having an after school job in a daycare wasn't glamorous, but I liked it, and it fit into my career goal of being a family therapist. I wanted to help other people get past the trauma I'd endured in my own family. My mother died of breast cancer when I was ten, my dad went into a deep depression and never really got over his grief, and my grandmother developed Alzheimer's. I had my older sister Isabelle, but when she got married I felt like everyone I'd ever cared about had abandoned me.

Carrie Denison was one of my favorite kids that I took care of at Miss Margaret's, maybe because she reminded me of myself at that age - seven years old and sort of lonely. Before I could even hang up my jacket, Mrs. Evans said, "Carrie's been asking for you."

"I'm on it." I went back into the play area and sure enough, Carrie was sitting at a table by herself, staring off into space. I got down to her eye level. "Hey, kiddo."

I'm gonna flunk. Can't do it can't do it can't do it!

Sounded serious. I pulled up one of the tiny chairs and sat down at the table next to her. "What can't you do?"

Carrie didn't even look surprised that I knew what she was thinking, maybe because little kids were much more accepting of weirdness like that. "Can't do this art project my teacher gave us." *Not getting it out of my backpack* she thought as she folded her arms across her chest and slumped down into the chair.

"Where's your backpack?" I glanced around the room and saw her pink bag with the kittens on it hanging from the peg where the coats were stored. I took it down and dug around until I found a blank piece of Manila paper with a note from her teacher attached. *Today students were asked to draw a picture of their family. Carrie didn't even try, so I'm sending it for homework.*

"Why don't you want to draw your family?"

Tears came to Carrie's eyes. "I'm gonna get a baby brother and then my mommy and daddy won't love me anymore."

"Carrie, your parents will still love you, and your little brother's gonna really need you."

"How do you know?"

"My sister's seven years older than me and I don't know what I'd do without her."

Carrie brightened up a little. "Really?" I nodded. "But how do I draw it?"

I reached into the bin on the back table where the art supplies were stored and handed her some crayons. "Draw your daddy, your mommy with her baby bump, and then put yourself right here, between them."

"What's a baby bump?"

21

I rounded my hands in front of my stomach and Carrie giggled. Once she was happily drawing I set out the snacks, graham crackers and apple juice, and checked on some of the other kids to make sure they were on task.

Out of habit, I pulled out my phone and checked my messages. This was the week before the fall Homecoming Dance, and the number of texts made my jaw drop. Even after reading Sara's article and giving me the cold shoulder today, some of those kids were willing to take a chance if they wanted something from me. I didn't know if I felt used, annoyed, or just relieved that I hadn't been ostracized, but I tapped on my phone and started reading the texts.

From Kendall Manheim: *Saw you talking to new guy Nick. Back off. He's MINE! I'll get a Homecoming date with him on my own!*

Sigh.

From Allison Baker: *That gorgeous new guy's in my Econ class. Heard he's 19! Wrangle me a date for HC dance!*

From Mary Bekins: *New guy Nick in AP French is SO cute! Rumor has it he's an undercover narc. I don't care – get me a date to the dance!*

From Katherine Howard: *I was going to overlook your sinful methods and ask you to hook me up for the dance with hottie Nick, who flunked out of private school, but since you were so rude after school, forget it.*

Fine by me.

From Hattie: *Word's out about Nick, but I've still got first dibs for Homecoming.*

From Sara Davis: *Forget that boy in the hall you knew about and forget Jeff Atwell, which you dug out of my head. I want a date to Homecoming with that new guy. Nick? He's in my English AP Lit class.*

I deleted that one.

And from Hank: *Since all the senior girls want to go out with newby Nick Knight, I guess I'm taking you to Homecoming.*

Well, at least I'd found out the new guy's last name.

Hank's invitation was less than romantic, to say the least. Hank and I have gone to the last three Homecoming Dances together, but I wished he'd treat it less as a matter of convenience and more like what it is, an important senior year event. At least he asked me instead of Rachel.

The last two texts were from identical twins Jane and Agnes Bates. They tended to dress alike, wore their short brown hair parted down the middle, and had identical beauty marks on the top of their lip. The only difference was that Jane had a tiny rose tattoo on her ankle which Agnes didn't have, and Jane usually wore contacts while Agnes preferred glasses, but even that wasn't a given.

Those two were real pranksters, too, so I called them my "frequent fliers." If I fixed Jane up with a date and she decided she didn't want to go, she sent Agnes instead, wearing contact lenses, and the poor guy was none the wiser. Or vice versa – Jane masquerading as Agnes wearing glasses. I was beginning to run out of guys who hadn't been on the receiving end of their "Bates and switch" routine, and for the life of me I couldn't convince them to quit doing it.

From Jane: *That new guy Nick's in my advanced art class. Get me a date with him for the Homecoming Dance!*

And from Agnes: *Saw my sister talking to Nick*

*what's-his-name. Heard he lives on his own- no parents.
If you fix me up with him I PROMISE to go!*

So they both wanted Homecoming dates with the same guy?

I reread all the different versions of Nick's pre-Melville life. I knew it was high school and we were teenagers, but still…How did all those rumors get started anyway? And what was the truth?

I didn't have time to puzzle out the answer to that or speculate on why I couldn't pick up on his thoughts when we met, since the daycare kids were begging for a story. I resigned myself to a reread of *Goodnight Moon* and settled into the beanbag chair on the floor, with the children all cross-legged around me.

I was hoping my sister could give me some advice about this Nick problem on the drive home tonight.

****

Real estate wasn't my sister's first career choice. At age twenty, Isabelle was happily taking courses at Community College and working on an associate's degree in interior design. She was really good at it, too. She could just look at a room and know how it should be arranged, with the colors, fabrics, and wall-hangings in just the right spot. But Dad couldn't afford to help Isabelle out financially, so she quit design school and enrolled in a real estate course, one she could complete in a matter of weeks. That meant she could get a job quicker, then find the perfect home for a client and offer her services as an interior designer.

After some impressive sales and the resulting commissions, Isabelle decided to move into her own apartment. I begged her not to leave, but she said having one less mouth to feed would take some pressure off

Dad, and anyway, it was time she lived on her own.

One morning my sister arrived at our house, sporting a bag of bagels and a big grin. *New client…Jonathan…condo…dinner…hot hot hot!* You know, stream of consciousness stuff, enough to clue me in that she'd met someone special.

I sat down at the breakfast table to enjoy the cream cheese bagel. "Isabelle," I said with my mouth full, "quit mooning over this guy and tell me about him."

She rolled her eyes, plopped down in the chair across from me and nibbled on her own bagel. "You're so smart," she said, "*you* tell *me* about him."

I wagged my finger in her face. "All I 'heard' is that he's cute. I can't pick out of your head what isn't there."

She shrugged. "Okay, he wants a two bedroom condo somewhere within easy access to his law firm on the north side of Indianapolis."

I groaned. "I don't care what kind of house he wants. What about him? "

Isabelle giggled like she was the school girl instead of me. "He's twenty-six, super-smart and sophisticated, tall…" Her eyes got all dreamy.

"And of course he's single," I teased. "New to town, doesn't know too many people…women. Right?"

The next week Isabelle found Jonathan the perfect condo on the south side of Melville, only about a ten minute drive across the county line to his office. She asked me to go with her on the showing. Since she wanted me to listen for his thoughts about her, I wasn't invited for the pleasure of my company.

We walked into the brand new end unit condo and looked around. It was stunning. Hardwood floors, brand new kitchen, a master suite upstairs plus two more bedrooms, and an attached two-car garage.

"I'm trying to convince him to buy this three bedroom, two bath instead of the two-one he thought he wanted." *Good for resale value.*

"Resale, yeah right," I said, then saw her eye roll. "Sorry. Where's your super-hot hunk of a buyer?"

Just as I blurted that out, someone behind us cleared his throat. I must have turned three shades of red, but I hoped Jonathan would chalk it up to me being a kid. He was definitely everything Isabelle said he was – tall, handsome, well-dressed. I sighed. I saw right then I'd be losing my sister to this guy. That thought immediately caused me some guilt, because on the one hand Isabelle deserved some happiness, but on the other hand, with Grandma sick and Dad working two jobs, Isabelle was all I had.

"Who's this?" Jonathan asked as he eyed me warily.

"My sister, Emma," Isabelle said, exchanging glances with me. *Play along* her thoughts read and her face pleaded. "She missed the after school bus, and I didn't have time to drop her home before our appointment."

I stuck out my hand. "Nice to meet you, Mr. Calloway."

Jonathan's face lit up as a lovely thought popped into his head. *Almost as pretty as Isabelle.* "Oh, please. Call me Jonathan."

I liked him immediately. As soon as he turned his back to walk through the condo, I gave my sister two thumbs-up.

Isabelle and Jonathan fell madly in love. I wrestled with the reality that my best friend, surrogate mother and confidante was starting a whole new life without me, but she was just so happy I didn't have the heart to lay a guilt trip on her. So I stuffed down my own fears and served as maid of honor at their beautiful September wedding a little over a year ago. After their honeymoon, Isabelle moved into the three bedroom condo she'd helped Jonathan buy.

My fear of living apart from Isabelle turned out to be unfounded, but not for the reasons I'd imagined.

****

Isabelle texted me that she'd gotten a last-minute house showing and couldn't pick me up after work, so I took a chance and called Hank to see if maybe he could give me a ride home from the daycare. He texted back that he'd just gotten home from debate club and his mom was walking in with gourmet carryout.

Okay thanks anyway I replied.

But a text bounced right back from him. *On my way.*

I sent him a happy face and realized yet again what a great friend he was. Would he ever be more?

"Thank you thank you thank you," I said as he pulled up in front of our condo to let me out. "I owe you big time."

"No problem." The hint of a blush spread across Hank's face.

I gave it a minute to see if he was thinking anything about me, or Sara, or Rachel for that matter, but I couldn't pick up on his thoughts. "So Hank..." Feeling the elephant in the room, or car, I gathered my courage and jumped in. "Did you read the Senior Feature today?" I had to hope Hattie was right and he didn't believe what Sara had written about me.

Hank winked at me. "Yeah. Miss Match. That's catchy."

"But what she said about how I do that…"

Hank shut off the engine, turned sideways in the seat, a serious expression on his face. "Was she right? Can you read minds?"

I was speechless, not to mention backed into a corner. I certainly didn't want to lie, but admitting I'd been hearing Hank's admittedly unromantic thoughts about me all these years could be a friendship-killer. "Uh…Sara was mad and…um, Hank do you believe…I mean, would you hate me?"

He burst out laughing. *I'm just messin' with you.* "Believe anything Sara Davis writes? Emma, you know me better than that."

I exhaled in relief. "Yeah, I do." I plastered a smile on my face. "Sorry about your dinner."

"That's what microwaves are for. Say, since your sister's not home, you're welcome to come to my house for dinner."

Was that a real invitation or was he just being nice? I hesitated, hoping I'd pick up something, but all I heard, literally, was Hank's stomach growling. My heart sank a little. "No, it's okay. I'm sure Isabelle will be home soon and I've got a ton of work to do." But not homework.

I hopped out of his car, waved goodbye, and stood there watching till he was out of sight. Once again I thought how nice it would be to hear him think something romantic about me, but I guess I wasn't on his mind. At least not that way.

I hurried inside, pushed my school bag aside and got totally wrapped up in responding to those texts I got earlier. My services were definitely in demand for date fix-ups, and with a guy like Nick at stake, girls were willing to overlook how I got results, so long as I did.

"I'm famished," Isabelle said as she dropped her heavy briefcase on the breakfast bar.

I hadn't even heard her come in. I glanced up at the kitchen clock and realized it was nearly eight o'clock. "Hi. Sorry. I didn't start anything for supper."

Isabelle moaned. "Jonathan's stuck at the office. I'll order Chinese." She dug her phone out of her bag.

"Moo goo gai pan," I said as I continued reading and responding to texts. Suddenly I stopped and gasped.

Isabelle's head snapped around just as she was about to punch in the speed-dial number. "Are you okay?"

I stuck the phone in her face and she had to back away a little in order to read it. "Is that from…?"

"Yeah, Dad, and this time he says more than 'Doing well. Talk later.'"

Isabelle sighed. "So is he still in New Albany?"

I shook my head. "Says he's left southern Indiana and is now staying with friends in Greenwood, back near Indianapolis but way far. He's working part time for one of those tax prep places." I tossed the phone on the counter and yanked out my ponytail holder in frustration.

"I wonder why he won't just come home." Isabelle closed her eyes and rubbed her forehead. *Come home to what?*

"Yeah, I guess there's not much left for him here." I sighed, and then I got mad at myself all over again. "I can't believe I didn't see that coming."

"Emma, I've told you over and over, it's not your fault. Dad was depressed and even he didn't know what he was going to do, so there's no way he would have been thinking about it."

Months ago, when he wasn't at his regular job as an accountant, Dad had been working evenings and weekends at a new age bookstore in Indianapolis. He seemed to be getting better about handling stress, too, or at least that's what I told myself. With me at school and my daycare job, we hardly saw each other. The week prior to Valentine's Day I'd been scrambling around trying to find dates for classmates looking for their soul mate, so when I got home from school on February fourteenth, I was totally fried. All these months later, I still blamed myself for not seeing or hearing what was right in front of me.

Isabelle and I rarely talked about Dad's vanishing act, so we sat in silence till the Chinese food arrived.

"Did Sara Davis's story come out in the school paper today?"

I winced. "Yeah. She called me a mind-reading 'Miss Match' and said kids better watch it around me."

Isabelle looked skyward and shook her head.

"I got a lot of dirty looks and mean thoughts, but then something happened. There's a new guy at school," I said as I dove into the white carton with my chopsticks, "really cute, and lots of girls want to go out with him. They're all hoping I can fix them up with a date to Homecoming."

"Emma," Isabelle sighed, "you spend too much time on other people's love lives. You should find your own boyfriend. Your job takes up enough time as it is." *Concentrate on Hank.*

I waved her thought away. "He doesn't think of me that way."

"Are you sure?"

I groaned. "That's just it. I'm not sure." I jabbed my chopsticks into the Moo goo gai pan and pulled out a lengthy bean sprout. "Did I ever say thank you? For taking me in when Dad left?"

Not necessary.

I nodded and turned around to fight back the tears that always threatened to fall when the subject of Dad's absence came up. "Should we go see Grandma this weekend?"

Isabelle frowned. "Sometimes she remembers me, but she never recognizes you anymore."

"She might."

You're in denial Isabelle was thinking. "We can go if you want to."

Maybe it was denial, but I still wanted to see Grandma, give her a big hug like I did when I had the family I remembered from my childhood. And even if she doesn't recognize me, I could talk about our mutual ability to read minds. A pretend conversation was better than nothing. "I'd like that."

Just then my cell phone pinged and I gave it a quick glance.

"More date requests?"

I nodded, put it on vibrate, and tossed the phone on the counter.

We did go visit Grandma over the weekend, and it was like Isabelle predicted. She eventually remembered her but kept calling me Stella, since I look more like our mom than my sister does. I tried to bring up the ability Grandma and I share, but all I got was a blank stare. More than ever, I knew I was on my own with this. It was a sad visit, but I was glad we went. Grandma Austin didn't have much time left.

****

It was Resource Period, a planned student study time that met every day. Kids were assigned to a teacher for record-keeping, but then all they needed was written permission to go somewhere else, like the library or to make up a test. I had a ton of neglected homework, so I was staying put in Miss Taylor's classroom. I settled into my desk and unpacked my book bag.

"Hey, Emma! Remember me?"

I looked up in surprise. Nick Knight sat down in the chair next to me and tossed his book bag on the floor between us.

"Um, yes…" I was totally flustered and told myself to get it together. Half the girls in this school wanted to date this guy. I needed to get my head in the game, except I was completely distracted by those gorgeous blue eyes and that killer smile. I forced myself to look away so I could focus in on his thoughts.

"I was hoping we'd have a class together," he said with a wink.

"This isn't a class, it's a study hall." I opened my literature textbook and pretended to be reading *Macbeth*.

He shrugged. "Whatever. I'm just glad to see you again."

I melted inside. He was smiling at me, making me feel like the only girl in the room. I briefly closed my eyes for a little romantic fantasy, and then returned to my efforts to hone in on some of his inner dialog. What was he thinking? I focused as hard as I could, but I was getting nothing except a headache. Maybe I was trying too hard. Yeah, that was it. I'd never before come up against a guy with that much charisma and I was sure it was throwing me off.

"It's good to see you again, too, Nick," I finally sputtered. "I was wondering…"

"Hey, Emma." It was Katherine Howard, and she

was giving Nick her best come-hither look. *Quit monopolizing the hunk.*

"Hi, Katherine," I said. "I think you've met Nick. You texted me about a date with him."

"Uh, nice to meet you," Nick said as he blushed a bright red.

Katherine's eyes got wide as she backed away. "I never said...Emma, really!" *Sara was right about you.* Embarrassed, she headed to the other side of the room and took a seat by the window, turning her back on us.

I felt a smug satisfaction in calling Katherine out, after what she'd said to me in Family Relations the other day. She couldn't have it both ways – call me names and then demand a date.

"Ladies and gentlemen, this is a study hall. Stop talking and get busy." Miss Taylor rarely raised her voice, but she appeared to mean business.

Nick smiled and whispered, "Maybe you and I can get together and...get better acquainted." He winked at me, then pulled out his laptop and got busy on...Well, from here it looked like he was surfing social media. Huh. I guess he needed to ease into his studies.

Wait. Get together with Nick? When I was supposed to be finding him a Homecoming date with any number of eligible bachelorettes, including my best friend Hattie? I squashed the thought that getting to know Nick would be fun for me, too, and went back to Shakespeare. Maybe reading about murder and mayhem would take my mind off Nick Knight.

****

After work I changed into sweats and running shoes, grabbed my music earbuds and hit the pavement, headed for the public hiking and biking trail not too far from

Isabelle and Jonathan's condo. But I never got there. Instead, I ended up in front of three seventeen Pendleton Place. The house I grew up in.

My parents bought this 1950s-era three bedroom, two bathroom home when my sister Isabelle was a baby. With two incomes and Grandma Austin taking care of Isabelle, and then me a few years later, things were going well. But then my mom got sick, leaving Dad with huge medical bills and no second income. A short time later she died, and Dad never seemed to recover. By the time I got to middle school he could barely make the mortgage payment.

Most folks in the neighborhood took pride in the appearance of their property, but our old house looked even more run down now than it did the last few years we lived there. The roof tiles were sticking up in a few places, which meant there was probably water damage inside. The formerly crimson front door had faded to a pinkish color; the shutters needed a new coat of black paint; the garage door was off its hinge on one side and hanging askew; and worst of all, the one flower bed I used to lovingly care for was nothing but weeds. Gone were the pretty geraniums and jonquils I'd planted to try and spruce up the exterior and bring a little joy to my dad. The entire house had deteriorated, and yet as I stood on the sidewalk, the only thing I could think about was those weeds.

"Whose house?" a voice behind me asked.

Startled, I pulled my earbuds out, turned around and looked up into the smiling face of Nick Knight. He was also dressed for a run, but his running shoes were new, name-brand, and his jogging clothes were top of the line expensive jersey material. My hands flew to my face to hide the blush that was spreading. Never mind that I was staring at a rundown, vacant house with a bank foreclosure sign in the yard, I was also sweaty in my well-worn grey sweatpants and mismatched hoodie. I could only hope he thought I was just overheated from my run. "What did you say?"

"Whose house is that?" he repeated.

"Oh. Well, it used to be mine, I mean my family's, where I grew up, but…" I swallowed hard and stopped rambling. "What are you doing in this," I waved my arm around, "neighborhood? I thought you lived…" I couldn't finish that sentence. "Where do you live anyway?" I tried to "listen" for his response but got nothing.

Nick smiled and shrugged. "I was trying to get to know my new town, but I kinda got turned around and here I am."

If the rumors were true, he lived in one of those McMansions over on the west side of town, which meant he was a long way from home. I concentrated really hard and tried for the third time to get a read on him. For the third time, nothing. Maybe my talents were fading. But that couldn't be, because I still heard other people's thoughts loud and clear. Wait. Maybe, just maybe, he was having romantic thoughts about me and that was why I couldn't pick up anything. That made me feel all giddy, but it also created major problems because I had a bunch of girls wanting to date this guy.

"Need directions? I've lived in Melville all my life."

"Nope," he said as he visually scouted out his surroundings. "I like to get lost. That way I get to see new scenery. I'll make it home just fine."

"Suit yourself." I turned to go.

"Emma." Nick put a hand on my shoulder to stop me. "What happened? This house, I mean."

I felt really uncomfortable. Yet he looked so sincere, like maybe he even cared about the answer. I shifted my weight from one foot to the other, crossed and uncrossed my arms, and finally said, "Well, my dad, he, uh, moved. I live with my sister and her husband."

Nick took my hand and gently pulled me toward him, as easily as if he'd known me forever. "I'm sorry that happened." He squeezed my hand. "Is there anything I can do?"

Not being able to read this guy made me wonder if he was really that nice, or if this was some new kind of flirting tactic. I hesitated a little too long before I retrieved my hand, but if I didn't get out of this neighborhood I was gonna burst into tears and really embarrass myself.

I forced myself to sound chipper. "What you can do is get together with me like you said, to discuss finding you a Homecoming date. I assume you read Sara Davis's article in the school paper?"

"Mel High's very own Miss Match, mind-reader extraordinaire," he said with a wink.

I groaned. "I hope you didn't buy into that part…" I didn't want to lie, because I can read minds, but I also didn't want to scare off the new guy who might be developing feelings for me.

Nick laughed. "Mind-reading isn't logical."

Okay weird, but back to business. "Maybe we can meet for coffee. Tomorrow after school?" I pulled my hoodie over my head to ward off the October chill and took one last glance at the house. *I wish I could've had a normal family, like everyone else,* I silently groused as I turned to resume my jog.

"It's not too late!" Nick called after me.

Too late for what? Coffee? Homecoming? *A family*? Oh. My. God. Did he just read *my* mind? No, it couldn't be. It just wasn't possible. I shook my head and focused on my run.

****

When I stood in front of my school, it was almost like I could feel the vibes from decades of graduates. Melville High School was a mashup of different architectural styles from different centuries. The main part of the school building was built in the early 2000s, with red brick and structural steel beams, lots of windows that let in the natural light, and a landscaped courtyard near the front entry. On either side of the main entrance were the older yellowing brick portions with few windows and a plaque in the wall that read 1975. The gymnasium in the back of the building has been there since the 1950s, although it's been renovated a couple of times since then.

The high school was just a couple of blocks up Main Street from what used to be empty store fronts and antique dealers, but had been renovated into trendy restaurants, specialty shops, music venues, a newly-refurbished public library, and an artsy-type coffee house, The Mellow Coffee Bean, a favorite student hangout. Yesterday when I accidentally ran into Nick Knight in front of my old house, he agreed to meet me for coffee. At least I thought he did.

I slowly sipped my white chocolate mocha latte and hoped he'd show. I glanced at the time on my cell phone more than once and drummed my fingers on the table in frustration. Pretty soon I'd to have to write this off as a lost cause, apologize to Mrs. Evans for being late to work, and tell Hattie I just couldn't pin this guy down.

"Mind if I join you?"

I looked up from my phone to see Nick standing there, smiling as always, a cup of steaming coffee in his hand. I exhaled and motioned for him to sit.

"I meant to be here sooner, but I was at the Service Project meeting and it went longer than expected."

"Volunteering?" I asked, and he smiled and nodded. This guy just seemed so different from the other boys at school. Hank was a selfless, caring guy, but I never remembered him doing volunteer work. "So what's this year's service project going to be?" I was trying to make small talk as if this was any other guy I'd known all my life, all while my heart was about to pound out of my chest. *Hattie, don't forget about Hattie,* I reminded myself.

"We're helping a bigger organization build a house for a needy family down in Indianapolis."

Are you for real? "Like Habitat for Humanity?" I took a huge swallow of my lukewarm latte. "I guess they need to get started right away, before the weather turns bad."

Nick took his khaki-colored corduroy blazer off and tossed it on the seat next to him. "Yeah, construction starts in a couple of weeks, and despite what you might think about me being the new kid, I really am planning to help."

I sucked in my breath, surprised at his intuitive response. "How do you do that? Respond to something I didn't even say?"

Nick smiled and gingerly blew on his coffee. "I'm just paying attention."

Huh. The old "paying attention" excuse, one I've often used myself. I shook my head in confusion and pushed my empty cup aside. "So I…" The words got stuck. I cleared my throat and tried again. "So. I was wondering if you'd let me fix you up for Homecoming with my friend Hattie Smythe."

Nick thought for a moment. "Is Hattie the basketball player?"

I nodded. I hoped he wasn't turned off by her total jock look.

"Don't get me wrong, I'm not afraid to date a jock," he said as my eyes widened in surprise, "but I can't go to Homecoming with her. I've already got a date."

Shock number one: he seemed to be reading my mind. Shock number two? "You've already got a date?"

Just then the coffee shop door opened with a blast of cold autumn wind, and in blew Kendall Maneater, uh Manheim, and whenever she entered a room she somehow managed to suck all the oxygen out. Frigid breeze notwithstanding. She was wearing black leggings and a tight brown leather jacket with a scarf draped fashionably about her neck. I wasn't surprised she looked stylish because of her part time job in a mall boutique, but I hated that she looked that good right now. *There's my man* she thought as she spotted us.

What? He's going to Homecoming with her? I groaned inwardly at the cliché – the hot new guy and the attractive, sophisticated serial dater.

Kendall winked at Nick. "Hey, Babe," she called over her shoulder as she went to place her order, "save me a seat."

Babe? "Please don't tell me you're going to Homecoming with her."

39

Nick shrugged. "Kendall seems nice, and being a man of the twenty-first century, I'm okay with being asked out by a girl."

This was a fiasco. Now I was going to have one angry best friend, not to mention a few gazillion disappointed girls who may or may not be willing to settle for their second choice. "Kendall Manheim?" I repeated. Well, she warned me.

"Yeah," he replied as he flashed her a big smile across the room. She in turn flipped her hair seductively, paid for her coffee and rejoined us.

"Is there a problem, Emma?" Nick peered at me closely. "You don't look so good."

"I don't think the latte's agreeing with me." Since I couldn't read this guy's mind, I didn't know if he accepted Kendall's invitation because he liked her or because she was the first to ask, but I was frustrated and disappointed. Wait. Why was *I* disappointed? Disappointed for Hattie, of course.

"I gotta go to work." I pulled on my jacket as Kendall swooped in and sat down dangerously close to Nick.

"Don't leave on my account, Emm," Kendall cooed. The way she said my name sounded like the Wicked Witch taunting Dorothy.

I narrowed my eyes at Kendall, grabbed my book bag and got the heck out of there.

Chapter 3

An anonymous entry hit the *Melville High Weekly Herald*'s gossip column on Friday before the big dance. *What senior girl with a little something extra let the hot new senior boy get snapped up for Homecoming by...???* There may not have been any name attached to that snippet, but it had Sara Davis written all over it.

I passed Sara in the hall between classes and got a wicked grin from her, not to mention a snarky *I'm on to your mind-invasion techniques.*

"Nice piece in the gossip page this morning," I told her.

The flicker of surprise on Sara's face lasted mere seconds. "You don't have any proof." She stuck her nose so far in the air I swear she'd drown if it was raining, and then she stomped off.

Kids could be petty and vindictive, but I'd thought by senior year we would have all matured. Not Sara. Her vendetta against me reached all the way back to ninth grade. At Freshman Orientation, I "heard" her admiring a cute boy from one of the parochial schools and then offered to set her up with him. I made the mistake of repeating back to her verbatim what she'd thought about him, and blurted it out right in front of both of them. Mortified, Sara's face turned red and then purple and she stormed off, vowing revenge. She'd had it in for me ever since, and her position as editor of the school newspaper suited her purposes perfectly.

I hadn't had a chance to talk to Hattie about Homecoming, since Nick was now taken. But I was pretty sure Hattie had read that oh-so-obvious gossip piece and was probably mad that I didn't get her that date with Nick like I promised. I had to do damage control.

Hattie and I once had a huge fight back in seventh grade over another new boy in school – Hank. Hattie thought he was cute and of course, I thought so, too, but she was too shy to talk to him. The only class all three of us had together was speech, and due to the teacher's insistence on alphabetical seating, Austin and Zimmerman were at opposite ends of the classroom, with Smythe seated closer to Hank. Even then she still wouldn't start up a conversation with him.

Turns out he did notice me, though, because he asked both me and Hattie to his Bar Mitzvah. I didn't understand the religious part, but the party afterward was awesome. I was the first girl Hank asked to dance, much to my delight and Hattie's chagrin. After he'd politely danced with Hattie and a few others, he spent the rest of the evening with me. I was flattered, but felt a little guilty because Hattie got stuck sitting at a table with an overweight girl with frizzy red hair from Hank's synagogue. By the way, that girl turned out to be Rachel Bomburg, now gorgeous and sophisticated.

Hattie refused to speak to me for days afterward, claiming I'd stolen her boyfriend. Pointing out that he wasn't her boyfriend fell on deaf ears. So she turned her attention back to her first love – basketball. Except for one ill-fated eighth grade romance with Robbie Martin, no one caught her attention until Nick.

Sure enough, an angry-looking Hattie cornered me

at the school's main entrance as I was headed out the door and off to the daycare. Kids were exiting the building, some in a hurry to meet rides or buses, some sauntering along chatting with friends. I glanced around us. "Can we walk and talk? Too many people around." I took off.

Hattie's legs were much longer than mine, so she didn't have trouble keeping up. "Emma, you promised! How could you let Nick get snared by Kendall? Why didn't you listen in on his thoughts?"

"Shhh." I glanced around to see if we'd been overheard. "I tried, but…"

She stopped in front of me, hands on hips. "But what?"

I threw up my hands in frustration. "I can't…"

"Hey ladies." Sara Davis slithered up out of nowhere, a smirk on her face. *This might be fun.* "What's going on?"

I could just see Sara salivating over a scoop about an argument between the school's star basketball player and its infamous matchmaker. More ammunition for another eye-catching editorial at my expense. I wasn't going to give her the satisfaction.

"Private conversation, Sara," I said.

Instead of moving on, Sara planted herself right between Hattie and me. "So who are you going to Homecoming with, Hattie?" *I can hook you up with my cousin Eddie.*

I opened my mouth to reply to that, but stopped myself before I made matters worse. "Have a nice day, Sara." I crossed my arms and glared at her.

With both Hattie and me towering over her, she shrugged and walked away.

"Okay, you can't what?" Hattie asked, once we were sure Sara was out of earshot.

I let out a huge sigh. "I can't hear Nick's thoughts. I've tried but I just can't do it."

Hattie blinked. "Seriously? Why not?"

"No clue."

She had to let that sit for a moment. "But you still could've fixed me up with him."

"I tried. You know how fast Kendall works."

Hattie frowned. "But you can read Kendall's mind."

"Yeah, but I can't follow her around all day. Some things are just out of my control." I clenched my teeth in frustration.

My inability to pick up on Nick's thoughts left him vulnerable to the Venus flytrap that was Kendall Maneater. Worse yet, I broke a promise I never should have made to someone I care about. Lots of girls besides Hattie were angry, too. They'd been tossing me dirty looks and angry thoughts all day. I was back to being the school pariah.

"I'm gonna be late to work," I said, checking the time on my phone. "I'm sorry about Nick, but..." I figuratively crossed my fingers, "...Kyle Robertson wants to go out with you."

Kyle Robertson? "But he's a nobody."

"He's not a nobody. He's president of the honor society."

"Great," Hattie sighed. She pulled the ponytail holder off her wrist and tied her hair back in that bun kind of thing she always wore for basketball practice, which was where she should be right now. "A date with a nerd who'll no doubt spend the evening spouting scientific theories."

"Just keep him dancing and he won't have time to talk. And don't forget, I'm going to the dance with another of those nerds, soon-to-be valedictorian Hank Zimmerman."

Hattie softened a little. "Yeah, okay, but at least you and Hank are friends, and you didn't even want to go out with Nick."

I swallowed hard. She was right about Hank and me, but as for Nick... "Hattie, please, just give Kyle a chance."

I could see she was relenting, so I made yet another promise I hoped I could keep. "Let me try again with Nick. I'll see if he's free next weekend."

It's your last chance! And with that thought missile, she stormed off.

Duly warned.

****

"Are you wearing that dress again?" Isabelle was standing behind me, frowning, as I checked my look in the full-length bedroom mirror.

"Duh," I said and rolled my eyes. Immature, yes, but Hank would be here any minute to pick me up for Homecoming and it was too late for a wardrobe do-over. "A new dress wasn't in the budget, so I decided to look fabulous in something I already own." I turned back to the mirror to finish adjusting the black jeweled clip that was encircling my long brown hair at the nape of my neck.

I reached for the string of pearls I'd borrowed from her, knotted them and hung them around my neck. Despite Isabelle's dubious expression, I didn't think I looked too bad. I've grown an inch or so since I wore this dress last year, so the little black dress now hit me mid-thigh, and instead of last year's heels, I was wearing a pair of black ballet flats. Hank and I were about the same height and I didn't want to tower over him.

"Well, if you're sure…"

I gave Isabelle's attire a once over. "Aren't you a little overdressed for a night of pizza and channel surfing?" She looked really pretty in a new tea-length reddish black polished cotton dress with a matching belt around her tiny waist, and diamond teardrop earrings which sparkled as she pushed her brown bobbed hair behind her ears.

We're stand-in parents.

I lifted an eyebrow. "When did the PTA press you and Jonathan into service as chaperones?"

Isabelle narrowed her eyes at me with that look that said "cut it out," just as the doorbell rang. "That must be Hank," she sang out as she left my upstairs bedroom.

I picked up my black faux-leather clutch bag, looked inside to make sure I had lipstick, student ID and house keys, and followed my sister down the stairs.

Jonathan, who was wearing one of his dark grey business suits, had already opened the door. "Hey, Hank." He offered his hand to shake and then motioned him in.

"Wow." Hank whistled softly as he saw me descending the last few steps.

I blushed, but honestly Hank looked pretty handsome, too. The Homecoming Dance wasn't formal, or even semi-formal really, so he was wearing a dark navy suit with a matching vest, a perfectly coordinated tie, black dress shoes, and he'd used enough product that his usually curly black hair was lying flat around his forehead.

"Hi," I said.

Hank grinned as he handed me a red carnation wrapped in tissue paper with a green ribbon tied around the stem. "I know it's not Prom or anything, but my mother says a man should never arrive empty-handed."

I was flattered that he went to that kind of trouble, even if his mother told him to. "That's so sweet. I'll just put it in water."

He likes her, my sister was thinking as I started for the kitchen to find a vase.

I gave her a wistful smile. The fact that Hank thought I looked pretty tonight was encouraging, but anything more was probably just wishful thinking on Isabelle's part. Mine, too.

"Only as a friend," I whispered as I walked past her. I opened several cabinet doors till I found a small bud vase, added some water, and put the carnation in. It looked really pretty and I didn't want to waste it in the kitchen, so I brought it back to the entry hall and set it on the table next to the door.

You kids have… Isabelle was thinking.

"You kids have fun," I finished for her with a wiggle of my eyebrows. "See you there."

Hank helped me into my navy pea coat, chivalrously offered me his arm, and escorted me to the car where he opened the passenger door to his mom's freshly-washed, late-model sedan.

Is Emma okay?

Not really, but it was nice Hank picked up on my emotions. I was dreading what might be waiting for me at the dance.

Hank slid into the driver's side and fastened his seatbelt. He started the engine and backed out of the parking pad that was set aside for condo visitors. "You seem to have something on your mind."

I settled into the passenger seat. "Lots of kids didn't trust me after reading Sara's story, but that didn't stop them asking for dates."

"Yeah, kinda hypocritical if you ask me." Hank adjusted his rearview mirror.

"And Hattie wanted to go out with Nick, but Kendall beat her to it." I fastened my seatbelt and leaned back against the headrest. "Hattie and every other girl in the senior class," I moaned. Then I sucked in my breath when I realized how that sounded. "Except me."

It was hard to tell in the dark, but I thought Hank blushed.

I wasn't a football fan, but the Melville Golden Eagles squeaked by the Harrington High Tigers last night at the Homecoming game, sixteen to thirteen. Kerry Thompson kicked the winning field goal from forty yards out – a school record – with mere seconds left on the clock. So hopefully Allison Baker was happy to have a date tonight with the hero of the game, even though he was an underclassman. Check off one less angry girl.

There was a line of kids waiting to get into the gym, so Hank and I joined it. To gain admittance into the dance, all students had to show their school IDs, being carefully checked by my sister as it turned out, and pass through a breathalyzer station, manned by an official-looking Jonathan. Anyone with alcohol in their system would be sent home on a school bus in total humiliation. Once students were inside the gym, anyone who left was gone for good. They were pretty strict about this being a safe place to have fun.

Unfortunately, the next person to join the line was

Sara Davis with Eddie Davis, her eleventh grade cousin. I loved the irony. Maybe since she didn't have to impress a date, she didn't care that her pale pink poufy dress completely overwhelmed her and clashed with her red hair.

"Where's Jeff?" I asked her.

"I turned him down." She sniffed. "He said you told him to ask me, but he waited till today, which was way insulting." *You're a fraud.*

Fraud? Sara was clearly crushing on Jeff. I reached out to him to maybe do something nice, or at least distract her, yet she turned up her nose at an arranged date and ended up at Homecoming with her geeky cousin. I turned my back on her.

The gym doors were open, giving us a view of the decorations, and we could hear the DJ testing his mike, preparing to spin tunes. From what I saw by craning my neck around the line of kids in front of us, they had dimmed the lights and had a cheesy disco ball hanging from the center light fixture. The gym was draped with streaming crepe paper in school colors of gold and purple, and across the entryway hung a huge banner which read *Congratulations Golden Eagles*. The bleachers had all been shoved up against the walls and replaced with some of the cafeteria tables, covered in paper tablecloths and sprinkled with lots of purple and gold confetti to form a refreshment center. Up for grabs were cans of soda and bottled water displayed in large plastic bowls atop mounds of ice. Bags of popcorn were next to plates of freshly-baked cookies, plus an assortment of bagged pretzels and chips. A junk-food lover's paradise, and all included in the somewhat inflated price of a ticket to the dance. This was the PTA's biggest fundraiser of the year.

The basketball goals were tucked up and out of the way to accommodate a dance floor, and there was a photo op section in the far corner near the athletic concession stand with an autumn-themed backdrop, ready to snap pictures of happy couples. Naturally, there was a fee for that, too.

Faith Barlow was having her picture taken with Marshall Everett, the school's star Mathlete. He'd asked if I could help him get the date with her. I don't know Faith well, but she was good friends with Sara, which meant I couldn't let Faith know I'd had a hand in any of it. I gave Marshall some hints about how to go about asking her. Must have worked.

Faith was staring off into space, thinking *Wish I was here with...* while Marshall was smiling and having a great time. I wished she'd finished that thought, because it seemed her heart was elsewhere and maybe I could help. I'd always just assumed Faith was too wrapped up in her creative writing to bother with little things like dates or boyfriends. Unlike Sara Davis's other bestie Katherine Howard, who disliked me as much as Sara did, Faith seemed different. More aloof, but maybe more open-minded.

Faith caught sight of me and waved with both arms. I half-heartedly waved back. "Hey, Emma! You hear anything from Frank? Mom told me to ask."

Thinking about my MIA father made me cringe, so I shrugged and turned my attention to my own date. "Hank, do we want a picture?" What they were charging for a souvenir photo was outrageous, especially when someone could just snap a picture with a cell phone.

To my surprise, Hank said, "Sounds good."

Something to remember our last Homecoming together.

That thought sent my hopes for a romantic relationship with Hank soaring. He took my hand and led me straight into the picture frame. I quickly wriggled out of my coat, looped my arm through Hank's and was preparing to smile adoringly at him, when the photographer sang out, "Say cheese!" and snapped the photo with a blinding flash of light. I didn't even know if I was facing the camera.

"Can we see?" I asked the photographer. I was prepared to demand a do-over.

"Fill out the card and I'll email you. Next?" He craned his neck around Hank and me, dismissing us.

Hank and I exchanged frustrated glances.

As our eyes readjusted to the darkness, I saw that Flip and James were the couple behind us, and now they were posing for their official party pic.

"I'll go hang up your coat." Hank pointed to the box office-turned coat check room that the PTA was also staffing. For another fee of course.

"Hey, girl," Flip said as he blinked from the camera flash. "Ready for the big night?" *Brace yourself, girlfriend.*

I turned to face him. "Meaning…?"

Flip shrugged. "Lots of girls on social media admiring Nick and grousing about not getting a date with him. And blaming you for it."

"Blaming me how?"

"Basically saying that if you're the psychic Sara Davis says you are, you're doing a bad job of it."

I groaned inwardly. "Remind me to stay off social media for a while."

"Ease off, Phillip," James said. "I'm sure Emma

tried. Kendall usually gets what she wants."

"Speak of the predator and she shall appear," Flip said with an exaggerated eye roll.

I turned to see Kendall flounce through the entryway, beaming as she clung to Nick Knight's arm and nodding at her adoring subjects. It was a chilly October evening, and yet Kendall was wearing a sleeveless red cocktail dress which was way too short, and no jacket. No jacket! I got the shivers just looking at her.

Nick was underdressed but he pulled it off, sort of preppy style in jeans and a blazer. Everyone turned to admire the handsome couple as they strolled into the gym.

Lucky girl.

He's SO cute.

First chance I get I'm cutting in.

What a hottie. She's okay, too.

I didn't bother trying to pinpoint where those thoughts were coming from. The opinions were all about the same anyway, and I was just as annoyed as everyone else that Kendall snagged a date with the new guy before I could do anything about it.

Hank was watching all this as he rejoined me from the coat check. "How does Nick do that?" He shook his head. "Attract attention like that?"

Nick was something of a mystery, for sure. "You know how it is in a small town. Fresh blood and all that. Don't you remember how much drama you stirred up in middle school when you transferred in?"

"I guess." Hank shrugged as he watched Nick schmooze with our classmates.

A stage had been erected on the home team side of

the gym and there was a banner off to the side that read *King and Queen*. The DJ, one of the kids from Mel High's broadcasting class, spun the first song and started his voice-over in a deep baritone. "Ladies and gentlemen, welcome to this year's Homecoming Dance, honoring past Mel High grads, including last year's King and Queen, Tyler Paulson and Lucy McKinney." He paused as Tyler and Lucy waved at the crowd from the center of the dance floor. "And of course the victorious Golden Eagles football team. Enjoy the music, food, and company. Presentation of the Homecoming court and members of the team will be in about an hour."

Oh, good, an hour before I'd be forced to watch Kendall Manheim stroll onstage with quarterback Greg Plowman and be crowned Queen to his King. Greg was here with Mary Bekins, who'd stopped me in the hall and wanted a date with Nick, but I encouraged Greg to ask her out. I thought he was a better match because Mary had a special interest in football – her brother was a rookie NFL running back.

Just then Hattie sidled up to me, Kyle trailing behind her. *I hate myself for fighting with you.* "Hey, bestie. Having fun?"

"Hey girl," I said, relieved that she was over her mood, and gave her a hug.

Hattie looked a little less like a jock tonight, wearing a black pantsuit over a lacy white camisole. I silently applauded her choice of black ballet flats over tennis shoes, and was pleased she was even wearing a little lipstick and mascara.

"Did you see her?" Hattie tilted her head in Kendall's direction.

"Kinda hard to miss."

"Not only does she get to be Homecoming Queen with the captain of the football team," Hattie harrumphed, "she still walks in on the arm of the best-looking guy here."

Gee thanks.

Nice.

Rude.

As if.

I saw a lot of disgruntled guys standing around with scowls or crossed arms, including Hattie's date Kyle. I guess they were feeling a little threatened by all the attention the new guy was getting.

"Wanna dance?" Hank offered me his arm.

I hooked my arm into his as we strolled toward the dance floor.

The DJ was playing the electric slide, the song where the lyrics call out the dance moves and partners weren't even needed. More and more kids were crowding onto the floor aka the basketball court, including some of the dates I'd arranged. Other than Sara, who was all frowns and left feet as her cousin continually stepped on her toes, maybe things weren't going so bad after all. Fraternal twins Sam and Darrin O'Brien were with the dates I arranged, Jane and Agnes Bates. The four of them seemed to be enjoying the dance, and so far no date-switching had occurred.

Hank and I pushed our way through the throng and staked out a spot to dance. Pretty soon I was having fun and forgetting about my Kendall-envy, my dread of Sara's retaliation, my uncertainty about my relationship with Hank, and my confusion over Nick.

I guess the DJ was trying to appeal to all musical tastes, because in rapid succession he spun vintage rap songs with clean lyrics, some heavy metal, and even a big-band style swing number. When he cued up "Thriller," everybody got fired up since it was almost Halloween. Hank and I were thoroughly enjoying ourselves and each other's company with every new song that came up.

All too soon the DJ handed over the mic to our school principal, Mr. Longstreet. "Ladies and gentlemen, the time has come to crown the Homecoming King and Queen."

Now was my chance to make good on my most recent promise to Hattie. "I'm gonna go say 'hi' to Isabelle and Jonathan," I whispered in Hank's ear. Just a little fib. He nodded and smiled at me as I hurried off.

Isabelle and Jonathan had long since closed their check-in stations, and I'd caught a glimpse of them dancing with abandon. They were on the other side of the gym now, watching the official presentation, so I scurried over.

"Having fun?" Isabelle asked.

"Uh-huh," I muttered, scouting the crowd to locate Nick and hoping he hadn't been snagged by any one of a billion lovesick girls.

Sorry I'm so boring.

"You're not boring, Isabelle," I replied, "but I've got to find…"

I spotted Nick over by the refreshment table, talking to a couple of guys. I took off without another word. Luckily the business of crowning the Homecoming King and Queen and then introducing the football team had the attention of most of the kids.

"Can I talk to you a minute?" I asked him.

Nick appeared engrossed in an intense conversation

with honor society members Marshall Everett and James Harrison, but when he saw me he flashed that disarming smile of his. "Hi, Emma. Great party, huh?"

"Seriously, can I borrow you?" He shrugged, set down his bottle of water, and allowed me to take his arm and lead him to…. I didn't know where. What with the principal on the microphone and periodic cheering from the student body, the place was too loud for any kind of conversation. I wondered if Isabelle might…I tried to catch her eye. I needed her permission to step outside, or Nick and I wouldn't be allowed back in.

"Maybe your sister will let us back in if we sneak out into the lobby," Nick suggested.

I turned to him in surprise. "How did you know that's what I was…that my sister was…?"

"A chaperone? I introduced myself to her when I checked in at the door and she told me."

Well, okay, that made sense. I finally caught Isabelle's eye and pointed to the lobby with my best look of desperation. She nodded back, so Nick and I stepped out. Once out of the noisy gym, the quiet in the hall made me feel a little self-conscious. There I was with the cute new boy in school, and I was about to ask him out on a date with another girl.

"What's up?" he asked with a grin.

"Well, you probably know by now that a bunch of girls wanted to be here with you tonight, and…"

"So they're all mad at Kendall?"

Mad? Green with envy was more like it. I refocused. "My best friend Hattie – Harriet Smythe - I told you about her, right? Well, she really wanted to go out with you from the first moment she saw you in the school cafeteria, but unlike Kendall, Hattie's kinda shy. Since I was too late to fix you two up for Homecoming, I told her I'd ask if maybe you'd, well…" *Spit it out Emma.* Geez. It wasn't like this was the first time I'd arranged an awkward date. But it would be a lot easier if he wasn't looking at me with that twinkle in his eye. I took a deep breath and got to it. "Would you be willing to go out with Hattie next weekend? There's a hayride coming up, a Halloween thing."

Nick's smile had melted away and he was wearing a serious, thoughtful expression, almost like he was peering into my soul and wondering if this was what I really wanted.

And I was wondering that, too. "Unless you don't like Hattie…"

Nick shrugged. "Sure, she seems nice. But I'd rather go on that fall hayride with you."

Me? Not Kendall, not any of the cute girls clamoring for his attention, but me? My heart started racing.

"That's right, I'd rather go with you," he repeated.

And there it was again. Another coincidence? It wasn't possible, was it? I studied him closely for a moment but I just couldn't figure this guy out. I'd tried to listen in on his thoughts so many times without success, but was he reading *my* mind? If so, it was unnerving and gave me a taste of how other people must feel when I did it to them.

And if I went to the hayride with Nick, what about Hattie? I couldn't do that to her again, especially after screwing her over for this dance. "Um, well…" I made a mental note to get Hank to take me to the hayride.

Nick folded his arms in front of his chest and frowned. "Oh, okay, you're already going with Hank."

Seriously! Again? "Are you reading my mind?" I

blurted out.

Nick's jaw dropped. "No. I already told you, mind reading isn't possible *or* logical."

Logical or not, it *was* possible. I took a deep breath. "So will you do it? Go out with Hattie? We can all four go together if you like."

"On one condition," he answered. "Dance with me, right now."

I listened to the silence coming from the gym and figured the ceremony was over, but the dance music hadn't restarted yet. What could it hurt? I came with Hank, a guy who hasn't given me any real romantic encouragement since seventh grade. So why not? One dance with this cute guy, just to get it out of my system, and then he'd go out with my friend.

"Sure," I told him as I took his arm and we walked back in. I waved to Hank, who was deep in conversation with fellow math geek Marshall, until he looked up and saw me on Nick's arm. Was that disappointment on Hank's face?

The music started again and this time it was a slow song. "I'd like to dedicate this to all the returning grads," the DJ announced over the first few chords, as a kind of nostalgic, wistful ballad cued up. Nick pulled me close and gently swayed me around the room. I was in heaven.

And really confused.

Chapter 4

The annual October thirty-first event on Melville's Main Street offered pumpkin carving, Halloween-themed karaoke, face-painting, candy handed out to trick-or-treaters by the area merchants, and a costume judging contest. And of course a haunted hayride.

A few blocks north of Main Street was an historic neighborhood with houses built in the late nineteenth century. One of those old homes fronted a four acre farm behind the downtown area. The homeowners sponsored the ride on their property via a tractor piled high with hay, complete with staged ghost and ghoul sightings and a visit from The Headless Horseman.

But I didn't have time to reminisce. I had work to do.

Yesterday at lunch I pulled up a chair next to Hank and leaned in. "Would you be my date to the Haunted Hayride Saturday night?"

He frowned. *I was just going to ask* you. "Hello to you, too."

He was going to ask me? I wish I'd known that. After all, hayrides under a full moon could be romantic, and it made me wonder...

"I'll pick you up at eight," Hank said. *Better check the weather, know what to wear...*

I sighed.

Next I needed to iron out the logistics with Nick. I'd

planned to talk to him during student resource period, but he wasn't there. Sometimes I wondered when the guy ever studied, because I've never once seen him crack a book. I asked Miss Taylor if she knew where he was, and she said he went to the special needs room. She wrote me a pass and I went to look for him, but I don't get it. Why would Nick spend all his free time volunteering when he was in danger of flunking his classes?

Turned out he wasn't in the special needs room either. I stood in the doorway thinking about what to do next when the teacher stepped out.

"May I help you?"

"I was looking for Nick Knight."

"Try the library," the teacher said before closing the door.

Well, good. Getting some homework done. I flashed my school ID to the student monitor at the library sign-in desk and scouted the large area. Off to one side were multiple rows of computers next to some study tables, and then the rest of the room was the usual library stuff. No sign of Nick.

Woof! Bow-wow! Grrrr!

My ears perked up. Dogs? What? I followed the sound to a glassed-in room next to the librarian's office. Inside were a group of small children and three dogs of various sizes and questionable pedigrees. Sure enough, there sat Nick on the floor reading a story to the kids, the dogs at his feet. He looked up from his story and smiled at me as I tiptoed in and huddled against the back wall.

"Hey, guys, this is my friend Emma," he told them.

"Hi Emma," a couple of them said.

"Hi." *What's going on?*

"Emma," Nick said, "these kids are from Grey Road

Elementary and they're here enjoying Doggone Good Book week." Just like he knew what had just flashed across my mind. Did he? If so, it was creepy.

I looked around at all the kids who seemed completely caught up in the story about a dog named Farley who was following his nose, and wished I had as much rapport with the children I worked with at the daycare as Nick did with kids I assumed he'd just met. I shook my head in confusion but motioned for him to continue reading.

He finished to thunderous applause, well, okay, a lot of finger snapping, and a couple of yips from the dogs. Afterwards, the elementary teacher took the children and the dogs outside.

"What is Doggone Good Book Week?" I asked Nick once we were alone.

"Something those Grey Road teachers thought up, a way to encourage their students to read. And who doesn't love dogs?"

Me. "Okay," I said, "but why are they here instead of at their own school? And whose dogs are those?"

Nick's face lit up. "I heard about the reading program from our school librarian and offered to read to the kids at the elementary school. But our library's bigger, so I convinced our librarian to have this special event here. I asked the pet shelter where I volunteer…"

"When do you have time to volunteer at the elementary school? And the pet shelter? Seriously, do you ever study?"

"Mostly I go on Saturdays," Nick replied, ignoring the part about the homework. "Wanna join me sometime?"

Unlikely.

"It's okay if you're not a dog lover," Nick said as if I'd said something out loud. "But if you change your mind, let me know."

I looked Nick in the eye. "I can't figure you out."

He grinned at me. "Then don't try."

Is he psychic?

"You must think I'm clairvoyant," Nick replied, inadvertently or not.

My eyes widened. "Well 'clairvoyant' wasn't the word I had in mind, but same thing I guess." I started to ask him how he knew what I was thinking, but I was losing hope of ever getting a straight answer. So I refocused on my reason for finding him in the first place. "I wanted to talk to you about your date to the hayride with Hattie."

"I'm still going," he replied, although he didn't sound too enthusiastic.

I shrugged. "Okay, great." *And Hattie owes me big for this.*

"I'm sure Hattie appreciates all your efforts," Nick replied, and again I got chills down my spine.

****

I only had one date request for the hayride, since most kids prefer to go out on Halloween with groups of friends. Jeff Atwell, with a *What the heck? It's Halloween and why not trust the psychic?* thought, asked for a set up with Agnes Bates. And Sara wasn't happy.

"Thanks a lot, Emma. I thought you were going to fix Jeff and me up." *Agnes Bates? That flake? Gimme a break.* Sara even treated me to an eye roll.

I crossed my arms and tapped my foot. "When I tried at Homecoming you nearly took my head off. By the way, did you have fun with Eddie?" I smiled when she winced at the reminder.

"You blindsided me with that one. But now that you've dug around in my head and know I really like Jeff, you go and set him up with one of those Bates twins. You know they're gonna switch dates, right?"

Oddly enough, she had a point.

Sara put her hands on her hips, got in my face and glared. "I've been thinking of doing a follow up to my Senior Feature article."

Just great. The rumor mill had barely died down from the last time Sara wrote about me. I'd had enough of kids giving me strange looks, wondering if I knew their deepest secrets, and then turning around to use me to get dates for them. "Sara, you don't have to threaten me. I'd be happy to try again with you and Jeff."

He's so cute and you promised is what she was thinking, but all she said was, "See that you do," and stomped off to class.

Oh, boy.

****

It was a cloudless October night with a full moon, no wind, and a temperature hovering just above freezing, enough to put the proverbial frost on the pumpkin. For such a casual event as a community Halloween hayride, Hank didn't need to come to the door to formally pick me up, so he just honked and I ran out and jumped in the car. I was wearing an old pair of jeans that I didn't mind getting covered with hay and hopefully nothing worse, a couple of layered long-sleeve t-shirts, and a thick NFL Colts hooded sweatshirt that I borrowed from Jonathan.

Hurry up hurry up hurry up, Hank silently urged me as he tapped the steering wheel. He checked the time on his dashboard, put the car in gear and zoomed off before

I even had a chance to fasten my seatbelt.

"What's the rush?" I asked him.

"The rush is *A* - timed tickets for the hayride, and *B* - we're meeting Nick and Hattie there."

Finding a parking spot anywhere on Main Street proved to be problematic, since it seemed like everyone in town had come out for this event. Hank circled around the block a couple of times looking for street parking, but nothing opened up.

"Hank, you're wasting gas. Just go park in the school's parking lot and we can walk."

Hank glanced over at me. "Okay, but it's a good three blocks." *And you're not wearing a coat.*

I waved away his unspoken concern. "It's not that cold. I'll be fine." I ignored his raised eyebrow.

Even parking at the high school looked iffy at first, but Hank finally spotted a father putting his small children into his car and staked out the spot, signal blinking, and waited with more toe tapping and steering wheel thumping until the dad finally backed out. We jumped out of the car and walked briskly, helping me generate some body heat.

"Where are we meeting Nick and Hattie?" I did a quick survey of Main Street, trying to locate them. The place was Halloween-central. There were scarecrows next to bales of hay strategically placed as barriers in the street to keep people from driving through, and possibly mowing down, pedestrians. All up and down the lengthy street, every storefront was decorated Halloween style. The merchants participating in trick-or-treating had official signs in front of their stores which read *Melville Safe Halloween Place,* and everywhere I looked I saw both kids and adults in costumes.

"We're supposed to meet them over at the pumpkin carving." Hank pointed across the street as he zipped up his fur-lined corduroy jacket and adjusted his stocking cap down over his ears. *I wish Emma had her coat,* he thought.

I wished so, too. I pulled my hoodie up over my head and stuffed my hands into the front pouch, making the best of my poor wardrobe choices. But then Hank surprised me by putting an arm around my shoulders and drawing me in a little closer. I smiled at him and he gave my shoulder a squeeze. I definitely felt warmer. I tried listening to his thoughts again.

We're going to miss our ride time.

I sighed. No romance. Hank was back to clock-watching.

We made our way through the crowds and across the street to the pumpkin carving area, where lots of families were in the midst of digging some crazy looking faces out of those gourds. Some of them were quite artistic, and others were just a mess. There would be prizes in a number of age categories, but I didn't envy the judges having to narrow it down. And then I spotted Nick, busily carving a jack-o-lantern masterpiece, with Hattie watching over his shoulder.

"Hey, guys," I said.

Hattie glanced up and tilted her head in the direction of Nick's pumpkin. *Cool carving, huh?*

I nodded and flashed her a look. It would've been nice if she'd complimented him out loud. Knowing how tongue-tied Hattie got around boys who weren't fellow jocks, or Flip, I hoped she was at least trying to make conversation with her date.

"Dude," Hank said, "if you're about done, our

hayride tickets say nine p.m., but we need to be in the line by eight forty-five." He pulled out his cell phone and flashed it at them. "In five minutes."

Nick left his unfinished pumpkin carving, but he didn't take Hattie's hand or behave at all like they were on a date. He was smiling, waving at folks he passed, and sort of bouncing as he walked. Hattie stared at the ground and shuffled along, never making eye contact with him or me.

Hank pulled the four tickets out of his wallet. "Queue line starts way over there." He pointed to a line of people that snaked down a long driveway and into the blocked-off street. The old house on the acreage was all lit up for Halloween and decorated with strings of pumpkin lights, cheesecloth cobwebs, bouncy plastic spiders, jack-o-lanterns, and someone on the edge of the driveway in a witch costume stirring a cauldron of dry ice. As we approached, she let out a creepy cackle that set the little kids in front of us squealing in fright. The four of us stepped in behind that family as I crossed my fingers they wouldn't get too spooked by things that go bump in the night.

This date was a BIG mistake. I jerked my head around to see a frowning Hattie.

Nick frowned, too, leading me to believe he either heard Hattie's thoughts or picked up on her mood. Maybe Hattie and Nick just needed to ease into the evening, starting with this romantic hayride.

Hope this hayride's worth the money. That was Hank's random thought.

"The ride's gonna be totally worth the high price of these tickets," Nick replied to Hank's unvoiced comment. "Riding through Farmer Brown's pumpkin patch with all that scary stuff should be fun."

"Farmer Brown, huh?" I chuckled.

The line was moving slow. Nick put his hand on Hattie's elbow to steer her along, and Hank, almost as if he was in competition, took my hand and led me along as well. I decided to take what I could get, so I squeezed his hand affectionately. I was rewarded when Hank smiled at me and thought *Emma is...*

"Hey, Emma!" Flip waved and shouted from behind us in line, interrupting my eavesdropping on what could have been a revelation from Hank. I half-heartedly waved back.

The rides were running a little behind, so after a half hour of standing in the line, in the cold with no shelter, I was shivering when it was finally our turn to board the hayride. The conveyance was actually a tractor with bales of hay doubling as seating benches, plus some loose hay filling up the center so if someone got bounced around, they wouldn't land on cold, hard, metal. We had to climb up a stile to get inside, and all twenty people they allowed on board seemed to be scrambling to get the best seat, which was in the back.

Hattie plopped down in a prime location at the back of the tractor bed, which provided an unobstructed view of the field and hopefully a first glimpse of The Headless Horseman. She looked expectantly for Nick to sit down next to her, but he somehow managed to get me seated next to Hattie, him on my left, and then Hank on the other end at Hattie's right. It was an uncomfortable arrangement in more ways than one, but it was a good spot to keep an eye out for what might sneak up behind us. And big bonus, the hay offered some protection from the cold.

"Are you having fun?" I asked Hattie in a whisper.

No, she thought. "Sure."

"What's wrong?" I asked her, but got *the look.*

Hattie adjusted her lightweight jersey athletic jacket and stuffed her hands in her pockets. Maybe Hattie wasn't so much unhappy as she was cold, and I could relate. I decided to watch and listen to see if I could figure it out. In the meantime, more kids were boarding the tractor, including Agnes Bates and her date Jeff Atwell.

"Hey, Emma," she said with a sly smile.

I narrowed my eyes at Jane. "Hi, *Agnes.*"

And then disaster hit. Or at least it was a fiasco as far as I was concerned, because next on board was Kendall, arm in arm with a guy I'd never seen before, and they made a beeline for the four of us. Kendall had the nerve to wedge herself between Nick and me, and pointed her date to the opposite end where he got stuck sitting next to Hank, who tossed me a *What the hell?* look. Kendall climbing up those steep steps and walking through piles of hay in spike-heeled boots and skin-tight jeans was mind-boggling, and yet she managed with ease. She looked like she was off to a very stylish rodeo instead of a community Halloween event. Despite all that, she was living up to her maneater reputation, arriving with a date only to abandon him when someone more interesting caught her eye.

Kendall reached out and patted Nick on the knee, smiling seductively at him. "Hey, babe, didn't expect to see you here tonight." Her poor date squirmed uncomfortably.

I tossed her a dirty look. "Kendall, I didn't know you were into hay and horse poop."

She tossed her hair and lifted her nose in the air, being careful to smile at Nick all the while. "Who doesn't like a romantic moonlight hayride?"

Nick casually moved her hand off his knee. "Introduce us to your college friend, Kendall."

College? *I* didn't even pick up on that one. "How did…?" I asked.

"Duh," Nick said, cutting me off before I could finish the question, and pointed to the guy's sweatshirt. "Ball State University."

Yeah, okay, I missed that. I looked longingly at the emblem of the school I'd wanted to attend practically all my life. And then the next two passengers stepped on board: Sara Davis and Katherine Howard. Could this night get any worse?

Sara sat down right next to Jeff, grinned at him, and thought *Agnes has straw in her hair.* Sara didn't know one twin from the other.

Katherine sat down in an empty space across from Sara, Jeff and Jane. *Halloween is the devil's day* kept roaming through her mind, making me wonder why she'd agreed to come to a Halloween hayride, but Sara could be pretty persuasive when she wanted something.

The last two people to climb in were Flip and James, who settled themselves near the front next to Katherine. Glad for the company of a couple of friendly faces, I stood up and waved at them as they took their seats.

Flip called out, "Hey, Emma, Hank."

"And friends," Hattie shouted back.

"Oh, Harriet," Flip said with a wink as he scooted down into the hay, "didn't see you there."

"Nice to see you, too, *Philip*!" Hattie laughed a little too loudly at her own joke, but her mood was still somber and I kept listening for her thoughts to find out why she was so unhappy.

Get outta my head.

"Sorry," I whispered. "Can we talk later?"

The stile steps were pulled away, the gate to the tractor bed was closed, and the engine revved. We took off on our ride, making a wide circle until we were facing due north, into the cold, so I slid down and shoved my feet under some loose hay.

There was a full moon out, adding to the eeriness, but that was the only light we had since the tractor's headlights had been shut off. While we were moving, Nick stood up to do one of those exaggerated stretches, and in response to the driver's "Everyone please stay seated!" managed to sit back down again between me and Hattie, nudging out Kendall. Nick stretched his arms over his head and they came to rest on the back rail of the tractor, one arm behind Hattie and one arm behind me. His right sleeve got pushed up a little and I got a better look at that tattoo I saw the first day I met him. It looked like Chinese, or maybe Japanese, or maybe just a bunch of hieroglyphics. I wondered if that chicken scratching meant something or if it was just a bad ink job. Before I could ask him, Hank leaned around me and scowled at Nick, who removed his tattooed arm from behind me.

I'm cold, he doesn't like me, I wish I'd never agreed to this... was what I was picking up from Hattie. I stole a quick glance in her direction, but she headed me off with *full moon, trick-or-treat, fall leaves, horse poop* and deliberately looked away. I was confused. She'd begged me to set up this date with Nick, and now she regretted it. When I glanced Nick's way I saw him staring off at the stars and not paying attention to Hattie either. I decided it was time for a strategic move. I checked to make sure the driver wasn't looking, then got down into the hay and scooted little by little until I made my way over near Hank, leaving Hattie and Nick sitting side-by-side again. Hank gave me a big smile when I settled in next to him.

I was happy to be on this ride with Hank, but some of my friends didn't seem quite as enthused. Nick seemed to be enjoying the ride but completely uninterested in Hattie, while Hattie was slumped down on the hay, her arms wrapped tightly around herself. Kendall kept resting her hand on Nick's knee, which he repeatedly pushed away, and poor college guy sat all alone, staring off into the distance. Jane and Jeff were huddled together, leaving a big gap between Jeff and Sara as she glared at him, and if looks could kill... I even felt a little sorry for Katherine, because she had her eyes closed, her lips moving, and I kept getting snippets of *deliver us from evil.* At least one couple was getting into the spirit of a moonlit hayride, though, because Flip's eyes were wide with anticipation as he reached over to clasp James's hand.

It was pretty quiet out, with the exception of a few giggles from the passengers and a dog howling off in the distance. Or was that a coyote? I shuddered involuntarily and Hank put a protective arm around me. Then, from seemingly nowhere, we heard hoof beats emerge from the edge of the nearby wooded area. Sitting atop a huge horse was The Headless Horseman himself, a larger-than-life rider with a cape concealing the top of his head and a carved jack-o-lantern stuck to the saddle's pommel, charging directly at us. Girls screamed and guys laughed nervously, and then he was right there behind us, the horse whinnying and raring up on its back legs, so close that I could feel the horse's hot breath on the back of my neck. The rider was a little too big and too real for my tastes. After a few more ghostly wails from our visitor, he vanished into the ether. Or rather, back into the woods. Hank gave my shoulder a squeeze before releasing me. I didn't want to be released.

Whoops and hollers went up from everyone on the hayride, and the tractor turned to make its way back to drop us off so it could pick up the next load of people eager to be scared out of their wits.

The tractor parked, the stile was reattached, and people began to disembark. As Hank was helping me down, I heard Sara's loud voice behind me.

"These tickets were expensive! Total ripoff," she groused to Katherine.

I turned around and forced a smile. "Did you and Katherine enjoy the ride?"

I would have except for Agnes canoodling Jeff. "It was lame," she harrumphed.

An idea came to me, one I wasn't sure would work, but I decided to try. I waved over Sara's head. "Bye Jeff, bye Jane! Hope you had fun."

Sara's eyes got wide, but her surprise was nothing compared with Jeff's. He turned to his date. "Jane? I asked Emma to fix me up with Agnes."

"Oops," Jane giggled.

"Not cool, Jane," Jeff said.

Sara and Jeff exchanged glances, Jeff glared at his faux date before stomping off ahead of her, and I wanted to shout "Hallelujah!"

****

It was the first Monday of November after Halloween, but I hadn't heard from Hattie so I didn't know what really happened between her and Nick. Or what *didn't* happen. I'd sent her a couple of texts over the weekend but she never responded. So I stood idly in front of my locker before school, killing time till she came by, hoping she'd spill.

"Look who it is. Miss Match." Hattie narrowed her eyes at me.

"Come on Hattie. I can set up dates, but how they go is out of my hands."

"Maybe you should do more than root around in people's heads before setting them up," Hattie retorted.

"If you'll recall, I didn't dig that information out of your mind. You asked, no, begged me to set up the date."

Her shoulders slumped. "Point taken."

"So what happened?"

Hattie sighed. "He was the perfect gentleman, picking me up in his car…"

"What kind of car?" I asked with a bit too much interest.

"BMW, like I care. Opening the passenger door for me, asking about family, basketball, yada yada yada."

"What's wrong with that?"

"Before I could answer, he started spouting a bunch of basketball stats right off the top of his head, and you'd think that would be a conversation starter, but I just froze." *After that, all he wanted to talk about was you.*

Well, that was interesting, the part she didn't say. I was sorry it didn't work out for them, sort of, but I wondered if maybe Nick really did like me. He'd told me repeatedly that he wanted to go on that hayride with me instead of Hattie, but since I couldn't read his mind, I couldn't be sure if he thought of me as a potential girlfriend or wanted to keep me in the friend zone.

And then there was Hank. Despite his thoughts being elusive, his actions always showed me that he cared. If only he would either think them or voice them out loud. But what if Hank and Rachel...?

Even though Nick was intriguing, I was hesitant to get involved with a guy who could potentially listen in on *my* thoughts.

I sighed. "Anybody else you're interested in?"

Hattie scowled and walked off.

Chapter 5

Final exams in mid-December were serious business to high school seniors. College acceptance letters didn't come out till early in the New Year, so failing first semester senior classes could get you kicked off a university's admissions list or see scholarship offers withdrawn. My scholarship was secure but limited, so I needed to forget about matchmaking for the time being and focus on my B average if I had any hope of being accepted into the school of my choice.

I was really the only person in school who'd gotten to know Nick even a little bit. I saw a lot of him during school hours, but never evenings or weekends. Actually, no one ever saw Nick outside of school unless it was at a volunteer event, like the pet shelter or that Habitat for Humanity build. Sometimes I would see him during student resource period, but he was never studying. He surfed the net or helped other kids, who then raved about his tutoring skills, so it wasn't like he was dumb or anything. I caught him doodling a lot in Miss Taylor's classroom, making me concerned about how his grades would turn out, which would limit his college prospects. Maybe the rumor mill had been right, that he got expelled from that private school up near Chicago because he wouldn't do his work. If so, he brought his bad habits with him.

"How are final exams going?" I asked him in Miss

Taylor's class.

Nick shrugged, grinned, and went back to whatever he was looking at online.

Occasionally I'd see him across the cafeteria during lunch, but he rarely sat with us at the senior table, preferring to work the room, socialize, and get to know more kids. He was always laughing and having fun with whoever invited him to join them. He was thoroughly enjoying all aspects of high school, except the part where he should be focusing on academics and graduation.

****

After exams were over and the semester ended, I could finally relax, confident that I'd made decent grades and my miniscule scholarship would remain safe. Isabelle was determined to make Christmas nice for her, me and Jonathan, which helped fill the void of Dad's absence. She bought me designer jeans and a white cashmere sweater she swore she got at a Black Friday sale, and wrapped it festively with lots of crinkly ribbons and pretty paper. I spent an entire paycheck from my daycare job buying her some expensive bath soaps and body lotions from the mall, and a coffee shop gift card for Jonathan. Still, all Christmas Day my mind kept replaying last year.

Dad and I never had a whole lot financially, but our family was together and that had always seemed enough. Little did I know last December twenty-fifth that my world would soon fall apart. After the holidays my father became more and more withdrawn, gave up caring about his appearance, and then I noticed he was hanging around the house a lot in the middle of the day. I asked him why he wasn't at the office, and he said he was working online to get ready for tax season. I accepted that explanation until I got home from school on Valentine's Day, and all I found was an empty house and a note.

So I breathed a sigh of relief when Christmas was over this year. I could forget about the past and concentrate on New Year's.

Usually New Year's Eve was considered an adult holiday, but teens liked to celebrate, too. With school out for winter break, a few kids had reached out to me for help finding a date for The Big Party being held at one of those McMansions on the west side of town. The house belonged to one of the Indianapolis Colts football players, Todd Bekins, who happened to be Mary Bekins' older brother. He was hosting the party not only for his friends but some of his sister's, too. To avoid party crashers or paparazzi, Mary deliberately stayed off social media and instead sent out personal email invitations that hit inboxes on the day school dismissed for winter break. Most kids were fried from final exams and had family obligations for Christmas, so buzz about the party didn't get big until afterwards.

Mary texted me that she'd wanted to ask Greg Plowman, but he was going to be out of town with his family, so she needed a date to her own party. Naturally she wanted Nick Knight. So did both Bates twins, Allison Baker, Jennifer Ward and Katherine Howard, who seemed to have gotten over her embarrassment from that day in student resource time. Even though I didn't hear from Kendall Maneater, uh Manheim, she never needed my help finding a date anyway, and for all I knew she'd already asked Nick on her own. I'd heard Sara Davis was out of town for the holidays, so I breathed a sigh of relief.

Hattie was conspicuously absent from the list of girls wanting to date Nick, but after their lackluster Halloween date I understood why she didn't want to try again. I wondered if she'd show up for the party stag, or would skip it altogether. I thought about asking Hank to be my date, but his family had their Hanukkah traditions and I rarely saw much of him in December anyway, so it didn't surprise me that I hadn't heard from him about Mary and Todd's New Year's Eve party. Since Hank was maintaining cyber-silence, it occurred to me that I could ask Nick to be my date, since he hadn't objected when Kendall asked him out last October.

I needed to find out if Nick already had a date before I went any further with my plans or my wishful thinking, but I realized I had no way of getting in touch with him. He wouldn't give out his cell number, and if there was a landline I hadn't been able to find it. I even tried stalking him on social media. He wasn't there either.

It was the day before New Year's Eve and I was getting desperate. I scrolled through all the texts I'd ever received about Nick, including the gossip about his supposedly nefarious past and speculation on how he spent weekends. (Reporting to his narc handler? Medical checkups for his terminal illness? Meeting with his probation officer? Private tutoring so he'd pass senior year?) I finally landed on a thread involving Hattie, Flip and James, where James mentioned he'd spotted Nick picking up carryout at a local Mexican restaurant and he'd been wearing scrubs. So, hospital volunteer? Yeah, that sounded about right. But before I went chasing off across town to St. Anthony's, I decided to check in with Hank. Maybe he'd planned to invite me to the party, assuming I'd be available at the last minute, and I didn't want to disappoint him.

I sent a text. *How was your holiday? You going to Mary's party?*

Great thanks, and yeah, with Rachel.

I gasped. Rachel Bomburg? Have they been seeing each other over the holidays? Of course they have. They attend the same Synagogue, and their parents are friends. That left me totally weirded out, thinking about him with that other girl he had so much in common with. I was both mad and hurt, but I typed in a breezy *See ya there.* So now I definitely had to find a date for myself, because it would be too embarrassing to show up stag. Date-wrangling for myself had always been a little tricky, since I could never be sure of a guy's feelings for me if he didn't voice them or think them on the spot, and I didn't like rejection any more than any other girl. What if Nick rejected me, too? I'd have to risk it.

St. Anthony's was a couple of miles away from the condo where we live, not an insurmountable distance, but late December in Indiana wasn't for sissies. Isabelle was out showing houses, I didn't drive, there was no bus service up here in suburbia, and after Christmas gifts and being off work for nearly two weeks, I didn't even have enough cash for a ride share. That left only one way to get there, and I'd have to layer on plenty of clothing if I was going to walk that far in the cold. I started with long underwear under my jeans, two long-sleeve shirts under Jonathan's thick hoodie sweatshirt, and then I squeezed all those layers into my heavy pea coat. I tied a scarf around my neck, pulled on some faux-fir lined boots, put on two pair of gloves and headed out the door.

By the time I arrived at the hospital an hour later, I was shivering and chilled to the bone. If I wanted to avoid frostbite, I'd definitely need to do some serious warming up before I started the trek back home. I pulled open the heavy glass doors and hurried into the warm lobby, stomping my feet and rubbing my hands together to get the feeling back, while I scouted out the overhead signs for directions. I planned to start in the gift shop and failing that, ask around to see if anyone knew Nick Knight.

"You're not sick are you?"

I jumped around in surprise to see Nick standing right behind me. He was wearing scrubs with a long-sleeved shirt underneath, not what I'd think a gift shop volunteer would wear, but what do I know. "No, I'm fine. Well, I'm kinda cold, but I'll warm up. James mentioned that…"

"That I volunteer here," he finished for me. "I was just on my way to the cafeteria. Come on, I'll buy you a coffee."

A hot beverage was just what I needed, so I gratefully trotted alongside him. Nick steered me down hallway after hallway through a maze of corridors, and pretty soon I smelled food. He sprang for two coffees, filled both with cream and sugar, and then we sat down at an empty booth. After a few swallows I was finally able to shed my coat.

"Better?" Nick asked.

I nodded as I inhaled the aroma of freshly brewed coffee and let the steam warm my face. *How do I act casual and still ask him without looking too desperate?*

Nick blew on his hot beverage. "What did you want to ask me?"

My head popped up and if I could see myself, I'd bet I had shock written all over my face. "How…?"

He smiled. "Well, I figured if you came all this way looking for me, you had something to ask me. Date night again?"

I rolled my eyes because he always had a way of making it seem so logical. "Mary Bekins' New Year's Eve party."

"I already have a date."

Ohmigod I have the worst luck! "Kendall?" I cringed.

Nick grinned at me, my disappointment dissolving into a puddle of mush. "Nope. Kendall and I didn't really hit it off."

Well that was a relief. "Then who?"

"Actually, I'm just hoping I have a date. I haven't actually set it up yet..."

Maybe there's still a chance...

"...and I hope I haven't missed my chance," Nick said.

Gulp. If this was just another coincidence, it was a bit much. He leaned in across the table and lowered his voice. "I agreed to go on that date with Hattie to make you happy, when all I really wanted was to go out with you. So will you go to the New Year's Eve party with me?"

My heart started pounding and my stomach did flip-flops. The hayride was a couple of months ago, so I figured he'd lost interest. "Me?"

"Yeah, you. I heard that Hank's going with some girl from his church, so I hoped you didn't already have a date. Sorry to be so late asking, but what d'ya say? Sounds like a cool party."

From what Mary told me, it was going to be awesome. "Um, well," I hedged, "Mary said something about wanting to ask you and I told her…"

Nick sighed. "I already told Mary I have a date, but I promised her you'd find just the right guy for her. Please don't make a liar out of me, on either count."

"Well, I guess…" *Did I just agree…?*

"You agree to go to the party with me?"

And there it was again. I was going out of my mind trying to figure out what he was doing. "Okay, you're reading my mind again, aren't you?" I tried in vain to tune in to his thoughts, but all I "heard" was something that sounded like scientific jargon. I glanced around at all the medical personnel in the vicinity and figured I was picking it up from one of them. And Nick looked so innocent. I've never met anyone else who could do what I do, and even though I wasn't completely sure that's what he was doing, I was still suspicious.

"We've had this discussion before," Nick said, eyeing me over the top of his coffee mug. "Mind-reading isn't a scientific possibility. It's all just body language and probabilities."

I rolled my eyes. "Yeah, so you've said." I took a sip of my cooling coffee.

Nick swallowed the last of his beverage and grinned at me. "You haven't answered me yet. About the party."

I relaxed and smiled back, sticky paranormal subject avoided. "Yes, I'll go with you." But, wait. *Who can I get for Mary?*

"By the way, I hear Greg Plowman's staying in town after all."

I lifted an eyebrow at him. Even if he thought hearing thoughts wasn't possible, he was doing it. Or some version of it. "How do you know?"

"Oh, I hear all the gossip," Nick said.

That didn't tell me how he was getting his info, but he was right about Mary and Greg. They hit it off Homecoming. Maybe Greg figured Mary had already gotten a date to her own party. Or maybe as a football player himself, he had a case of nerves at the thought of being around Todd Bekins and the other professional players. I pulled my phone out and sent Greg a text. My phone pinged right back with a text from Greg accepting the date, so I fired off one to Mary and stashed my phone back in my pocket.

"So now that that's settled," Nick said, "I'll pick you up at nine."

I smiled to myself. I couldn't believe that I was the one getting the date with Nick Knight. There would be lots of jealous girls there, but for once I didn't care. "Sounds great."

"And if you can wait around for about an hour till I'm finished here, I'll drive you home. It's like ten degrees outside."

I tilted my head. "What is it you do here anyway?"

He let his eyes wander around the room, avoiding eye contact with me. "Oh, this and that." He stood and gathered the empty mugs. "So can you wait?"

I nodded, thinking how cold it was outside, but then I wondered what I was going to do for an hour.

"There are a bunch of magazines in the lobby," Nick said.

I shot him a look as we parted company.

Chapter 6

"You're going where?" Isabelle was incredulous.

I pulled my pea coat out of the hall closet. "To a New Year's Eve party at Todd Bekins' house. I know his sister Mary from school." I was trying to sound nonchalant, but seriously, I was pretty psyched about getting to hang out with actual NFL players, plus arrive on the arm of the hottest guy at Melville High. I was wearing the sweater and jeans Isabelle gave me for Christmas, and I thought I looked pretty good in them. Maybe Hank would even be a little jealous, unless he only had eyes for Rachel.

Isabelle shook her head. *No supervision I bet.*

"Isabelle," I said rolling my eyes like a little kid, "Todd's an adult, plus some of his teammates and their wives will be there. Plenty of supervision."

My sister narrowed her eyes at me. "Are you sure? No sneaking champagne at midnight?"

"Yes, I'm sure. Mary says her brother doesn't even drink during football season, so they'll be passing around sparkling cider."

Isabelle let that sit a moment before something popped into her head. *That PGA golf tournament!* Huh? She must have known I was reading her random thoughts, so she grinned at me. "Todd Bekins lives near that country club with the famous golf course, right?" I nodded. "Those million dollar houses rarely come up for sale, and the only way a realtor gets a listing is by referral."

"Okay, so…?"

She opened a drawer in the entry hall table and pulled out a handful of her business cards. "Here, just in case any of those pro football players are looking to buy. Or sell."

I doubted the subject would come up, but since I owed Isabelle big time, I stuffed the cards in my pants pocket just in case. I peered out through the narrow glass window in the door to watch for Nick.

"Is Hank coming to the door for you this time, or just honking?"

"Hank's got a date with someone else tonight," I told her as I continued watching the parking lot from the door, "so I'm going with Nick."

The hot guy from the Homecoming Dance?

"Yeah, him."

There was a knock at the door and Isabelle heaved a huge sigh of exasperation as she reached around me to open it. "Hi, Nick." She smiled at him and motioned him in. "Good to see you again." *Lucky girl. Hope he's a good kisser.*

I blushed. Then I looked at Nick. Was he blushing, too, or was his face red from the chill outside?

"Nice to see you again, Mrs. Calloway." Nick helped me on with my coat.

"Oh, please. Call me Isabelle. What time will you two be home?"

I tossed her a pleading look. "One?"

She pretended to give that some thought but I could tell she was okay with it. "Make sure you've got your key, Emma. Jonathan and I may be out a bit later than that, so text me when you get home."

"Have a nice time at your husband's company party," Nick said, and opened the door for me.

Isabelle and I glanced at each other in surprise. *Did you tell him?* She silently asked me. I mouthed a silent "no." She turned her gaze on Nick.

Nick shrugged. "I mean, I just figured. You wearing that nice cocktail dress, big law firm like Mr. Calloway's must be throwing a New Year's Eve party."

It couldn't be that simple. Could it? Again Isabelle and I exchanged meaningful glances, but I didn't have a logical explanation for this.

Nick held open the passenger door to his late-model, shiny white Beemer with its luxurious leather seats, slid into the driver's side, and we were off.

****

"Are we late?" I asked Nick. Todd's driveway was four deep in cars and more were parked all up and down the street of this tony Indianapolis neighborhood.

The time on the dashboard read nine seventeen p.m. "I guess everyone else was more punctual," Nick said. He ended up parking a half a block away and we had to hike back up a hill in the frigid night air. As we exhaled, the condensation hung like a vapor cloud.

I looked around at the neighboring homes that sell in the upper six digits and understood why Isabelle would want a listing or sale here. Some were built mid-twentieth century, some much newer, and each one had a unique architectural style and expansive landscaped lawn. Todd's house appeared to be one of the newer builds.

I stomped my feet on the porch trying to get some circulation going when someone finally answered the doorbell. It was Todd Bekins himself, and maybe I was a little star struck, but he looked even better in person than as a receiver on the field at Lucas Oil Stadium. The grey silk shirt he was wearing was stretched taut over his bulging biceps, and his black Polo leather belt accentuated his trim midline, which in turn drew the eye down to his well-defined quads. Todd was a rookie, first round draft pick from Notre Dame University, rich, single, and very handsome. He and Mary looked a lot alike. Mary wore her thick black hair tied back in a ponytail most of the time, and like her brother she was short with a muscular build, but her sport of choice was gymnastics. They both had light caramel skin since they were the products of a mixed marriage.

"Welcome," Todd said, inviting us in with a flourish of well-toned arms. "Coats go in the guest bedroom down the hall."

Nick helped me off with my coat. "I'll take them."

I stepped out of the entry area into a very large living room and took a good look around. There was a reason these houses commanded such high prices, because every inch of this place seemed to be constructed with the highest quality material. But this was definitely a bachelor pad. There was only one small, beat up sofa facing the flat screen TV over the gas fireplace, a secondhand coffee table with a faded and stained Notre Dame area rug under it that looked like it came from Todd's dorm room, and two worn, brown leather recliners. In the kitchen all I could see were some bar stools pulled up to the center island, and a Keurig coffee pot next to the built-in stainless steel oven. I was pretty sure Todd could afford to furnish the place if he wanted to, so I wondered why he hadn't hired someone. That was when I remembered Isabelle's business card tucked into my pocket. I'd be sure to give one to Todd.

The lack of furnishings made me wonder where everyone was going to sit tonight, because I knew Mary was expecting a large turnout. However, the only people I saw were Jane and Agnes Bates standing in front of the faux fire, chatting it up with fraternal twins Sam and Darrin O'Brien.

Mary was flitting around the kitchen setting out food trays. Her email invitation said her brother was having the party catered by an expensive Italian restaurant in Indianapolis. I watched as Mary pulled dishes of antipasto and salad from the double-sided fridge and set them on the center island. Then she artfully arranged the homemade Italian bread slices on a large platter, next to several choices of steaming pasta dishes in warming pans on the marble kitchen counters, and lastly she uncovered a dessert concoction that was drizzled with chocolate squiggles and smelled of brandy. Greg Plowman was standing helplessly by, watching her work. Mary elbowed him out of her way and pulled a stack of decorative paper plates out of a solid-wood cabinet, then opened a drawer where you'd expect to see silverware, but in true bachelor style, contained plastic cutlery. She set all those items on the counter next to the food and stepped back to admire her handiwork.

"Emma," Mary squealed when she glanced up. She took Greg by the arm and dragged him across the room with her. "Where's Nick?" *That guy's a hunk!*

"He took our coats." I wondered what was taking Nick so long, but I felt pretty smug about being here with him. "Nice party," I said as my eyes drifted to the food. I realized my stomach was growling.

Who cares about Nick what's-his-name? The rookie quarterback's favorite receiver's around here somewhere and I'm stuck talking to girls. Greg was leaning against the kitchen island, arms folded, scowling.

I smiled. "Hey, Greg, you shouldn't be stuck here with two high school girls. Go talk to some of those professional athletes."

Greg gave me a brief look of surprise but then breathed a visible sigh of relief. Without another word, he was off in search of more stimulating conversation.

Come to think of it, as I looked around the large living space, I realized there weren't very many people here at all - only the two sets of twins, Mary, her brother Todd playing host at the front door, and Greg who had disappeared. But there were all those cars outside. I opened my mouth to ask Mary where everyone was hanging out, but I didn't get my question out before the doorbell rang again. Seemed someone was even more fashionably late than Nick and I.

Todd opened the door and motioned in the new arrivals. I couldn't help noticing the once-over he gave Kendall as she flounced in on the arm of some cute guy I didn't recognize, maybe another college student. She gifted Todd with a beaming smile and a flip of her mane, and then did a quick survey of the room. *Where are the rest of the football players?*

Huh. She arrived on the arm of one hot guy, had the party host gawking at her, and was disappointed that other hot guys weren't around to ooh and ahh over her grand entrance. I resisted the urge to roll my eyes as Kendall removed her tight leather jacket to reveal a black sweater shimmering with sequins hanging off one shoulder, exposing a lacy red bra. I had to face facts, she was gorgeous and I was jealous. I just hoped she kept her hands off Nick tonight and focused on her date. I glanced his way and felt bad for him when I heard *What did I get myself into?*

As I turned away from Kendall, I saw Hank in the kitchen and followed him in. "I'm glad to see you," I said with an affectionate squeeze of his arm.

He smiled at me warmly as he dished food onto his paper plate. "I'm starved." He popped a black olive in his mouth and took a bite of pasta.

"Where's Rachel?"

Hank took his time chewing and swallowing, while I eagerly awaited his thoughts.

"Talking to Hattie, last I saw," he said.

Hattie? "I didn't know she was coming tonight. Does she have..."

"A date?" Hank shrugged. "I think she's meeting someone here."

And speaking of dates..."Hank, what made you invite Rachel tonight?"

"Oh, her other plans..."

"Hey, tiramisu!" Darrin O'Brien spotted the rich dessert that Mary had just set out and made a beeline across the room, cutting off our conversation as he reached right between Hank and me to grab a plate.

Frustrated, I stepped aside and let Darrin dish up an ample portion of dessert. I scouted out the room as it dawned on me that Nick never returned from dropping off our coats. I hadn't seen Hattie at all, and Kendall and her nameless date were now gone, too. Even the Bates twins and Darrin's brother Sam were MIA. In fact, this room was looking pretty empty, and I didn't just mean the decor.

"Where did everyone go?" I asked Hank.

"There's a pool table in the basement," he said as he forked up another bite of lasagna. "That's where you can find your less-than-attentive date."

I slapped my forehead, metaphorically of course, as I spotted the open doorway that revealed a flight of stairs. "C'mon, let's go!" Hank reluctantly shoved his plate aside and allowed me to lead him down the basement steps.

Now I saw where the party was happening. There was another whole house down there, complete with a second living room, a full wet bar, pool table off in a far corner, and from my vantage point at the bottom of the stairs, I spotted a couple of bedrooms and a bathroom down the hall. This must be where all Todd's furniture money went, because everything down here was new and modern. Flip and James were parked on a luxurious brown leather sectional sofa watching some sporting event on the biggest flat screen TV I'd ever seen. Agnes and Jane were with Sam O'Brien as his brother Darrin, dessert plate and four forks in hand, rejoined them. Greg Plowman had cornered a guy who looked beefy enough to be a pro linebacker, and Kendall was working the room, flirting with every man in sight and seemingly oblivious to the glares from their women. And seated at two barstools with their heads together, I was shocked to see Sara Davis and her partner-in-crime, Katherine Howard. Guess more than one family changed their holiday plans.

It was a really crowded space and frankly a little too warm. It was also pretty loud, what with the volume on the game turned up, an iPod blasting a succession of rap or R&B tunes, and all the excited jabbering as people whooped it up over a football play on TV or cheered on the guys playing pool. I hoped Sara and Katherine wouldn't notice me.

Mary jumped up onto the bar and shouted, "Two hours till midnight," which was received with several "whoo-hoos."

Nick was at the pool table in the middle of a game with Todd. "Over there," I shouted to Hank.

I put Hank between me and the two girls I wanted to avoid at the bar and got close enough to watch the pool game for a minute. Nick was playing with the skill of a hustler. He lined up his shot, looked up and caught my eye, winked, and without missing a beat sank the ball in the pocket. Todd groaned and racked 'em up for another game.

I felt a tap on the shoulder. "Hey, bestie."

Hattie looked really pretty, like she was out to impress someone. Who, I wasn't sure. She'd abandoned her jersey workout pants in favor of a plush grey sweater over blue jeans, and her hair was shoved behind her ears to reveal a pair of diamond studs I'd never seen before. Plus she'd put on a little mascara and lipstick, which I hadn't seen her do since Homecoming.

I gave her a quick hug as she scooted past me, allowing me to see that Hank now had his arm draped casually around Rachel. My stomach lurched. The girl looked even better than her social media pictures, and tonight she'd traded in her contacts for stylish glasses that made her look really smart and sophisticated.

I tried not to frown at Hank and Rachel as Hattie sidled up to a tall, dark-haired guy who looked vaguely familiar, and slipped her arm through his. "Oh, Emma, you remember Robbie Martin, right?"

Robbie Martin? I sucked in my breath. Wow! He had definitely improved in the looks department since I last saw him in eighth grade. He was dressed in grey trousers and a pullover sweater, his black hair pulled back in a man-bun. Robbie had probably grown a foot taller, and was now eye-to-eye with Hattie.

"Yeah, I remember Robbie," I said through clenched teeth.

Back in middle school, once Hattie finally accepted that Hank was a lost cause, she started having mushy thoughts about Robbie Martin. He was a nerdy-looking violin prodigy, and *his* only thoughts were about Mozart. She went to all his concerts, sitting front and center and applauding wildly. He, in turn, never went to any of her basketball games, always claiming he had rehearsal or a private lesson or something. But Hattie liked him and she was my friend, so I tried to be supportive. When his parents decided to transfer him to St. Malachi across town to further his musical education, Hattie was distraught. She begged Robbie to stay in touch, but of course he never did. And now there he was, looking hot and sophisticated, and there was Hattie all love-struck again.

"Robbie's parents are long-time friends of the Bekins' so Mary invited him," she explained, gazing up into his eyes. *Isn't he adorable?*

"Hattie, can I talk to you?" I didn't wait for an answer but dragged her past the stairs and around the corner to an empty bedroom. "Robbie Martin of all people? Hattie…"

She shrugged. "Don't worry, I'm not dating him. But it's just so good to see him again." She giggled and pushed past me.

Between seeing Hank with another girl, my best friend crushing on an emotionally-unavailable guy, and being ignored by my date, I suddenly didn't feel so good. Was it something I ate? Oh, yeah, I hadn't eaten anything at all. Maybe that was the problem. Nick and Hank were both occupied, Hank with his arm still around Rachel watching Nick the pool shark. So I headed upstairs alone to the kitchen, which was now completely deserted. I thought about the events of the evening as I filled my plate and took a few slow bites. Things weren't working out very well.

I decided to take my food back to the basement, hoping to either lure Nick away from the pool table or distract Hank. Unfortunately the pool game was still on, and Hank and Rachel had moved to the sofa, laughing and talking. Sara and Katherine hadn't moved and were either ignoring me or waiting to pounce, and Hattie had her arm looped through Robbie Martin's. I didn't know what was up with my appetite, but suddenly I wasn't hungry at all. I tossed the paper plate and all its contents into a trash bin.

Todd lost another game of pool and handed the stick to Kendall's boy toy, who stepped up to try to beat the reigning champ, Nick Knight. Kendall wasn't paying attention to her date because she was too busy working the room.

Man she's HOT! was what I picked up from somewhere, and then whoever he was chided himself with *Cut it out. Jailbait.*

I followed the direction of those thoughts and saw Todd eyeing Kendall with an appreciative eye. That was the second time he'd noticed her, uh, charms, so I sidled up to him and whispered, "She's almost nineteen."

Todd looked at me, surprised on more than one level. "Yeah, but she's in school with my sister."

"Kendall usually dates older guys," I told him with a tilt of my head in the direction of her date. "Let me introduce you." I headed her way, glancing back to make sure he followed me across the room. He did. "Kendall, Todd wants to meet you."

"Ohhh," she cooed, "I've been hoping to talk to you. I just love watching you on TV." At that she put her hand with the long manicured fingernails on his bicep and squeezed just a little as Todd grinned and blushed.

Before I left Kendall to work her new prey, I remembered my promise to Isabelle. "Hey, Todd," I said as I placed one of her business cards in his free hand, "my sister's a realtor and she also does interior design. From what I saw upstairs…"

"Yeah yeah," Todd said, not taking his eyes off Kendall. "Mary keeps bugging me about that." He shoved Isabelle's card in his pocket before turning his full attention to the maneater. Well, I could truthfully tell my sister that I tried.

I hadn't spent any time with Nick the entire evening. He finally finished playing pool to let other, less skilled players have a turn, but before I could make my way over to him, he got waylaid by some twentysomething woman with a big rock on her left hand.

Nick reached up and over a few people to take my hand and drew me near him. "Emma, have you met Reese Fowler? Her husband's a rookie running back."

"No." I turned to face her. "Nice to meet you."

How can I snag you for the charity fashion show was what Mrs. Fowler was thinking as she sized Nick up, but what she said was, "Your pool playing is very impressive, Nick."

Before she had a chance to sign him on for her volunteer project, I jerked his arm and pulled him away. "Nick, are we on a date tonight or what?"

He smiled at me. "Of course we are. But when Todd asked me to join him for a game of pool, I couldn't say no. He's the host."

"And you didn't tell him you're a pool shark."

Nick shrugged with a wickedly cute grin. I melted.

It was five minutes till midnight and everyone was scurrying around getting ready for the countdown. Todd turned the TV to the channel that broadcasts from New York City where they drop the big glass ball from some skyscraper in Times Square, and Mary and Greg were rushing around filling everyone's glasses with sparkling cider. Todd put out noisemakers and poppers on top of the bar, and everyone grabbed a handful and paired up with their dates or significant others, planning to ring in the New Year with a kiss. I reached behind me to clasp Nick's hand and – shocker – he was gone again.

"One minute to midnight," declared the TV announcer. All eyes in the basement were glued to the television as the last seconds of the old year ticked down. But where had my date gone? A quick glance around the room made me want to cry because Kendall had thrown her arms around Nick's neck. "Ten seconds, folks," said the TV guy. "Five, four, three, two, one. Happy New Year!"

Auld Lang Syne played on TV, and everyone in the room kissed someone. Everyone except me, Sara and Katherine. How awful was it to get lumped in with those two? First I spotted Hattie kissing Robbie a little too enthusiastically. I hated that she was getting her hopes up again. Jane was kissing Sam while Agnes kissed Darrin. Okay, that worked. Mary got a quick buss on the lips from Greg, while Todd clinked glasses with some of his teammates and their wives. I watched as he glanced around the room, probably trying to find Kendall, but unfortunately for both Todd and me, Nick and Kendall were in a lip lock. Seriously? Todd shrugged, but tears flooded my eyes. Nick begged me to come with him tonight, yet there I stood, all alone at midnight while he kissed another girl. And not just any girl. Kendall. I checked across the room and watched Rachel peck Hank on the cheek before going over to toast with Mrs. Fowler. Not exactly a romantic scenario. Were they just friends, or did Hank want more? I still didn't know.

"I saw what you did," Sara said.

I rolled my eyes before turning around. "What are you accusing me of now, Sara?"

"You listened to Todd's thoughts and then introduced him to Kendall. Didn't work out too well, though," she snickered.

I glowered at her. "Body language, Sara. Didn't you see the way he was eyeing her?" That wasn't an exaggeration, and I couldn't be the only person who noticed Todd's attraction to Kendall.

To avoid all the amorous revelers, put distance between me and Sara with her unfortunately accurate observation, and get even with Nick, I climbed across the sofa and planted a big kiss on Hank. Oddly enough, he kissed me back.

The noisemakers were cranked and poppers went off, everybody toasting with their cider and shouting, "Happy New Year!"

"Happy New Year," Hank whispered in my ear, giving me goose bumps.

I was really confused. After all, Hank blew me off to bring Rachel to this party. I thought I was so lucky that Nick invited me to be his date, and yet I just shared an incredible kiss with Hank.

Suddenly Nick was by my side. "I'm so sorry," he said, his face in a scowl. "Kendall grabbed me and kissed me before I realized what was happening."

Yeah, a gorgeous girl sucks face with you and you don't fight her off. Shocking. But before I could say anything, Nick pulled me close and belatedly gave me a long, slow, romantic kiss. "Forgive me?"

"Why should I?"

Out of the corner of my eye I spotted Kendall kissing Todd, which gave me a little satisfaction, until I saw a dejected Hank climbing the stairs, alone. That was like a stab to my heart.

I was about to go after him when Nick kissed me again, and this time he didn't release me so quickly. I glanced into his big blue eyes and almost forgot I was mad, but something was niggling at me. I'd just kissed Hank and felt an unfamiliar yet incredible sensation, but then Nick kissed me not once but twice, and nothing. Shouldn't I have felt all tingly or something?

"As first dates go, this one kinda sucks," I told Nick.

He grinned and gave my arm a playful punch. "I'll make it up to you, I promise."

I needed to do some serious thinking about all this.

Chapter 7

I got a text from my school counselor the first day back from the holidays. Mr. Moore wanted to see me immediately, before first period. I could think of any number of things he might want to discuss, none of them good, so I presented myself at the Counseling Office before I even went to my locker.

"Emma," Mr. Moore said, "come in." He indicated a chair in front of the desk in his tiny office.

I squeezed myself in and glanced around. Nothing had changed since the last time I was here at the end of junior year. The walls were covered with college pennants - Indiana University, Purdue, Ball State, Notre Dame, University of Southern Indiana, and his alma mater Northwestern – and the rest of the wall space was taken up by posters with Chinese fortune cookie-type motivational quotes. *If you can dream it you can do it.* The ever-popular *Don't stop when you're tired, stop when you're done.* And the one every teacher in every school I'd ever attended had on their wall, *Aim for the moon. If you miss, you will land among the stars.*

"I wanted to discuss your SAT test results," he said.

Gulp. "I checked the scores online. They didn't look that bad."

Mr. Moore leaned his elbows on his desk and tapped his index fingers together. "Most of your scores were slightly above average, but your essay writing score was a four. Right in the middle of the range from two to eight."

I'd never been a very good writer, so that didn't surprise me. "Do I need to retake it?"

He shook his head. "What I'm suggesting is enrolling you for second semester in a Creative Writing class here at Melville High. It will help improve your writing skills and better prepare you for college. Are you still hoping to attend Ball State?"

I nodded. "Unless something changes." Social isolation came to mind. Or rejection from my number one choice.

"Your scholarship is somewhat limiting," Mr. Moore continued, "and there are only a handful of schools in Indiana that are willing to meet the criteria they set out. With your current writing skills, Ball State may hesitate to offer you admission. If we can show them improvement, your odds go up. If not…"

"Community College," I mumbled.

Mr. Moore peered at me over his glasses. "Community College has less stringent scholastic standards."

I nodded. "It's just that Sara Davis keeps spreading rumors about me, lots of kids believe her, and if my social life dwindles any more…"

He nodded. "I've seen some of Sara's handiwork. Shall I speak to her?"

"No!" My eyes widened. "I mean, no, I'll handle it. What about that writing class?"

Mr. Moore handed me a paper with my schedule change noted on it. "Mr. West's Creative Writing class. It meets second period."

"What about Student Resource?"

"That's a sacrifice you'll have to make. Do your homework before or after school." Mr. Moore wrote me a pass and sent me on my way.

I didn't know how to feel about this sudden addition to my schedule. My counselor's suggestion that I improve my writing skills made sense, but the idea of being in Mr. West's class with serious writers and journalism students like Sara gave me the quivers. I made a quick stop at my locker, and instead of hanging around to socialize, I headed straight to Family Relations, someplace I always felt safe. I was the first one there.

"Happy New Year, Miss Taylor." I walked into the room and took my usual seat. I liked Miss Taylor, but sometimes, like today, she seemed distracted.

I watched as she riffled through her desk drawers, looking for who-knows-what. Maybe she was still mentally on winter break. Fair enough. A lot of us kids were, too.

*What did I do with...*I wished she'd finish that thought, because maybe I could help find whatever it was she'd misplaced.

Hattie arrived. She took off her denim hooded jacket and hung it on the back of her chair before she plopped down in the seat next to me. A quick glance told me she was back to basketball apparel. She pulled out a notebook and pen from her book bag.

I hadn't talked to her since New Year's. Now I was afraid to bring up the subject at all, since it was possible that another rejection from Robbie Martin was the reason she'd abandoned her more stylish look for the safer athletic gear. "Ready for our last high school semester?"

"Mmmm," was all she said, if you can call that a

reply.

I concentrated really hard but Hattie was keeping her thoughts to herself. "Have you heard from Robbie?"

She gave me a withering look.

I squirmed for a moment before getting out my own pen and paper. Soon my attention was drawn back to Miss Taylor, who'd left off searching her desk and was rummaging through the file cabinet. "What's up with her?" I whispered to Hattie.

Hattie glanced over at the teacher and shrugged. "Too much partying?"

I never really pictured Miss Taylor as the partying type, but then students rarely think of teachers as having any kind of social life outside of school. She was in her early thirties and usually wore drab pants paired with nondescript sweaters. I didn't get it. If she'd wear some stylish boots instead of tennis shoes, do something with that frizzy black hair besides stick it in a pencil bun, and apply some makeup, she might even be attractive.

Other kids filed into the room, chatting with each other or on their cell phones, and took random chairs despite their first semester seat assignments. The tardy bell rang and everybody quieted down to wait for the teacher to start the lesson. But she was still looking for… whatever.

"Um, Miss Taylor?" I called out to her, followed by snickers from classmates. Even that didn't get her attention.

Where's that change for the coffee machine? she was thinking.

Oh okay. She must be jonesin' for some caffeine. "Want me to go get you some coffee?" Yeah, I know, she didn't say that out loud, but she was wasting valuable class time hunting for loose change.

Ben loaned me that money, and again I didn't know what that was supposed to mean, or who Ben was. But Miss Taylor shook her head no, took a deep breath and was finally ready to start class. "Welcome back, ladies and gentlemen. I assume you all have your textbooks with you?" There were a few groans from some forgetful students, but I had my book front and center. "Those of you without a book, you'll have to look on with someone or pull it up online. We're starting with Chapter seven, page three hundred and ten."

I opened my textbook and saw that this chapter was on parental responsibility. I frowned because that hit a little close to home. I was beginning to wish I'd gone to get the teacher her coffee after all, even if she didn't ask.

"This is a long chapter," Hattie whispered, thumbing through the pages.

"Yeah." Judging by the title, it was looking to be a very long chapter.

****

With great trepidation, I headed to my new second period Creative Writing class, in a far wing of the building I almost never went to. The idea of toiling in a class I knew I'd be bad at already had my stomach tied in knots, but as I rounded the corner near the classroom, I saw Hank and Nick having what looked like a serious discussion. I inched a little closer.

"So is it you and Emma or you and Rachel?" Nick asked. "And why were you kissing my date New Year's Eve?"

"Why were you kissing Kendall?" Hank shot back.

The two of them glared at each other, and although neither was the type to get into a hallway scuffle, they

103

both looked angry.

Hank tossed his book bag over his other shoulder as the warning bell sounded. "Look, Nick, you seem like a nice guy, but I don't think you should be leading Emma on."

Nick lifted an eyebrow. "Who says I'm leading her on? I could say the same to you about Rachel."

Now it was Hank's turn to scowl. *Rachel? What*...He glanced at the hall clock. *Can't be late to Trig*...was all I was able to get, which was no help whatsoever. Was he serious about Rachel? Was I just his good friend or something more? I quit hiding in the shadows and walked right up to them. "Hey, guys. What are you talking about?"

Suddenly Nick was all charm again. "Hank's just looking out for your best interests." He gave me a wink before heading off for class.

I got in Hank's face, blocking his exit. "What best interests?"

Hank shrugged and wouldn't look at me. "I don't think Nick's right for you."

"Then who is? You?"

Hank shifted from one foot to the other. "Well, as long as we've known each other…"

I waited for the rest of that sentence, but it didn't come. I sighed. "Right. But what about Rachel? You two seemed pretty cozy New Year's."

Hank looked puzzled. "Rachel?" He blinked. *I really wish*...But the tardy bell rang, and without another word or thought Hank took off. What did he wish? Did it have to do with me or Rachel? Another unfinished thought. I wanted to scream.

I was not only rattled from the argument with Hank

but tardy to class, so I hoped the teacher would let it slide on the first day. There were about twenty other kids in the classroom, most of them future journalism majors, and they were already engrossed in writing something. Mr. West frowned at me and tilted his head in the direction of the clock.

I slinked in, took an empty seat toward the back of the room, and then checked the whiteboard for the assignment. "Write about something unusual or unique that happened over the holidays." *Oh great. What I did on my winter vacation.* I took out pen and paper and then stared at the blank page. Just what was I supposed to write about? Isabelle trying a little too hard to make Christmas nice for all of us? Not getting so much as a Christmas card from my dad? My big date with Nick that ended with him kissing another girl at midnight?

How did you get in this class? My head whipped around to see Sara Davis next to me, writing furiously while she peeked at me from the corner of her eye.

"Oh, hey Sara," I whispered. "Did you hear from Jeff Atwell?"

Sara's eyes widened. "What are you talking about?"

I shrugged. "Well, it's been a while since Halloween. Want me to talk to him?"

"Ohmigod, Emma, you're so…" Her face turned red as she glanced at the teacher, who was frowning. Sara scowled at me and hunched over her essay.

"Miss Austin," Mr. West said. "We're doing a quick-write so I can assess your abilities. Care to join us?"

"Okay." I wracked my brain for something to write, and the only thing I could come up with that I would actually let him read was about meeting Colts player

Todd Bekins. I started jotting down thoughts, scratching through them, rewriting…

How did Emma get in this class?

Another naysayer? My gaze drifted to the seat on the other side of me where Faith Barlow was sitting. Great, first Sara, now her friend Faith. My poor writing skills must be legendary. I turned to her with a half-hearted wave. I've seen her during lunch, her headphones on and her focus divided between Sara, Katherine, and whatever she was scribbling in her notebook, but I didn't know what sort of skills she had. Maybe she was as bad as me and just wished she could be a writer.

"Heard from your dad?" she whispered.

I could always count on Faith to ask about Frank. A few years ago when my dad took a second job at the New Age bookstore to try to supplement his income, Faith's single mom Monica used to shop there. After Dad started working in the store, Monica showed up a lot more, chatting him up and even buying him the occasional cup of tea. What few conversations I've ever had with Faith always centered around her mom's friendship, if that's what you call it, with my dad, and how sorry Monica was to hear that Frank had left town. Faith and I had nothing else in common. I shook my head, put my fingers to my lips to indicate quiet, and pointed to the teacher who was about to address the students.

"Who would like to read their piece aloud?" Mr. West asked.

I gulped and put my hand over my chicken-scratching as I looked around the room, hoping someone, anyone, would volunteer. No one did.

"Well, then, what about you, Miss Austin?"

I opened my mouth to speak but nothing came out.

Then I picked up on Faith's thoughts. *She sucks. No way she's reading in front of everyone.*

That made me mad. "I'm not ready, Mr. West," I said, "but I think Faith is." Served her right for those snarky thoughts.

Faith scrunched up her face.

"Miss Barlow? Will you share with us?"

She stood up and, with a sideways glance at me, cleared her throat and began reading her impromptu writing assignment.

"Unique occurrences are an anomaly in my otherwise ordinary life. But on Christmas Eve I witnessed a remarkable and awe-inspiring event, one worthy of the solemn occasion we were celebrating. Walking into church with my mother and grandmother, we noticed that someone had painted graffiti on the side of the building. Outraged church members were gathered around, whispering among themselves, things like 'how dare he' and 'no respect.' But I couldn't understand why they were all so angry, because instead of vandalism, I saw beauty. The rich colors and clean lines exuded a feeling of joy and pure love. I looked upon a rainbow, a cross, a dove, and a message which read Peace on Earth. Soon a change came over the crowd as anger turned to amazement. Someone started singing the first strains of *Silent Night* and as everyone joined in, we understood this artist had brought us together in love on that holy night. Isn't that what Christmas is all about?"

The room went silent as Faith sat down. If I was wondering about her talent, my question had been answered. Even Sara Davis was looking at her with newfound respect. Finally Mr. West said, "Very nice."

An understatement if I ever heard one.

****

At lunch, I went to the salad bar and piled the veggies, cheese, bacon bits and croutons high on my plate and headed to the senior table where Flip was already sitting.

"Where's James?" I asked him.

Strep throat, flashed across Flip's mind, but his mouth was full of cheeseburger so he just shook his head.

"Sorry he's sick."

Naturally that elicited a scowl from Flip. I sat down next to him and tucked into my salad.

Hank showed up, food tray in hand. "Mind if I join you?" I beamed at him, relieved he'd gotten over his spat with Nick earlier. Flip and I scooted our chairs around to make room. "Can you move over one more? Hattie's right behind me."

"Sure." I'd hoped to talk to Hank a little more about the argument he'd had with Nick, but when Hattie appeared, she set her tray right between Hank and me. I tossed her a look that she ignored.

Hank smiled at Hattie with an almost imperceptible glance my way. "It was good to catch up with you over break."

"Yeah, good talk," Hattie said.

Catch up? When? How? The idea that two of my best friends were excluding me caused me to swallow hard and choke on a piece of cucumber.

"You okay?" Hank asked, reaching around Hattie to pat me on the back.

"Yeah." I coughed and reached for my water. After an eternity and several gulps from the bottle, my throat finally unclenched.

It was just a couple of phone calls Hattie was

thinking as she squeezed ketchup all over her fries.

As far as I knew, the only talking Hank and Hattie did was a few words at Todd's New Year's Eve party. "What were you two talking about?" I asked.

"Hank called me New Year's Day. We talked about the Indianapolis Pacers. You know. Basketball? Statistics? That stuff." Hattie winked at Hank and smirked at me as she took a bite of mac and cheese. *Guess I'm not so boring after all,* she thought.

I gave her my "I heard that" look. It had been years since Hattie had that crush on Hank, and somehow I didn't think she'd suddenly rekindled it after spending New Year's Eve with Robbie Martin. But the knowing looks passing between them and the shared secret was making me crazy jealous. Was Hank interested in Hattie now? What about Rachel? What about *me*? I sipped some water while I collected my thoughts.

Hattie turned to me. "Have you started that homework assignment in Family Relations?"

"I'll have to do it at home now that Mr. Moore took me out of study hall and stuck me in that new class." I stabbed my salad with the plastic fork.

"How hard can it be?" Flip asked. "It's a fluffy elective course."

I narrowed my eyes at him and he threw up his hands in mock surrender. "Excuuuse me."

Hattie waved a French fry in my face. "Seriously, Emma. What are you going to write your Family Relations essay about?"

Hank had been watching this exchange between Hattie and me, but no thoughts revealed what he was really thinking. "What's the assignment?"

I leaned around Hattie and smiled at Hank. "We're

supposed to write a response to the section in the chapter on parental responsibility, and I'm…" stumped, paralyzed with fear, flummoxed, you name it.

"I just did some debate research on that topic, so I have lots of material if you need ideas," Hank offered. *Maybe we could get together after school…*

I was thrilled that Hank was again showing interest in me, thinking about getting together, even if it was only to help me with my homework. I was about to jump on that offer when someone said, "I'll help you."

Everyone turned around. Nick was standing there with a tray of pizza and angling for an invitation to join us, something he rarely did. I noticed that the table next to ours was filled with giggly sophomore girls who were tossing him flirty looks and would have been happy to scoot over for him. *He's so cute. Wish I was a senior. Wish I was allowed to date.* Random thoughts from random girls, reminding me that Nick was still that handsome guy all the girls swooned over back in October. But I was still mad at him for kissing Kendall. Hank dug his fork into his mystery meatloaf while Nick put down his food tray, straddled the chair and bit into the pepperoni slice before he even got seated.

"I thought you were off saving the world someplace," I muttered.

"Nope, just stuck in the long lunch line." Nick swallowed his food and wiped his greasy fingers on the napkin. "I meant what I said. I can help you with your homework after school today." He glanced at Hank, who didn't look up, and then turned back to me. "An essay about parental responsibility sounds interesting."

To you, maybe. "I have to work after school. You know, earn money?" It must be hard for a rich kid to comprehend that sort of thing.

"Oh, I forgot about the daycare. When's the assignment due?"

In a fit of immaturity I opened a package of dry crackers and stuffed them in my mouth. That prevented me from saying anything. It also caused another coughing fit. I reached for my water, but suddenly...I felt like I couldn't breathe, couldn't move. Instinctively my hands flew to my throat.

Nick was up in an instant. He got behind me, yanked me upright, wrapped his arms around my midsection, thumbs facing my sternum, and pumped until I spat cracker crumbs all over the table. Flip and Hank jumped up to avoid the mess. I slumped back down in the chair as Nick handed me my water and looked me in the eye. "You okay?"

I swallowed a few gulps and nodded. "Where did you learn to do that?" I managed to squeak out.

"Heimlich maneuver?" Nick shrugged, sat back down, and addressed his pizza. "CPR, at my old school. You should go see the nurse."

I shook my head no, willed myself to calm down, and sipped my water. Nick was eating, but everyone else was staring at him in surprise.

Just like a pro Flip thought. I had to agree.

"Friday," Hattie told Nick. "Assignment's due on Friday."

"Okay," Nick said, "then what about after school? We can go to the library before you have to be at work and get it started."

"Don't you have some work of your own to do?" I snarked, still embarrassed from having to be rescued.

"I already offered to help Emma," Hank told Nick

in a measured voice.

"Emma," Nick said, ignoring Hank and looking me in the eye, "I really want to help. Maybe writing this essay will help you deal with the thing with your dad."

"Thing?" *The "thing" where my dad went bankrupt and then sneaked out of town.* I felt a little foolish, two guys vying for my – homework? And after Nick just saved my life. But what was that look on Hank's face? I listened to his thoughts and all I got was *Nick's got a lot of nerve.*

A lot of nerve doing what? AARRGGHH!

Nick gave me a warm smile, spoiling my concentration. "Just say yes."

"Yeah, do it," Hattie urged me. "You need a good grade on that assignment. You gotta keep that A to balance out…"

I put up my hand like a traffic cop. "Don't remind me. Creative Writing."

Hank had gone back to eating his food, but after a wistful glance at me, he scooted in a little closer to Hattie.

It didn't look like Hank was going to make his homework offer again or finish his thought. "Fine," I told Nick. "I'll meet you in the library."

****

I went to the library right after the final bell and scouted out a place to sit, but it turned out there was no need, because Nick had already staked out a table at the far corner of the room and was waving me over. I had to wonder how he got there so fast, unless he cut his last period class.

Wish I had a study partner that cute thought a girl next to us.

I glanced over to see her batting her eyes at Nick. She blushed when he grinned back at her. "Forget her, she's…"

"Fourteen. Yeah, I know. So about your essay…"

I groaned and pulled out pen, paper and my textbook. "Here's the section of the chapter I have to respond to." I pointed to it with the pen.

Nick flipped through the ten or so pages in the book in a matter of seconds. "It's all about when parents separate or start divorce proceedings, what their responsibility is to their kids."

I looked up at him in shock. "How can you read that fast?"

He ignored the question. "Your parents didn't get divorced, so…"

I sighed. "Even though my mom died, I can still relate to the feeling of abandonment. By both parents."

Nick leaned in a little closer. "When did your dad leave?"

"Almost a year ago. On Valentine's Day if you can imagine. He'd been working two jobs and was never home. His job wasn't going well for reasons I didn't understand, and he kept talking about quitting. Then apparently he did quit but didn't tell me or Isabelle."

"Then what happened?" Nick prompted.

Simple question with no easy answer. I focused my attention on the book to keep Nick from seeing the angst I knew my eyes reflected. "He got an out-of-town job offer."

Nick shook his head. "It had to have been more than just the job. Maybe he was scared, or confused, depressed…"

Maybe. Probably. I hadn't thought of it like that.

"Dad could have made better choices."

Nick took my hand across the table. "Well, maybe the two of us can come up with an essay that won't bring up too many bad memories."

I pulled my hand back. "Unlikely." I pretended to reread a page in my textbook. "Besides, there is no 'two of us.'" New Year's Eve flashed through my thoughts and I got mad all over again.

"Emma, come on…"

I sighed. "Since you're clearly not into me, how 'bout I fix you up with someone else? There are at least a dozen girls still begging for a date with you. Just name one."

"I don't want to date anyone else. I like you. I want to spend time with you."

"Seriously? You sure have a funny way of showing it. I don't have your cell number, I don't know where you live, I don't know anything about your family, and you spend our one and only date playing pool with guys and kissing another girl."

"While you were kissing another guy," he reminded me.

I crossed my arms and leaned back in my chair, a scowl on my face. "Your point?"

He winced at my reaction and tossed up his hands in surrender. "Okay, so to make up for my bad behavior, what if I ask you to dinner and invite my parents so you can meet them."

I was pretty sure my jaw dropped. To the best of my knowledge, I was the only girl – heck, the only person – Nick had offered to introduce to his family. I was definitely not letting this opportunity go by, if for no other reason than bragging rights. But I tried to play it off as no big deal. "Sure, whatever."

"Great."

My phone pinged with a text and I pulled it out for a quick glance. It was from Hank. *We need to talk.* I hit "ignore" and stuffed the phone back in my pocket.

"Hank?" When I didn't say anything, Nick shrugged and pointed to the assignment. "Your thesis for this paper should be – write this down – 'Children of divorcing parents may be confused because they don't understand their parents' emotions.'" He looked up. "Sound okay?"

I was getting whiplash changing the topic from dating to dinner to homework, but his topic sounded really good, so I wrote down what he said.

"How 'bout I pick you up from the daycare on Friday. You like Mexican?" More whiplash, but Nick was smiling at me and I was going all mushy again.

Chapter 8

"Where are you going at this ungodly hour?" I asked Isabelle. I pulled the halves of my bagel out of the toaster and tossed them on a plate.

At seven a.m. on a Friday, the only thing I wanted to think about was my breakfast. Isabelle was in the kitchen fully dressed for work. She smiled at me before snatching half my bagel and smearing it with grape jelly.

"Work, where else?" she replied with her mouth full of chewy toast.

My sister was wearing crisply starched jeans and her corduroy blazer with the Hayes Real Estate logo on the pocket. But she rarely got to work before nine. "Why so early?"

Isabelle grinned and tapped her forehead. "You mean you haven't already picked it out of my brain?"

"Too early in the morning." I made a territorial grab for the other half of my bagel and went to the fridge for some cream cheese.

VERY important client...

"Okay okay okay," I exclaimed. "Just tell me about your client."

Isabelle smiled and started making a pot of coffee. "It's Todd Bekins, so thank you for that. I'm meeting him at his house, not my office." She pushed the button to start the coffee brewing and while she was waiting, rummaged through the cabinets. *Where's my...*

"Your travel mug's still in the dishwasher."

She opened the dishwasher and set the mug next to the gurgling pot. "Todd wants to meet at eight a.m. because he's got to leave later this morning for a flight to… wherever their playoff game is."

"Houston." I took a bite of bagel. "At least something good came out of that disaster of a New Year's date."

Isabelle stopped mid-pour to face me. "Disaster?"

I guess I'd never mentioned how badly that evening went for me. I gave her the condensed version.

"Oh, Emma, I'm so sorry." She put the coffee down and came over to give me a hug. "Why didn't you tell me?"

I pulled away and took my plate to the sink. "Forget it. It's over, and that's what I get for being stupid. I thought Nick really liked me."

"Are you sure he doesn't?"

I winced. "Well, no. And since I can't hear any of his thoughts…"

Isabelle's eyes widened. "You can't?"

"Nope. Every time I try all I get is jumbled up nonsense. But at school a few days ago he made a big deal out of apologizing for New Year's."

"That's good, isn't it?"

"Maybe. So after I let him grovel awhile," I said, knowing I was putting my own spin on it, "I agreed to let him pick me up from work tonight and take me out for dinner. And he's going to introduce me to his parents."

You'll be the envy of Mel High, she thought, which made me giggle. "Wow. Be sure to take notes, because this I gotta hear." Isabelle checked her briefcase on the kitchen counter to make sure she had everything, picked up her coffee and glanced at the time. *Seven thirty.* She tossed me a look.

"Yeah, I hear you. I gotta hurry or I'll miss the bus." I gave her two thumbs up. "Todd Bekins seriously needs your help. Right now that living room looks like frat boy central."

Isabelle laughed as she headed out to the garage. I raced to the front door, pulled my coat from the closet, tossed my book bag over my shoulder and ran outside just in time to hop on the school bus.

****

I'd only been enrolled in Creative Writing class for five days, and already I was behind. Today's assignment was an argumentative essay. Mr. West said we were to argue for or against a current events topic, and to make it clear in our thesis statement which side we were on. Last night I'd wracked my brain trying to figure out a topic, and every single one I came up with was either lame or would take too much research.

And then it hit me. Why not use the essay that Nick helped me write and let it do double duty? So I dug it out of my book bag, sat down at Jonathan's computer and tweaked it. I retitled it Children of Divorcing Parents Don't Understand Adult Emotions, leaving out the confusion part. When I reread it, I decided I had a pretty good essay. Well, at least worth a C.

I arrived a minute or so early for class, the first time I hadn't been tardy all week, and put my printed essay on my desk, ready for the teacher to collect.

Plagiarism, someone was thinking. I glanced to my right to see Sara Davis craning her neck to read my work. I'll admit I used a lot of Nick's ideas, and for a kid who didn't do much schoolwork he was amazingly good at writing, but I didn't cheat.

I slammed my hand down over my paper. "I didn't…" I stopped myself before I repeated her thoughts out loud. That was how this whole thing with her started back in ninth grade, me saying exactly what she'd been thinking. I decided to switch tactics. "Can I read your essay? I'm sure it's good, you being in journalism and all."

Flattery apparently didn't work on Sara. She stuck her nose in the air as she booted up her laptop. "I always get As in this class."

I sighed. This was only the first week, and yet it looked like I'd be treated to an entire semester of Sara's nasty behavior. I turned sideways in my chair and said, "Sara, why do you have it in for me?"

Her jaw practically dropped. *How can you not know?* "I don't have it in for you," she lied with a dismissive wave of her hand.

The last thing I needed was for Sara to use me as a punching bag for the rest of senior year. "We'll be going our separate ways in a few months. Can't we bury the hatchet?" Preferably not in my back. "What if I set you up with Jeff Atwell? I hear he's…"

"Don't do me any favors, Emma," she snapped.

I blew out a puff of air and faced the front of the classroom.

****

"Hey, bestie, got any plans tonight?" Hattie walked up to her locker and spun the lock.

I stared into my own locker, trying hard to focus on weekend homework, but I was too giddy with excitement about my date tonight with Nick. "Why do you ask?"

*Hank and I…*Hattie was thinking.

Suddenly on high alert, I turned to give her my full attention.

"Hank and I are going to that new DiCaprio film and you mentioned you wanted to see it."

After I'd ignored Hank's call when I was in the library with Nick earlier in the week, he and I texted back and forth a few times, but he'd been busy with debate club stuff every day at lunch. Maybe he was going to tell me he had decided to date Hattie after all and wanted me to hear it from him first. I didn't want to hear it at all. "You and Hank, huh?"

Hattie shrugged. "It's not like we're a couple." *No word from Robbie.*

"Haven't heard from violin-obsessed Robbie Martin, I see."

Hattie put her hands on her hips. "Let's agree to disagree about Robbie, okay?"

I should feel bad for her since Robbie hadn't been in touch, but she was my best friend and I hated to see her get hurt. Again. "Hattie, come on. I told you back in middle school that Robbie would never commit to anything that didn't include a full orchestra."

"Spare me the 'I told you so's'," she sniffed. "Do you want to go with Hank and me to the film or not?"

Hank and Hattie. Two names I never thought would be linked. "You sure you want a chaperone on your date?"

"Date?" Hattie at first looked stunned and then burst out laughing. "No, a bunch of us are going. Flip, James, Mary, Greg...I don't know who all, but everyone's meeting at the Metroplex. Hank's swinging by to pick me up. Need a ride?"

I breathed a sigh of relief, but felt a little guilty. "I've got plans," I told her, "with Nick."

That two-timing jerk? Hattie just glared at me.

I opened my mouth to answer, but before I could get a word out, I was waylaid by both Jane and Agnes Bates.

Date night date night date night... I couldn't figure out which one's thoughts were which, but obviously they were looking for the same thing. "Hi, ladies."

"Emma," Jane said with a knowing look at her sister, "I know it's short notice, but we need dates to a family wedding tomorrow night. It's going to be totally boring if we have to hang out all night with our younger cousins, so…"

"…so find us a couple of cute guys pronto!" Agnes finished.

I frowned. "I thought you two were seeing Sam and Darrin."

"Were," Jane said. "The boys got miffed when we switched dates on them one too many times."

"Imagine that," I muttered.

"Any ideas?" Agnes asked. "We're desperate."

"I'll get back to you." The warning bell sounded and I headed off to class, making it a point to casually eavesdrop on people to see who might be dateless this weekend. And it had to be two guys who hadn't already been on the receiving end of the Bates and switch. *And* who were willing for their first date to be a wedding where they wouldn't know anyone but the twins. But, hey, I was up for the challenge.

****

No potential dates for Jane and Agnes presented themselves during the morning, so I was hoping I could solve the problem during lunch. I chose a bowl of tomato soup, picked up some crackers, reconsidered after I'd nearly choked on them a few days ago, and chose a bag of chips instead.

"Coming?" Hank was right behind me, his lunch tray in hand, tilting his head in the direction of our usual table.

I grinned. "Of course." I pulled out a chair to sit down, and then my heart sank as I watched Hank pull up a chair next to Hattie instead of his usual spot next to me. Disgruntled, I took a seat on the other side of Hattie. While I was opening my bag of chips, Sam and Darrin O'Brien set their trays down across from me, and an idea popped into my head.

Hank avoided eye contact with me as he picked the skin off the fried chicken wings. "You joining us tonight?"

I was about to reply when I "heard" one of the O'Brien's thinking, *Great. Dateless all weekend.* That was my chance.

"Um," I said to Hank while eyeing the twins, "I've got plans with Nick for dinner, but we should be able to…" I'd like to pretend I didn't see Hank's frown, but I did. I pulled the plastic lid off my Styrofoam soup bowl and took a tentative bite. "Hey, Darrin, so you and Sam are free this weekend, right?"

Sam looked up from his burger in surprise. "Bad news travels fast."

But Darrin was quick to jump in. "We're not charity projects, Emma."

"Oh, I know. It's just that, well, if you're interested, I've got a couple of ladies looking for a double date tomorrow night."

The guys exchanged looks and then Darrin shrugged. "Whatever."

"Great. I'll text you the details. You won't need to pick up your dates."

"Who are…?" Sam asked.

"To be announced," I told them, and then turned to Hank with a big smile. "So tonight…?"

Hattie craned her neck over Hank to lift an eyebrow at me, but I shrugged and focused my attention on Hank, who unfortunately focused his attention on his food. I decided right then that Nick and I would join our friends for the movie after dinner. I was eager to meet his folks, of course, but I was determined to get to the bottom of this newfound "relationship" between Hank and Hattie.

I was on my way to return my lunch tray when I saw Jeff Atwell also headed that way. Maybe it was me trying to do something nice, or me attempting to get back into Sara's good graces, if I'd ever been there, but I called out to him.

"Can I talk to you a minute? I never got to apologize for Halloween."

****

Nick picked me up after work as promised. "Hungry?"

I climbed into his already-warm Beemer, because after walking only a few steps from the daycare to the car, I was shivering in the mid-January cold.

I fastened my seatbelt. "Yeah, I'm starved." That bowl of tomato soup for lunch didn't stick with me, and even though I munched a piece of cheese from the tray that I served the daycare kids, my stomach was rumbling. "Where are we going?"

"Castillo Authentic Mexican Restaurant," he told me. "It's just a few blocks away. Ever been there?" Nick pulled out of the daycare parking lot and made a right onto Main Street.

I shook my head. "Jonathan doesn't like Mexican, so Isabelle tends to pick up pizza or Chinese, or else we go to a steakhouse."

"Then you're in for a treat, because the food is awesome!"

We were there in like five minutes, and Nick must have been right about the food because the place was crazy busy. The restaurant only had one tiny parking lot which was full, but luckily on his third pass through the lot, Nick found a spot when an SUV pulled out. I was relieved we didn't have to park a block away, because once the sun set, which is very early in January, the temperature would drop even farther than the already sub-freezing temps we were currently enduring.

"Sorry you're so cold, but at least we didn't have to walk the block," Nick said as he opened the restaurant's glass entry door for me.

Maybe I was getting used to him repeating my thoughts aloud, but I just said "Thanks" and let it go. We stood around for about ten minutes near the door, shivering as people came in with blasts of cold air, and drooling as hot plates of savory food came out of the kitchen.

"How many please?" asked a young man at the concierge stand. He was Hispanic, medium height, really cute, and looked like he could be our age. But I knew I'd never seen him at school.

"Hi, Miguel," Nick said. "Emma, this is Miguel Castillo. His parents own the restaurant."

"Nice to meet you," I said.

"How many did you say?" Miguel asked as he surveyed the crowded dining room.

"Oh, sorry," Nick said. "Four. My parents are joining us."

Miguel picked up four menus and led us to a table at the back of the restaurant and away from the ever-opening front door. "Enjoy your meal." He left the menus on the table.

I hung my coat and scarf on the back of my chair and took a seat. "I get that you eat here a lot, but how do you know that guy?"

Nick grabbed a chip from the bowl a waiter placed in front of us. "From St. Malachi."

St. Malachi was a huge Catholic church on the far north side of town that operated a well-respected college-prep school. Their fine arts program was top-notch, and their football team was a force to be reckoned with.

I picked up the menu and started flipping through it. My idea of Mexican food was bland tacos, so all the items listed were literally foreign to me. "What's good here?"

"Everything, really. But for a Mexican food neophyte," Nick said with a grin, "I'd go with something basic, like tacos."

Neophyte, huh? I folded up my menu and set it back on the table. "I eat enough of those in the Mel High cafeteria."

"No comparison." Nick must come here so often that he didn't have to consult the menu because he never even opened his, and instead was intently studying its outside cover. "See this?" He pointed to the drawing of a bullfighter dressed in traditional Spanish clothing and red cape, in an arena ready to fight a bull. "Miguel drew it. What d'ya think? Pretty good, huh?"

I picked up my copy of the menu and studied the art

work. "Very good."

Nick grinned, closed the menu and set it on the edge of the table. "I've seen some of his other drawings, too. St. Malachi has a bunch of them on display in their lobby, along with work by their other visual arts students. You should go sometime and have a look."

I shrugged. "That school's on the opposite end of town." *And I have no transportation.*

"I'd be glad to give you a ride."

I looked at him warily and opened my mouth to demand an explanation, but got interrupted.

"Hi, Emma." Faith Barlow was walking past our table as Miguel was showing her and her mother Monica to a booth.

"Oh, hi, Faith." I opened my menu and pretended to be reading it again. The last thing I needed was one of Sara Davis's crew hovering around, collecting gossip.

Monica's head snapped around. "Emma Austin? It's so good to see you. Have you heard from your…?"

"Hi, Faith!" Nick said, cutting off Monica as if in response to my unspoken angst. "Ever been here?" Faith nodded. "It's Emma's first time. And hey, look at this." He pointed to the drawing that we were just admiring and then tilted his head at Miguel. "I guess you already know Miguel, right? From church? He drew it."

Faith blushed and hurried to catch up to her mom who was already seated. I watched Faith giggle and blush even more as Miguel handed her a menu. It was obvious to me, and probably anyone with eyes, that Faith was crushing on Miguel, and hoping they weren't already dating, I was about to suggest…

"Hi, Mom." Nick stood and pulled out a chair for an attractive woman in what looked like an expensive business suit. "Hi Dad," he added with a grin. "Glad you're here. We're hungry."

I'd been so busy watching Faith and Miguel that I didn't notice Mr. and Mrs. Knight walk up to the table. I could see where Nick got his good looks. His mother's eyes were the same piercing blue, and his dad had the same color of sandy blond hair, which parted in the same spot as Nick's.

Mr. Knight extended his hand. "You must be Emma."

I nodded and shook his outstretched hand. "Nice to meet you, Mr. Knight." I turned to his mother, "And you, too, Mrs. Knight."

"Well, technically, it's Dr. Knight," she replied.

"Mom's a psychiatrist," Nick said, "and Dad's an Architectural Engineer."

Those well-paying careers explained the expensive car Nick drove and the rumored nice neighborhood they lived in, but that still left me wondering why they moved to small town Indiana from Chicago.

"Dad's been working on that performing arts center over in Belford right from its planning stages, commuting back and forth every week to Chicago," Nick replied in answer to my unvoiced question."

Dr. Knight patted her husband's arm and turned to me. "And I have patients in both Indianapolis and Chicago, so now I commute in reverse." And to my shock she added, "That's how I met your father, Emma."

I sucked in my breath. Dad had been a patient of Dr. Knight's? But wouldn't that be sort of unethical of her to mention it? "You know my dad?"

"I assumed you knew, since Frank said he'd told his family about some of the concerns he was having."

Like my mom's death. And his inability to get past his grief, or hang on to a job, or…

She gave me a sympathetic look. "Nick tells me Frank is working out of town right now."

"That's one way to put it," I mumbled. Without a job or insurance, Dad must have had to quit seeing Dr. Knight. If he had been able to continue, maybe he would have gotten a handle on his problems and not bolted the minute he got the foreclosure notice on our house.

"Have you decided what you want?" Thankfully the waiter appeared just as I was starting to squirm.

I looked up from my menu and saw everyone waiting on me to order. Determined to prove to Nick that I could be adventurous, I said, "Enchiladas supreme. With extra red sauce."

Nick smiled. "I'll have the same."

The food at Castillo's was every bit as good as Nick said it would be, except maybe a little spicier than I'd anticipated. After the meal his parents paid the check, said their goodbyes and left. Nick helped me on with my coat, but instead of heading out to the parking lot, he took my hand and directed me to Faith's table. Their empty dishes sat waiting to be picked up, and Faith was writing something in her ever-present notebook. Thankfully Monica wasn't there at the moment, probably in the ladies' room or something, so I didn't have to endure more grilling about my father.

"Hey, Faith," Nick said, "I was thinking maybe you could use an illustrator for that story you're writing. Maybe Miguel would be willing…" Faith slapped a hand over her work, but before she could open her mouth to question him, Nick shrugged and said, "Think about it." He gave her a warm smile and steered me out of the restaurant.

Once outside we were hit with a biting wind, so we ducked our heads and made a beeline for the comfort of his car. I jumped up and down to keep warm until Nick beeped it open and held the door for me. He hurried around to the driver's side and got in. "And I thought Chicago winters were bad," he muttered, rubbing his hands together. "Can't wait to get..." Nick abruptly stopped himself and turned on the engine.

"Can't wait to get what?" I prompted, but Nick just smiled and winked at me. I sighed as I wrapped my arms around myself while the car heated up. That had been a very revealing dinner and I had a lot to think about. My father had been seeing a psychiatrist, who turned out to be Nick's mother. Despite the rumors at school, Nick's mom and dad had simply relocated for their careers, and Nick was a pretty well-adjusted kid. But none of that explained how he was able to read my mind. *Oh, great Emma, you're one to ask* that *question.*

Nick stretched out his hands in front of the heating vent, turned sideways in his seat and took my gloved hand in his. "Still think I'm mind-reading, huh?"

I jerked my hand away. "How do you do that?"

Nick grinned and gently pulled me in for a sweet, lingering kiss. "I already told you. I pay attention."

"Nick..." Yeah, it was a nice kiss, but he couldn't distract me that easily.

"Okaayyy," he said, leaning his back on the driver's side door. He shifted around uncomfortably, adjusted the heat control up then down, and finally made eye contact with me. "I'm a genius."

"Huh?"

"Genius." He tapped his forehead with a finger. "IQ

one sixty-eight. That's how I can read body language and predict what people are going to say or do."

I burst out laughing. "Nice try."

But Nick was staring at me with a very serious expression, his body language telling me he didn't appreciate my skepticism.

I blinked a few times. "Genius? You sure you aren't just psychic?"

Nick laughed. "I tell you I'm a genius and that's your takeaway?"

"It's just a little hard to…"

"I know. My mom was worried about me when I was little, thinking I might be autistic or something. She finally took me to a colleague of hers and had me tested." He waved his arms in a grand gesture. "Tah dah. Genius IQ."

I sat back against the seat and stared at the ceiling. "I don't care how you spin it, you're still reading my mind. And other people's."

Nick shook his head. "It's all mathematical calculations."

I sat up straight. "What is?"

"Non-verbal signals. In my head, I do a quick calculation of all the possible responses to any given situation, evaluate which one is most likely, and then respond in kind. It takes about two seconds."

My eyes widened. "So you're doing math problems in your head to figure out what people are going to say or do?"

"Oversimplification, but yes."

Was that why I'd never been able to read his mind? Maybe there was just too much going on in there. That day in the hospital cafeteria when I picked up all that scientific jargon. Was that Nick? I decided to give my theory a try. I focused really hard and listened to his thoughts. What I got was flashes of things like *probabilities...odds x equals binomials cosign...*I quit listening. Too much math, way over my head.

Okay, so Nick wasn't reading my mind or anyone else's, he was just doing really fast brain work. "So why are you at Melville High? Shouldn't you be at some private school for the uber-gifted?"

"I've never gone to public school before. When Mom and Dad decided to move here, they offered to let me stay in Chicago with friends, or enroll at St. Malachi, but I wanted to try public school. Besides, Mom knew your dad, so I figured I could make at least one friend at Mel High."

I took a few deep breaths. This wasn't what I thought he was going to tell me, but I was starting to understand. Poor guy. He'd probably had to spend all his time studying at Colson Academy, so public school took the academic pressure off while he made new friends. Maybe that meant I didn't have to be so creeped out anymore when he completed my thoughts, but I'd have to pay more attention to my body language. He could definitely read that. "You must be really bored in school, since you're so smart."

Nick shrugged as he put on his seat belt. "The work's easy, but I'm finally getting to have a social life."

"Wow. An honest-to-goodness genius. I guess Hank's got competition for valedictorian." I laughed as I squeezed his hand and released it. But Nick wasn't laughing. Actually he looked kinda serious. Maybe he felt bad coming in new and taking away Hank's hard-earned spot. I decided to lighten the mood. "Hey, a bunch of kids are seeing that new film at the Metroplex. Wanna go?"

****

We were a little late for the eight o'clock showing of the movie, but luckily it wasn't sold out. Nick bought two tickets and, being stuffed with Mexican food, we bypassed the concession stand and headed straight into the theatre. I squinted and waited for my eyes to adjust to the dark. Once they focused, I realized only a few seats were left and only on the front rows, but I spotted our friends down on the front two rows, so we joined them.

We got plenty of dirty looks and grumbling from classmates as Nick and I tried to get them to slide over so we could sit together. Wasn't happening. So Nick pointed to the empty seat next to the aisle for me, and he climbed over legs and feet to reach the only other vacant spot in the middle of the front row. Just as I was grousing to myself about how unromantic this date was, I glanced to my right to discover I was sitting next to Hank. He smiled at me, I smiled back, and then I saw Hattie waving at me from his other side. Awkward.

And where did Nick land? Right next to James and between Flip and Kendall, who was on a date with some guy not from Mel High, and that guy was sitting next to Mary Bekins who was holding hands with Greg Plowman. Jeff Atwell had his arm on the back of Sara Davis's chair and she was leaning her head on his shoulder. *You're welcome,* I thought. The opening credits rolled and wouldn't you know it? Kendall quietly put her hand on Nick's knee. Ugh. I started to reach for Hank's hand like I always do, but then I pull backed when I saw Hattie scowling at me.

****

"Did you like the film?" Nick asked as he walked me to my front door.

"Yeah, except for the part where we sat on different rows and Kendall manhandled you."

"And did you see me remove her hand, or were you too awestruck by DiCaprio?" Nick wiggled his eyebrows and leaned down to give me a goodnight kiss. "Forget Kendall. Anyway, she's seeing someone."

Wait. What? I was the matchmaker and I didn't even know that. "Who? Not that guy she was with tonight." I blew on my hands and started to shiver again. It was too cold out here to talk about Kendall.

"I don't want to talk about Kendall." Nick must not have noticed my eye roll when he pulled me in close. "Can we go out again?"

Suddenly I forgot all about the maneater. "Yeah, I'd like that. Text me, okay?" I still didn't have his number, but optimistically I handed him my phone and he actually keyed in his number. "Tell your folks I enjoyed meeting them," I said as he strolled off down the sidewalk to his parked car.

Isabelle was sitting on the bottom step in her bathrobe. "Did you have a good time?"

I closed the door behind me. "Yeah, but I'm too old for you to wait up for me. Didn't you get my text?"

She nodded. "I can't sleep." *I need some herbal tea.*

"I could use some of that tea, too. Oh, don't give me that look. I've got something to tell you." I took off my coat and boots. "Did you know Dad had been seeing a psychiatrist?" Isabelle blinked. "Turns out it was Nick's mother."

She was quiet a moment. *Wish he'd stuck with it.*

I nodded silent agreement. "Tell me about your

meeting this morning with Todd Bekins."

Isabelle smiled and hugged her knees to her chest. "You were right, that main living area is a disaster. I took some measurements, did some sketches, and then gave him some ideas of what I thought we could do. He's out of town for a few days, but I told him I'd email him next week with some virtual designs."

"Cool."

"Emma, did you know he has a girlfriend?"

I sat down on the step next to her. "It's got to be a recent development because he was single New Year's Eve. Does it matter?"

"Maybe. Todd told me said girlfriend has very specific ideas about how his house should look."

"Great. A backseat interior designer."

We both burst out laughing, but she put her fingers to her lips and pointed upstairs, indicating Jonathan was trying to sleep. We got up and started to tiptoe to the kitchen for that tea when the doorbell rang.

We exchanged looks.

"Did Nick forget something?" Isabelle looked out the peephole, gasped and flung the door wide open. "Dad!"

Chapter 9

I rushed to the door, looked out onto the porch and nearly fainted. I glanced at Isabelle, who was standing in the open doorway, her mouth hanging open.

"May I come in?" Dad asked. "It's cold out here."

My sister stepped aside. Dad didn't look good. He'd lost a lot of weight and had dark circles under his eyes. Everyone always used to say he looked younger than his fifty years, but it was like he'd aged ten years. He must have shopped in a second-hand store, too, because his jeans were worn and hanging loose on him, he was wearing loafers without socks, and he had only a faded grey hooded sweatshirt for warmth. No wonder he was cold.

Dad stepped on to the entry hall mat and shook the snow off his feet before setting down an overstuffed duffel bag next to the coat closet, where it landed with a thud on the hardwood floor.

Where do I start? Isabelle threw a pleading glance my way.

"We can start," I told her with a knowing look as I turned to my father, "by asking 'where have you been'?" I couldn't yet identify the swirl of emotions I was feeling, but my pulse was racing and sweat was forming on the back of my neck.

Dad turned his hands up in supplication. "I sent cards, texts."

Isabelle crossed her arms and leaned against the stair railing. "Generic messages with no real information. Emma and I deserve an explanation."

The color drained out of my father's face. "Didn't you read the note I left on the fridge? I thought for sure you did."

"Yes," I snapped. "You lost your job and then had to face bankruptcy and foreclosure. I read it. So did Isabelle."

Dad looked miserable. "I just couldn't take care of you, Emma, or our house." Tears sprang to his eyes but he quickly wiped them away with the back of his sleeve. "I'm sorry."

Sorry? Did he think that made up for the shock of coming home from school on Valentine's Day to an empty house?

"What's going on?" Jonathan stood at the top of the steps in his bathrobe, running his fingers through his bed-head hair and yawning as he peered down the stairs. *Holy crap!*

I guess he just figured it out.

"Sorry to wake you, Jonathan," Dad said. "I didn't know how to announce my arrival, so I guess I took Emma and Isabelle by surprise."

I frowned. "Ya think?"

Let him talk Isabelle silently warned me.

I crossed my arms in front of my chest and tapped my foot. "Okay, Dad, talk."

Dad sighed and looked like the weight of the world was on him. My righteous indignation started to melt.

"I left to take a job in southern Indiana, in New Albany."

"Eleven months ago," I reminded him.

"I had such high hopes for a fresh start, thinking I could send for you when I got settled."

My jaw dropped. "How did you think that would work out? I've lived in Melville all my life."

"I know, I know. I didn't think it through. But after a couple of months it didn't matter anyway, because I got laid off right after tax season. So I hopped a northbound bus to Greenwood, where a man I'd met on that New Albany job lives. He let me crash at his apartment, and I got a job at one of those big box retail stores till I was able to save up enough money to come home."

"I would gladly have driven down and picked you up, if I'd known where you were." Isabelle was starting to tear up, too.

"So why now?" I said.

Dad glanced from me to Isabelle and back. "I missed my family."

That hung in the air for a moment, and the silence got really uncomfortable as Isabelle and I each shifted from one foot to another. Dad seemed unable to make eye contact with either of us. Finally Jonathan spoke from the top of the stairs. "What are your plans, Frank?"

"Could you perhaps pay the cab? The meter's running." Dad looked chagrinned as he tilted his head in the direction of the waiting taxi.

Jonathan's jaw was set firm as he disappeared back upstairs and returned with a credit card in hand. He pulled a coat from the closet and stepped out the front door. He was back in record time, blowing on his hands to warm them up.

Dad shoved his hands in his pants pockets. "I was hoping I could prevail upon my daughters to let me stay here a few days. Just till I can get an apartment."

Isabelle rolled her eyes. "And how are you going to pay for an apartment?"

My father sighed, stuffed his hands in his pockets and stared at the floor. "I've spoken with the manager at the New Age bookstore in Indianapolis and he agreed to let me come back part time. And I'm hopeful I can get hired on with a tax prep place." He glanced up and smiled. "April fifteenth is not that far off, you know."

"I get that you found yourself in a financial bind," Isabelle said, "but why didn't you come to me? Or Jonathan?" She glanced at her husband, who nodded. "Instead of just walking out on Emma, on all of us?"

I was too ashamed. Dad poked at the throw rug with his foot. "I'd always been the breadwinner, but when I lost your mother…" He shrugged. "After that, nothing seemed important."

I remembered my conversation with Dr. Knight earlier and how it had shed new light on the whole thing with my dad. In my anger at being abandoned, it never occurred to me that my father was hurting, maybe even needed medical treatment. I fought back the tears that were threatening to tumble down my cheeks in torrents. Part of me wanted to reach out and give my father a hug, admit that I missed him and was glad he was back, but I just couldn't swallow my pride. If my newlywed sister hadn't insisted I move in with her and Jonathan, I could have ended up in foster care. So instead of that hug, I turned and ran up the stairs, slammed my bedroom door, and threw myself on the bed, sobbing freely.

After what seemed like hours but was really only a few minutes, I sat up and brushed away the tears running down my face, which was now a black sticky mess judging by the mascara smudge on the back of my hand.

I grabbed a tissue and blotted off the runny makeup and blew my nose, and then dug my phone out of my pocket to punch in the number that Nick just gave me. I could have called Hattie, or Hank, or Flip, but I called Nick. His line rang a bunch of times and just as I was sure it was about to go to voice mail, he picked up.

"Hey, Emma." He sounded sleepy.

"My father just showed up on our doorstep."

"Um, what?"

I glanced at the clock and realized how late it was. "Oh, sorry, I didn't mean to wake you. It's just that…" I tapped my foot on the floor with excess nervous energy. "How can Dad possibly expect to just walk back in like nothing ever happened? I'm just so…"

"Angry," he finished for me. "Yeah, I get that. Is there anything I can do?"

I tried to think, but it was late, I was tired and my mind wouldn't focus. "Do you think you could ask your mom for advice?" I hated to ask a guy I barely knew for a favor, but I didn't know where else to turn.

"No problem."

We ended our conversation and I tossed the phone on my bed as I lay on my back staring up at the ceiling. I could hear loud voices coming from downstairs, but I couldn't make out what they were saying and I didn't care. I forced myself to close my eyes and eventually drifted off to sleep.

****

I woke up with sunlight streaming into my bedroom. It was after eleven a.m., much later than I ever slept on the weekend. I tiptoed to the bedroom door, listened and heard nothing, so I bravely peeked out into the hall. On Saturdays Jonathan had a standing racquetball game at the gym and Isabelle usually went to her real estate office to snag any walk-in clients. I hoped they'd stuck to their routines.

I was still in my clothes from last night, so I tossed them in the laundry hamper. I went into the bathroom, showered, and washed the residual makeup off before tiptoeing down to the kitchen, unsure of what I'd find.

"It's okay, the coast is clear," Isabelle said from the kitchen table.

I exhaled as I poured myself a bowl of cereal, got a spoon and some milk and sat down at the table across from her. "So I didn't dream it? He's really back?"

She nodded as she flipped the page of the design catalog she was poring over.

I poured sugar all over my pre-sweetened cereal, knowing but not caring how bad that was for me, and took a huge bite. Of course it was too sweet but I kept eating anyway. "I'd ask what happened after I went upstairs, but..." I let that die as I poured more milk to cut the sugary taste.

"Dad slept on the foldout sofa in Jonathan's office, but we just don't have room here for a fourth person." Isabelle shook her head. "That's asking a lot of my poor husband."

I nodded and swallowed. "But Dad doesn't have any money. No house, no job..."

"Jonathan drove him to one of those extended-stay hotels and paid a week's rent."

"That was nice of Jonathan, but what do we do after that?" I tapped the spoon against the bowl while I thought.

Isabelle glanced up. "We?"

"I want to help," I insisted. "Despite my temper

tantrum last night."

She set the interior design catalog on the table and rubbed the back of her neck. *I wish I had a good solution.*

"You're looking for a solution, and so am I. Maybe getting Dad some help is what we need to do."

"Again with the 'we.'" Isabelle sighed. "Let's face it, Emma, our only parent is in trouble." *But you're just a kid. This isn't your problem.*

"I'm seventeen and a half," I exclaimed.

In spite of the seriousness of the moment, Isabelle chuckled. "You sound like you did when you were eleven and a half and insisted you were old enough to go to a PG-13 movie."

I smiled at the memory. "This is my problem as much as yours. I called Nick last night, and he said he'd talk to his mom about Dad. Maybe she can recommend a more affordable doctor or treatment program. Or something."

The sickly sweet cereal was suddenly very unappetizing, so I shoved it aside. Isabelle walked over and wrapped her arms around me. "I know this is frustrating, Emma, but we'll figure it out."

I held tight to her arms. I was lucky to have her.

****

Apparently the blind date I set up with Jane and Sam and Agnes and Darrin, or however they paired up at the cousin's wedding, went fine after the initial surprise on both sides. When the guys first walked into the country club and saw the Bates sisters all dressed and waiting, they knew they'd been had. But then they admitted they were glad I'd arranged it and all four of them sent texts thanking me. I congratulated myself on pulling it off.

I couldn't concentrate on my studies all week

because I was so worried about my father. I sought out Nick, hoping he'd talked to his mom and she had some sort of solution to offer. Since he and I no longer had Resource time together, I had to track him down during the school day. I caught up with him mid-week just as he was coming out of AP Literature class carrying a somewhat empty-looking backpack, and walking alongside Sara Davis of all people.

"Nick, can we talk?"

"Why do you need to talk, Emma?" Sara rolled her eyes. "Just read his mind." She snickered at her own joke.

I had more important things to worry about than Sara's pettiness. "Run along, Sara. I'm sure you have blind notices to post in the Herald."

She opened her mouth, closed it, and said, "Maybe I do." With a knowing glance at Nick, Sara turned and left.

When she was out of earshot, I asked, "Did you talk to your mom? About my dad?"

Nick gave me a cute grin as he dug into his book bag and fished out a business card. "She told me to give this to you and your sister."

Indianapolis Low Cost Treatment Clinic, it read, with an address not far from the bookstore where Dad used to work. The card listed a phone number and a website, and a couple of doctors with a string of letters after their names. I glanced up. "Does she think they could help him?"

Nick nodded. "Mom said she will gladly forward Frank's records to the clinic if he wants to make an appointment there."

I thanked him as the warning bell sounded and then

headed off to my next class. I was definitely going to talk to Isabelle about this.

At the end of the week in that hotel room that Jonathan had paid for, Dad called Isabelle. He told her the bookstore in Indianapolis had given him an advance, so Isabelle helped him move what little belongings he had to a small furnished apartment near the bookstore. After stocking his fridge with food, his bathroom with toiletries, and his kitchen with a few cooking utensils, she gave him the business card of the clinic, insisting he call for an appointment. I hoped he'd follow through.

Chapter 10

It was fast approaching Valentine's Day. Part of me dreaded it, because it was the anniversary of the day my father left. The other part of me was hopeful that now that Dad was home, we were on the path to a fresh start.

Bigelow's Pizzeria on Main Street was hosting a special Valentine's Day event. They were offering heart-shaped pizzas for two, karaoke, unlimited soft drinks, chocolates and red carnations, and all for what they claimed was the bargain price of fifty dollars per couple. The restaurant had a big party room in its basement that could only hold about a hundred people, so everyone was scrambling to line up a date and make reservations.

Adding to the excitement of the romantic holiday, everyone in school was all abuzz about the love telegrams, something that had never been done before. Mr. West thought up a fundraising idea for his student publication, and got the principal to approve it. For a mere five dollars, anyone at Mel High could order a Special Delivery Love-a-Gram and choose either a pre-written message or write their own, then have it delivered to the object of their affection by a member of the newspaper staff. The idea caught on fast, judging by all the chatter among students and love thoughts in kids' heads. Enough pre-ordered Love-a-Grams would probably raise enough money to put the rest of this year's newspaper budget in the black.

Another blind entry showed up in the special Valentine's Day edition of the Mel High Weekly Herald. *Send a Love-a-Gram to your significant other, or just ask a certain senior girl to read your beloved's...note.*

Since I'd almost dared Sara to post something about me, I sort of blamed myself for that one. But, still, would she ever let it go?

Hattie walked up to me in the hall before school, all nervous tension, and thrust a plastic baggie in my hand. "Hey, bestie. Mom baked these." *Haven't heard from Robbie...*

Even though I was salivating over Mrs. Smythe's heart-shaped sugar cookies, I put up my hand to stop Hattie's thoughts. "Tell me you weren't hoping for a Valentine's date with Robbie Martin."

Hattie looked the tiniest bit surprised before shrugging. "We've been in touch."

"Between symphony performances?"

Hattie crossed her arms and glared at me. I could almost hear her harrumphing. "He's busy. So am I. The Lady Eagles are headed to the county championship playoffs."

"Yeah, I know. Congratulations, by the way."

But for once Hattie's mind wasn't on basketball. "Emma, should I ask Robbie to meet me tomorrow night?"

"Where?"

She rolled her eyes. "Bigelow's of course. Everybody's going."

I put my hand on Hattie's arm and looked her in the eye. "Hattie, it's my professional opinion that you should wait to hear from Robbie. If you're too pushy..." I started to say she would scare him off, and then I thought that might not be so bad. "Just let things play out."

Hattie let that advice sit for a minute. *Yeah okay.* "What about you? You going to Bigelow's?"

That was a good question. I had hoped Hank would ask me, but I hadn't heard a word. Maybe he'd decided to go out with Rachel instead. My heart sank. I thought about Nick, but I wasn't sure if we had the kind of relationship you need for a romantic holiday. "I don't have plans yet."

Hattie's jaw dropped. "What? It's almost Valentine's Day."

I stored the cookies safely in my locker and then made a big show of taking some late homework out of my book bag to avoid any more probing questions. "Forgot to turn this in yesterday."

Before Hattie could say another word, or think one, I ducked into Miss Taylor's classroom to hand in my late assignment. She seemed distracted as usual, but this time I deliberately eavesdropped.

Maybe I shouldn't have sent that Love-a-Gram was going through her mind.

Huh? If she sent one it meant it was to someone here in this school. Seriously? Who could Miss Taylor be crushing on? And did grownups get crushes? Normally I didn't mess with adult relationships unless it was family like Isabelle, but I liked Miss Taylor and I'd be glad to nudge it along if I knew who to nudge. But that was all the info I got. "Sorry this is late, Miss Taylor." I put the work on her desk and backed out of the room. I didn't think she even realized I was there.

Today in Creative Writing, our homework was to write a love sonnet in the style of Elizabeth Barrett Browning's *How do I love thee?* Ugh. I couldn't write any kind of poetry, let alone copy a classic. I spent a couple of hours last night agonizing over it, and still came up with nothing.

"Hi, Emma," Faith said as she slid into her seat. "I heard your dad's back."

I blinked in surprise. "How did you hear that?"

Faith smiled at me. "Well, you know Mom and Frank were friends before…"

"Yes, I know."

"Well," she said as she dug through her book bag, "Frank's started working again at that bookstore Mom likes."

"Yes. *I know.*" What was her point? I honed in on her thoughts.

Faith shrugged. *Mom's seen him there a lot.*

Huh? Okay, so Monica's been shopping, but what was Faith getting at? I didn't know, but I had a more immediate problem. "Did you do your homework?" Faith probably had a killer sonnet written.

"Of course." She opened her notebook and read over her poem. *I wonder if Emma did her assignment.*

"I tried writing that stupid sonnet, Faith," I said as her face registered surprise, "but I just can't do it." I almost immediately wished I could take it back, because she'd probably run to Sara with more tales of my unique abilities.

The tardy bell rang and Mr. West was ready to start the class, but before he could begin and force me to admit I hadn't done my homework, in walked some of his star journalism students, Sara Davis leading the pack. Judging from the huge boxes stuffed with messages they were juggling, Sara and her fellow staff members were going to be busy making Love-a-Gram deliveries all morning.

"One for you, Mr. West," Sara said with a snicker. She put it in his hand and giggled as he turned about three shades of red.

I never expected the teacher to get a message. I listened intently, hoping he'd give away who it was from, but instead of opening it, he tossed it in a desk drawer.

But I'd have to figure out that mystery another time, because I was dying of embarrassment. The only two people in this class who didn't receive Love-a-Grams were me and Faith.

Sara sidled up to me. "You mean you didn't read some guy's mind to find out if he liked you. Tsk tsk."

"I can't…" I stopped myself. *I can't lie.* I clamped my mouth shut and glared at her.

Sara plastered a smug look on her face, winked at Faith and a few other students to be sure they appreciated her victory, and then sailed out of the room with her fellow journalism colleagues.

I tried to shrug off my embarrassment and disappointment as I watched all the other kids open their messages and pass them around. I was miserable. Why didn't Hank send me a Love-a-Gram? Why didn't Nick? Did they forget? Not care? Send one to someone else? Then I asked myself why I didn't send one to either of them. I could've done that.

While all this chaos was swirling around me, Faith slipped a folded paper onto my desk. I couldn't imagine why she'd be passing me an old-school note, but I opened it anyway. To my surprise and great relief, it was a sonnet.

"I had a couple extra," she whispered, "so just

pretend you wrote this one when Mr. West calls on you."

Gulp. That was probably the nicest thing anyone ever did for me. I turned and mouthed "Thanks" with two thumbs up. For whatever reason, Faith just saved me a big fat F on the homework assignment.

After class, Mary Bekins cornered me in the locker bay. "Is Greg Plowman going to ask me out for Valentine's?"

I was a little surprised, given that she hadn't mentioned wanting me to fix them up, but I'd assumed they were handling it on their own. "You mean he hasn't yet?"

"No." She folded her arms in a pout.

"I overheard him yesterday saying he was planning on it," I told her. Well, okay, I heard his thoughts, but same thing. "He's already made reservations at Bigelow's and he's going to surprise you today."

"You sure?" Mary sniffed. "Nothing like waiting till the last minute."

"Trust me."

****

After Faith did me that favor this morning, I decided I owed her one in return, so I looked for her at lunch. I knew she'd be with Sara and Katherine, headphones on and scribbling in that notebook of hers. After a few weeks of sitting next to Faith in Creative Writing and seeing how talented, and yes, sweet, she was, I felt bad for treating her like a pariah. Yeah, I knew all about "the company you keep," but maybe Faith thought of Sara and Katherine more as lifelines than friends. I could have been nicer to her, but I'd never taken the time, and now I felt bad about that. It was time for me to be as generous to Faith as she'd been to me this morning.

She was at their usual table in the corner of the lunchroom with her headphones on, head down, writing away, all alone for the moment. I hurried over with my lunch tray.

"Hey, Faith, wanna come sit with us?"

She pulled off her headphones and gaped at me. "Is this a pity invite? 'Cause Sara and Katherine will be here."

"I'm trying to say thank you for the save in class today. I'm sorry it's taken me all this time to…" *To be a friend* was what I was thinking, but I didn't finish my sentence. "Come on." I started walking, glancing over my shoulder to see if she was following. After a moment of hesitation she did. I headed over to where Hank and Hattie were sitting side by side, and James and Flip were chowing down on burgers and dipping their fries into the same pile of ketchup.

"Move over, Hattie." I deliberately set my tray down between her and Hank. "We gotta make room for Faith."

Hattie scowled. "There are plenty of other empty chairs at this table, Emma." But when I gave her a little shove she grudgingly got up and moved over one seat. "Did you say Faith? Barlow?"

I sat down in her vacated chair next to Hank and liberally squirted ketchup out of tiny packets onto my French fries. "Faith did me a huge favor in class this morning."

Everyone turned to see Faith standing behind me with her food tray, headphones dangling around her neck. "Sit here." I patted the chair on my other side.

"What favor?" Hattie asked with a sideways glance at Faith. *What's so important I had to give up my spot next to Hank?*

150

"Faith wrote the most amazing sonnet," I said. "A few of them really."

"And?" *This better be good.* Hattie took a tentative bite of her meatloaf, made a face and tossed her fork down.

"I just helped out a fellow student." Faith took a bite of her own meatloaf but seemed to enjoy it.

"So, Emma, did you get a Love-a-Gram from Nick?" Hattie asked.

Hank dropped his burger mid-bite and turned sideways in his chair to face me. "Yeah, good question."

Awkward. I didn't like being reminded that I'd been ignored by the two most important guys in my life. "No," I told them.

"In that case, if..." Hank started, stopped himself, saw Hattie smiling at him, and thought *Should I?*

Should I what? I sat on the edge of my seat, figuratively speaking, waiting for Hank to finish his thought or at least his sentence.

"Hey, Faith," Flip said from across the table, interrupting Hank's spoken and unspoken words. "I saw your name on the list of teen mentors for the Saturday night lock-in at St. Malachi."

I tossed an angry scowl at Flip, who got my meaning and shrugged apologetically.

"Yeah, I offered to help out," Faith told him. *Nothing else to do.*

"That's nice," was all I could think to say. Let's face it, I didn't have any Valentine's Day plans either. I turned to Hank, hoping against hope that he'd resume his thoughts, or words, or something.

"Hattie, you got plans tomorrow night?" Hank asked.

I shoved my food tray aside.

****

"Emma, someone wants to talk to you," Mrs. Evans called out. She'd been manning the front desk at the daycare and answering phones while I got the snacks ready for the kids.

I couldn't imagine who'd call me on the landline at work, since just about everyone had my cell number. I set the over-filled tray out on the big table in the playroom. "Tell whoever it is I'll call back."

"Uh, it's not a phone call," a male voice said.

I peeked my head around the corner to see Nick standing in the doorway, a single red rose in his hand. Huh. I smiled and gave him a hesitant wave, and then hurried to serve the apple juice, string cheese and heart-shaped cookies to the daycare kids. Except for our brief conversation in the hall, I hadn't heard from Nick all week. I motioned for him to follow me into the kitchen.

"I didn't get a chance to see you at school today," Nick said.

Didn't get to or didn't want to? I opened the fridge to store the extra juice and cheese.

"I really wanted to, but I was signed up to go to the special needs room at lunch," he replied.

Now that annoyed me. Not the part about his genius mind doing calculations on my body language. The part about him forgetting Valentine's Day while doing more volunteer work instead of studying. I set the service tray in the sink and turned to face him, my arms folded in classic defense mode. "Okay, you're here now, so…?"

Nick smiled, his big blue eyes all twinkly, and handed me the rose, which smelled terrific by the way. "I know how you feel about Valentine's Day, and I

152

didn't think you'd want to go to that big party at Bigelow's tomorrow night."

Maybe, but a girl still liked to be asked.

"So I have a suggestion. I signed up to be a teen mentor at St. Malachi for the…"

"Yeah, I heard about the middle school party."

"You did? Great! They're gonna have games for the kids and then a movie with a love theme. I was hoping you'd go with me and we could hang out. It'll be fun," he cajoled with an elbow jab to my shoulder.

Well, I rationalized, since he came from an all-boys academy, maybe he'd never had a girlfriend before and didn't know what was expected of him romantically. I sighed and thought about the alternative – staying home by myself. Even Isabelle and Jonathan had dinner reservations at some fancy restaurant. "Yeah, okay, what time?"

"Great," Nick exclaimed. "Pick you up at six."

****

Spending Valentine's chaperoning a bunch of middle schoolers would keep my mind off all the happy lovebirds at Bigelow's, even though I set a lot of them up. I especially didn't want to watch my best friend Hattie spend the evening with Hank.

I purposely put on a black sweater with my jeans, avoiding any red that might suggest I was dressed for the Valentine's festivities. Nick came to pick me up wearing a Northwestern University Wildcats hoodie sweatshirt. No clichéd holiday clothing for us.

Nick whipped his Beemer into a space on the back row of the huge church parking lot behind the building. "Ready?" He beeped the car locked and we went in through a side entrance.

The church had a full gymnasium for the use of both parishioners and the school, complete with basketball courts and bleachers, and that was where the party was being held. Everywhere you looked you could see the St. Malachi Catholic High School Crusaders symbol, a white shield like the ones knights of yore carried into battle with a slanted blue cross in the middle. It was proudly displayed on banners, the backboards, the bleachers, and the floor. And since this was a Valentine's Day party for twelve and thirteen year-olds, somebody hung up a painted and extremely artistic-looking mural with creative images of hearts, cupid, candy, and red carnations, and draped it between two of the basketball goals.

The mural stopped me in my tracks. "Wow."

"That's Miguel Castillo's handiwork," Nick said. "I told you he was good."

Even with something as simple as a holiday mural, the guy's talent shined through.

Wish I had the nerve to compliment Miguel in person, I heard someone thinking. I did a quick visual search, and saw Faith Barlow standing on the other side of the gym, gazing up at the mural.

Nick saw her, too, and he took me by the hand to walk me over. Faith was lost in her own world, so she was both surprised and a little embarrassed to see us standing in front of her.

"Cool drawing," I said.

I didn't even mention Miguel's name, just his work, and that still made Faith blush. "I gotta go set up the Twister game."

"Was it something I said?" I asked Nick as I watched her duck down a hallway and disappear.

Nick laughed and squeezed my hand. "I know you're itching to set her up with Miguel."

"It's not over till it's over," I replied.

The place was humming with activity: adult church volunteers running around setting up refreshments on a cafeteria-style table festooned with red, white and pink ribbons all sprinkled with candy hearts, while a couple of teenage guys were hooking up the big screen TV projector under the basketball goal.

"What kind of movie do they show preteens in a church?" I asked as I watched all the busy-ness.

"Valentine's Day," Nick said.

I groaned. "Yeah, I get that."

Nick shook his head. "No. *Valentine's Day* the movie, rated PG-13."

Giggly little kids with backpacks and sleeping bags were pouring in through St. Malachi's gym door, boys trying to look like high-school kids in jeans and Mel High hoodies, and girls wearing red or pink in honor of the occasion. They were all smiles and chatter as they rushed in and dumped their belongings in a corner of the gym. Was I ever that young and silly?

I remember when I was in seventh grade and there was a lock-in at the middle school on New Year's Eve. I don't think I even bothered asking Dad, but went straight to surrogate parent Isabelle, who dug into her savings for the fee and signed the form. That lock-in was held in the school cafeteria with various areas sectioned off for activities, and the wildly outnumbered chaperones were trying to establish order as we kids came streaming through the doors, laughing and calling out to one another. I was a little nervous about spending the night away from home, but Isabelle was sure I'd have fun and promised to pick me up promptly at eight a.m.

Hank was there that night. He'd only been living in Melville a few months and was still that geeky kid that no one knew very well. I was supposed to be meeting Hattie at the party but she was running late. Hank was sitting on his bedroll all by himself in a corner, playing a game on his phone while periodically pushing his thick glasses back up his nose.

I sat down next to him. "What're you playing?"

"Angry Birds," Hank replied without looking up.

That impressed me. It was a difficult game, so I figured he must be pretty good. "Winning?"

Hank tossed me a "duh" expression. "Do you play?"

"Heck no," I told him. "But I brought a deck of Uno cards if you wanna play that instead." I fished them out of my backpack.

The two of us played Uno till nearly midnight, only taking a break when the pizza arrived, and then gathered around the TV just before midnight to watch the ball drop and usher in the New Year. Twelve year olds don't kiss at midnight, but I felt a tingle go down my spine when Hank squeezed my hand at the stroke of midnight. Sort of the same chill I got when he kissed me for real this past New Year's Eve.

"So here's the game plan," Nick said, bringing me back to the moment. "Games like Twister, Monopoly, Golf Trivia, all located in different Sunday school classrooms, then pizza, then the film." He winked at me. "Gotta keep these kids from playing spin-the-bottle."

I smiled at his joke. It was nice that this church had arranged for an evening that was fun but well-supervised. It provided me with a distraction from...*from what? Hank and Hattie? Wondering where*

I fit into Nick's life? Worrying about my dad? All of those, I guess. "Thanks for bringing me tonight."

Nick squeezed my hand and then hurried off to help with the setup.

Chapter 11

I had passed along the business card for that free clinic to Isabelle, who said she would take it to Dad. After Valentine's Day, I asked her about it and she said she hadn't had a minute to go see him.

"Then let's do it now. Together." She'd just picked me up from work and we were headed home. It was mid-week and I had a lot of homework, and I knew Isabelle was probably tired and hungry, but if Dad's former psychiatrist thought it was important for him to continue treatment, I wanted to make sure he had the information. What he did with it was up to him.

Isabelle glanced over at me and then craned her neck to look at the sky. "I heard that a winter storm's coming our way."

"All the more reason to go see Dad now," I said.

She turned the car around and headed south to Indianapolis, instead of north to our condo. After a short drive on Eighty-sixth Street, Isabelle turned off onto a side street lined with apartment buildings, and drove till she came to the last building at the street's dead end.

Isabelle parked the car and turned off the engine. "This is it. Dad's apartment."

I surveyed the run-down building with its flashing neon sign that read V lley View Apartments, the "a" burned out. There was no valley and certainly no view. I took in the overflowing dumpster parked at the edge of the parking lot. "This is it?" I shivered. My sister had cranked her car heater up as high as it would go, but it wasn't just the cold causing my reaction.

"It's all he could afford."

"Do you think he's home?" I almost hoped he wouldn't be, since I had no desire to venture into that building.

Isabelle pulled out her phone and fired off a text. After a few agonizing minutes, an answer pinged back. "Yeah, he's inside." She glanced over at me. *I know you don't want to see Dad living like this.* "I'll run the business card in to him and be right back."

She was right that this was unsettling. It would be hard enough if I was an adult, but as a kid, I didn't want to think about my father living in such reduced circumstances. But this was my idea, so I shook my head. "No, I'm going in."

We knocked on the door of Number Four A and Dad let us in. The apartment building had probably been built in the nineteen seventies and it didn't look to me that anything had changed in all those forty years. It was an efficiency apartment, one room with a bed, a tube TV, a small table and two chairs, a tiny bathroom, and a kitchenette. The electric stove only had two coil burners, and the fridge door was held together with duct tape. My heart sank.

Dad hugged Isabelle and then me. "To what do I owe the pleasure?" He went over to the TV and manually turned it off.

"How's work?" Isabelle asked. She dug through her handbag until she located the business card I'd given her weeks ago.

"I'm getting a few more hours," Dad said. "Oh, and

I might get the opportunity to study Reiki. I always wanted to learn about it, and the bookstore offers training classes."

"Rei...what?" I asked

Dad smiled. "Reiki. Japanese healing. One of my coworkers did a few healings on me and I feel better..." he stared up at the ceiling, "...about things. I might be able to help other people feel better, too."

Dad does seem more upbeat. Isabelle and I exchanged knowing glances. "Speaking of..." She handed him the clinic's business card. He perused it with a puzzled look on his face.

"Dr. Knight gave it to me," I said. "Well, Dr. Knight's son Nick, who goes to school with me, he gave it to me. She thought..."

Dad nodded and shoved the card in his pocket. "So you met my psychiatrist, did you?" He walked to the window and peered through the thick drapes. "Storm's coming."

"Dad," Isabelle said. "Call the clinic."

We each gave our father a hug and left. Once outside, I wrapped my arms around myself, shivering uncontrollably.

****

SNOW DAY!

Sure enough, the predicted snowstorm hit late that night. In fact, it got so bad that they had to call off school today. We woke up to six inches of snow on the ground, more falling, and visibility so low that it was slowing down the snowplows and salt trucks. That meant I had an entire Thursday free. My homework got a reprieve, and I didn't have to go to work since the daycare always closed when schools did.

However, bad weather didn't necessarily mean all businesses shut down.

I yawned as I stumbled into the kitchen, glancing at my sister in her work attire. "Tell me you aren't planning to drive around town showing houses today."

"No," Isabelle said as she stuffed a few items into her briefcase, "but I do have to go to Todd Bekins' house to oversee delivery of the new furniture and accessories."

"Today?" I peered out the kitchen window to assess the accumulating snow. "Can't you reschedule?"

Isabelle smiled. *Aww, she's worried about me.* "The store assured me the delivery guys could make it. If I postpone I have no idea when they could get me back on their calendar." Isabelle glanced at me. "Since you're not doing anything today, you're welcome to come along. Maybe you could text Mary and get her to join you at her brother's house. If she can get there."

Sounded good. I'd much rather watch Isabelle work her design magic at a pro football player's house than sit around the condo in my pajamas and surf social media all day. "Can you wait while I take a shower?"

"Make it quick," Isabelle said. "I'm supposed to be there at ten and I don't know how long it'll take to make the drive."

Isabelle and I arrived at Todd's house at nine fifty-five, after nearly an hour in bumper-to-bumper traffic on icy roads. *Wonder where that delivery truck is.* She craned her neck up and down the street.

"Can you text them?"

Isabelle gave me a disapproving look. "No. I only have a number for the store, not the delivery guys."

Speaking of texts, my phone pinged with one. "It's Mary. Says she's not going anywhere in this weather." I shrugged. "Well, then, I get to see Todd's redecorated house before his sister does."

A strong wind was blowing the top layer of powdery snow all around, giving the neighborhood a white-out appearance. I pulled my stocking cap down over my ears, hugged my pea coat tightly around me, tucked the hem of my jeans into my boots, and waded through drifting snow to reach Todd's front porch. Isabelle was a little slower because she was wearing black leather boots that were more stylish than practical, black leggings that looked cute but couldn't possibly keep her warm, and a wraparound coat that wouldn't stay tied. I rang the bell and jumped up and down trying to keep warm, hoping Todd would answer ASAP.

He didn't. Isabelle and I were both freezing and I was about to suggest we go back to the car when Todd cracked the door open an inch to peek out.

Wha...? He was thinking, like Isabelle wasn't expected.

"Good morning, Todd," Isabelle said. "Remember we spoke yesterday? The furniture's scheduled to arrive today. Soon, unless they're stuck in traffic or a snowbank." She stamped her feet to kick the snow off her boots. "May we come in?"

Todd opened the door wide to let us in. He was wearing grey sweats with the Colts horseshoe logo down both legs, a matching blue Colts hoodie, and his feet were stuffed into scruffy house slippers. "Excuse my appearance, but I thought because of the weather..."

"They deliver rain or shine – or snow," Isabelle sang out as she visually took in the mostly empty room she was about to transform. "That," she said, pointing to the worn sofa and wrinkling her nose. "It's going to the trash heap, right?"

"Got a charity coming by this week to pick it up. I'll move it to the garage for now."

"By yourself?" I gulped. I knew he was strong and all, but that was a heavy couch.

"If we offer the moving guys a tip, I'm sure they'll help." Isabelle gave Todd a pointed look. She set her briefcase on the kitchen counter and pulled out her phone, punched some keys, and then started walking around the room, double-checking her calculations.

"Hey, babe, where's that coffee?" a voice called from the basement.

Isabelle cringed. *The girlfriend's here.* My sister was probably worried that the girlfriend would start dictating furniture placement, and according to Isabelle's digital room diagram, everything was already planned to perfection.

"We've got company," Todd called back before turning to Isabelle and me. "I was just about to make a fresh pot. Can I offer you ladies some?"

Before either of us could answer, the girlfriend bounded up the stairs from the basement. My jaw dropped.

"Kendall?"

Ohmigod Emma! Kendall was definitely dressed for a day indoors in her pink sweatpants with a Colts horseshoe on the butt and matching pink Colts athletic jacket. Plus she was in her stocking feet like she'd been snuggled up on the couch, making herself at home.

Isabelle lifted an eyebrow but continued with her measurements. *Interesting.*

No, it was astonishing. "Kendall?" I repeated.

Kendall recovered quickly. "Hi, Emma. Got a new

job as gopher?"

"Hey Kendall, remember me? Emma's sister?" Isabelle waved from the corner of the room.

Great. The decorator is the matchmaker's sister. "Oh, hey, Isabelle," Kendall called out with fake sweetness as she walked across the room to look over my sister's shoulder. "I had some ideas about a few things."

Of course you did, Isabelle growled internally. "Well, let's just wait till everything's here and let Todd decide if he wants to make changes."

I went into the kitchen to get out of the line of fire, pretending to see how Todd was coming with that coffee. "So. Kendall?"

He blushed deeply. "Thanks for introducing us New Year's," he said as he set the pot to brew. *Awkward!* He sighed and turned to me with a sheepish grin. "I know it's weird. Kendall's graduating high school with my sister."

It was weird all right, but Kendall was definitely old enough to date a guy Todd's age if she wanted to. When I introduced them I thought Todd would just take her to a nice restaurant or something, not have her sitting casually in his house early in the morning, voicing opinions on decorating ideas. It must have gotten serious pretty fast. Then I remembered last month at the Metroplex, and Kendall with mystery guy number three.

"Just be careful," I warned him. "Kendall's got a reputation..."

For what? He lifted an eyebrow.

"...for dating lots of guys," I finished.

The delivery people finally arrived around noon, after an awkward couple of hours with Kendall alternately cooing over Todd or making suggestions about the decorating scheme, none of them of any value judging by my sister's thoughts and facial expressions. In short order Isabelle had the old sofa out to the garage, the new pieces in, the accessories in place, and everything arranged beautifully. Of course after we left, Kendall might try to convince Todd to move things around to suit her tastes. I hoped he'd say no, because the newly-designed living room looked good enough to be featured on the cover of one of those house decorating magazines.

****

Since school was called off yesterday, I'd happily avoided Creative Writing. One less day sitting in class with Sara glaring at me and shooting thought-darts, and Faith offering to help me out. I alternately felt like a pariah or a charity case.

Today in Family Relations, we were supposed to be discussing traditional family roles versus twenty-first century roles. I read the assignment last night and I was ready to contribute.

"This chapter focuses largely on two-parent families," Miss Taylor said as she opened the class discussion. "Any comments?"

"The book was published in 2002," Hattie said. "The information's way outdated."

"Not necessarily," said Katherine Howard. "My dad just preached a sermon on this topic last Sunday. He said that we as a society should return to the traditional family structure."

"And because a minister says so, we have to agree?" Hattie asked.

What would Miss "I worship" sports know about it? Katherine scowled, a firm set to her mouth.

"This isn't 1955," I said, coming to Hattie's defense. "Times have changed. Women take on different roles than they did back in the day. Besides, sometimes parents aren't married, or they divorce, or die, or…" I shook my head and breathed. "That doesn't mean a different kind of family isn't valid."

I knew my family was anything but traditional, but I was grateful for a caring sister who'd stepped up when I needed a surrogate parent. If it were up to me, my mom would still be alive, my dad would be emotionally stable, both parents would have good jobs and a nice house in the suburbs, and Grandma Austin wouldn't be sick. But I couldn't make my family look like a TV sitcom.

"I didn't say 'invalid.'" Katherine turned her back on Hattie and stared me down. "It's just that everything works better when there are two committed parents in the home."

"My mom died!"

"And your dad…" *is a loser who abandoned you.* Katherine's words but not her thoughts were interrupted by a steely glare from the teacher.

"My dad is back from his out-of-town job," I said with a sniff. "And I heard your minister-father was accused of…"

Katherine's face turned red, her eyes blazed, and in one motion she bolted across the room and clenched her fists. "Shut up, you crazy psychic," she growled.

Okay, I admit I "heard" that rumor about Reverend Howard by what I'd picked up from Katherine's troubled thoughts over the last few days, gossip on social media, and from the thought-rumors around school. Add all that to her reaction just now and I was convinced there was truth to it.

Hattie was on her feet, about to rush to my defense, but the teacher took control, stepping between Katherine and me and motioning Hattie back to her seat.

"All right, all right." Miss Taylor glanced between the two of us with a stern look and a *Start a fight and you're both expelled* mental threat. "I believe we're getting off track here." Miss Taylor waited till Katherine returned to her seat and both our tempers had cooled somewhat before she continued. "Let's just agree that roles once played by the father and the mother are sometimes taken on by others in the twenty-first century."

"Like big sisters." Hattie tilted her head at me, with a glare at Katherine.

"Yes," Miss Taylor replied, "and therefore we can conclude…" The teacher stopped mid-sentence when my cell phone pinged with a text. Oops. I forgot to put it on vibrate.

It was from Isabelle. She never sent me messages during school hours, so immediately all kinds of scary thoughts popped into my head. "Excuse me, Miss Taylor, but I have to take this." She waved me away and I hurried into the hall, glad to be out of that pressure cooker.

I pulled up the text. *News from Dad. Later!*

What? Isabelle gave me no clue, and I couldn't text her back right now, so I turned off my phone and figured I'd just have to wait till this evening. I returned to the classroom and took my seat.

"Ladies and gentlemen," Miss Taylor was saying, "This classroom should be a safe environment. We can disagree with one another, but insults and physical violence are not the answer in either the classroom or in society. This course is Family Relations, and we need to be mindful that every one of you comes in here with unique perspectives. Therefore, I'm scrapping my original assignment and asking you each to write an essay, to be titled Home is a Learning Center. Personalize it as necessary, and turn it in tomorrow." The teacher lifted her eyebrow as a few students groused about the change in her syllabus.

I started jotting down notes, but I knew this would be a difficult topic for me. What exactly had I learned from my family? Could I even write about it without choking up?

If I had a husband and child, I'd never leave them, I picked up from someone. I honed in, thinking it was Katherine, but it wasn't. It was Miss Taylor. Maybe being a single career woman wasn't all it was cracked up to be.

When the dismissal bell rang, everyone quickly left the room. Everyone except me, since I wanted to apologize to Miss Taylor for the argument with Katherine and the phone interruption. As I approached her desk, I spotted Nick sauntering into the room, early for the next period class. He rarely came to Student Resource anymore, preferring to use his free study period for volunteering or tutoring, so I was surprised to see him today.

"Slumming?" I asked him.

Nick grinned at me and headed for his usual seat. I followed him and sat down next to him, one eye on the clock. I couldn't be late to Creative Writing. Again.

"I'm glad to find you still here," Nick said. "I wanted to ask you about tomorrow, Saturday."

I got some unexpected stomach butterflies. Was he

asking me out on a bona fide date? We hadn't really had one that didn't include marathon pool games, parents or groups of kids. "What about tomorrow?"

"I need to run an errand down to Indianapolis and I don't really know my way around the city, so I was hoping you'd help me out."

Okay, not asking me for a Saturday night date. I stood up and adjusted my book bag on my shoulder. "That's what your GPS is for." I turned to go.

Nick put a hand on my arm to stop me. "Yeah, I know, but I'd rather have a personal tour guide. You free?"

Now he had me curious. "Where is it you need to go?"

Nick avoided eye contact with me and instead made a big show of retying a shoe lace. "One place I'd like to go is that shop where I hear they have killer chocolate desserts." He executed the perfect knot with a flourish.

I wasn't buying the excuse that all he wanted was chocolate. "That's over on Ditch Road. Not too hard to get to from here."

"True." He straightened up again and ignored my lifted eyebrow. "But there's also a bookstore nearby I want to check out."

I studied his face a minute, hoping to glean more information, but as usual it wasn't forthcoming. *I wish I knew what he was really up to.* "Yeah, sure. What time?"

"I'm not up to anything," he replied with a smirk.

"Cut it out, Nick," I warned him.

"I've got the homeless pet shelter in the morning, so I'll pick you up about four." With that, he pulled a notebook and pen out of his backpack, concentrated, and then – started doodling. When does that guy ever do homework?

****

I was still concerned about that text I got from Isabelle this morning. She was sitting in her car outside the daycare waiting for me when I got off work, nervously drumming her fingers on the steering wheel.

"So?" I climbed in and fastened my seatbelt. "About Dad?"

"So…" Isabelle said, "You'll find out when we get home." She pulled the car into the street. *Fabric choices, new action adventure film, spring wardrobe, call the condo maintenance…*

Great. She was blocking her thoughts. "Come on…" I begged.

At that, she popped in a CD, cranked up the volume and started singing loudly off-key.

We arrived home and Jonathan's car was already there. Usually he didn't get home till after seven, since he liked to go to the gym after work, so that got the wheels in my head turning even more.

I hope Jonathan picked up the Chinese, Isabelle was thinking. She turned off the engine and gathered her things from the backseat.

"Me, too. I'm starved."

Isabelle and I walked into the living room where Jonathan was sitting on the sofa, shuffling through some legal papers. And sitting in Jonathan's recliner watching TV was Dad. No wonder Isabelle wouldn't let me eavesdrop on her thoughts. After seeing him only a couple of days earlier, I was surprised he was there, and even more curious about what was going on. Isabelle sent me a quick thought. *I picked Dad up this afternoon. Big news he wanted to deliver in person.*

Dad aimed the remote at the TV and switched it off as he stood up from the chair.

"What's going on?" I asked.

"Well, to begin with, I called that clinic," Dad said. He shoved his hands in his jeans pockets and smiled. "It's a short bus ride from my apartment, so I went in for an appointment with a psychologist, a Dr. McNair. He seems to think we can pick up where Dr. Knight and I left off."

I nodded encouragement. "So that's the good news?" I looked to Isabelle for confirmation.

"It is, partially," Dad said.

Isabelle jumped in. "Dad's been offered a full time job. As a CPA."

Okay, that wasn't what I expected. Actually, I don't know what I was expecting, but after realizing what Dad had been going through for a long time, ever since Mom died in fact, I was hopeful. "Really?" I'd been tied up in knots lately, alternately worried about my father's situation and yet still angry about the past year. "So why couldn't you tell me that earlier?" I asked Isabelle.

She tilted her head at Dad. "I was going to let him tell you himself, but I guess I stepped on his moment."

Dad grinned at Isabelle. *No problem.* "Emma," Dad said to me, his voice catching a little, "I want so much to make amends. I know I hurt you."

I opened my mouth to speak, but I couldn't get any words out. Yes, I'd been hurt, but I understood it all much better now.

Maybe now Dad can get out of that rundown apartment.

I rolled my eyes at Isabelle. "Rundown" was an understatement.

Dad smiled at me, hands in his pockets as he rocked back on his heels. "Once I get a couple of paychecks under my belt, I'm going to buy a used car and then look for a house to rent in Melville." *You and I could start fresh in a new home.*

I swallowed hard as it dawned on me what he was suggesting. I turned to face Isabelle. "Do you think I should move in with him?"

I listened closely for thoughts telling me if Isabelle thought it was a good idea, or thoughts from Jonathan that I should take Dad up on his offer. When I didn't pick up anything, I turned to my sister. "Maybe I should give you and Jonathan your privacy."

No one said anything. It was so quiet, in fact, that Isabelle cleared her throat a few times, Jonathan went back to shuffling papers, and Dad shifted uncomfortably from one foot to the other.

Crickets.

I swallowed, took a deep breath and then a leap of fate. "Dad, I'm happy for you, but…" I turned to my sister, "if you guys don't mind, I'd prefer to stay here."

Isabelle nodded and gave me a big hug, and Jonathan reached around Isabelle and squeezed my shoulder. "Thank you," I whispered. "Both of you."

"Hey, can I get in on this?" Dad took a tentative step towards me and I allowed him to embrace me. I remembered the discussion in Family Relations today, and even though I'd always known that the Austin family was less than traditional, somehow we were making it work.

Enough of this emotional stuff. "Where's that Moo goo gai pan?" Isabelle asked with a knowing glance in my direction. "Let's eat."

****

Maybe it was the Chinese food, maybe it was the good news that my father was getting a fresh start, or maybe it was the idea of another sort-of date with Nick, but I didn't get much sleep last night.

Nick said four o'clock and that was exactly when he showed up. After the snowstorm that closed school two days ago, the weather had improved dramatically. Today the sun was out, the snow was melting, and the high temperature was expected to be near fifty. Pretty normal for the end of February.

"Do I need a coat?" I asked Nick, poking my head out the door. I had on aqua blue athletic pants with a matching jacket over a long-sleeve t-shirt. Nick was only wearing a corduroy blazer.

"It's up to you, but it's pretty nice out."

The air was so mild it was giving me spring fever, so I decided against taking my heavy coat. Nick turned off the car's heater and cracked the windows down a little. He also turned off his GPS, claiming he was relying on my sense of direction.

"Um, the bookstore is that way," I told him when he missed what should be our turn. "Aren't we going to…?"

"That's not the only bookstore in town."

I frowned and peered at him closely. "So where are we going?" Once again I was concentrating like crazy, trying to figure out what Nick was thinking, but as usual his mind had a *no trespassing* sign on it.

"You'll see," he said with a twinkle in his eye. "Do you like Katy Perry?" He plugged in the music.

I shrugged my indifference as we drove along listening to the music. "Hey, I know this neighborhood." Nick pulled his car into the parking lot of the New Age bookstore where my dad worked and snagged a space near the entrance.

"Why are we here?"

He hopped out the driver's side and pocketed the keys. "I told you I needed a book. Ready?"

What kind of book could Nick possibly want that would come from a bookstore like this one? Metaphysical stuff? I guess I really didn't know this guy at all, if he was into that and never mentioned it. Come to think of it, he rarely mentioned anything that interested him outside of volunteer work.

I wasn't quite as eager as Nick to go inside. If Dad was working, I didn't know how I felt about popping in on him unannounced. And of course there would be the inevitable stares and uncensored thoughts from his coworkers who knew the whole story about his year-long absence. I hesitated as Nick opened the large glass door.

"What's wrong?" he asked with what sounded like genuine surprise.

"You're the genius, you tell me."

Nick was still holding the door open and he looked down at me with a smile and a wink. "Okay, Mom told me your dad works here, but I'll bet he isn't even here today."

Dad's work schedule hadn't come up over Chinese last night, but he'd made it clear he wasn't giving up this part time gig. He needed the money and he wanted to study Reiki. "Maybe I'll just window shop at some of these other stores while you browse inside."

"Oh come on," Nick said with an impatient eye roll. He opened the glass door wider and waited while I continued to waffle, but a couple of people just inside the store were giving us dirty looks because we were letting in a draft. Nick reached back across the threshold, firmly took my hand and practically dragged me all the way to the book section at the back of the store. Once there, he released my hand and started browsing the shelves like he was a regular, which for all I knew he was. That was when I started "hearing" voices.

Isn't that Frank's daughter? Uh-oh. I caught a quick glimpse of a saleswoman I thought I recognized.

Does Frank know she's here? No, but I felt sure someone would tell him.

Whoa, nice looking guy! Okay, I should've expected that because Nick was hot.

And then…*Emma?* "Emma!"

I turned around and there was Dad. I blushed.

"Emma, you didn't tell me you'd be coming by today." Dad started to give me a hug, but then glanced around self-consciously at the other employees watching him, and settled for a quick squeeze of my shoulder.

"I didn't know," I mumbled with a scowl at Nick.

Nick was immediately all charm and good manners and offered his hand. "Nice to meet you, Mr. Austin. Nick Knight, classmate of Emma's."

Dad shook his hand. "Eleanor Knight's son, right? How can I help you?"

Nick ran his fingers along the book bindings. "I'm interested in Reiki."

Surprised, I turned to Nick. "Seriously?"

Nick nodded. "I had some free time so I did some research."

What free time was he referring to? He was taking all those advanced classes and, even though I knew how high his IQ was, I'd still never seen him do any homework. Yeah, yeah, the work was too easy for him, but it still had to get done. Before I could form my question, Nick opened his mouth and spouted off some stuff that went way over my head.

"'Reiki is classified as an energy therapy based on the belief that disturbances in energy fields in and around the body result in illness, and that improving the flow and balance of energy can improve health and wellbeing.' At least that's what I read."

Dad and I both gaped at him.

Dad recovered his composure first. "Yes, that's true." He perused the shelf, selected a book and handed it to Nick. "Here, this is an excellent choice. Say, would you two like a cup of tea?" Dad indicated the coffee bar where they also sold exotic teas. "I could take a break and join you."

I was still speechless, trying to digest the genius-speak that had flowed so easily out of Nick's mouth.

"Thanks, Mr. Austin," Nick said, "but Emma and I are headed to that dessert cafe down the street."

"Rain check then?" Dad sounded disappointed, and I felt a little guilty. He was trying so hard to be a father to me again.

Nick stepped to the cash register and paid for his book with a credit card. "Nice meeting you," he said to my father.

I was almost out the door, but then impulsively I turned around, hurried back over to where Dad was standing with a wistful look on his face, and gave him a quick hug. Then I left without a word.

In the parking lot, Nick put an arm around me and pulled me toward him. "Now was that so bad?"

Okay, it wasn't. "You should have warned me, that's all."

Nick steered me toward the car. "Come on, let's hit that dessert bar. Nothing brightens a day like chocolate."

Chapter 12

"Go Hattie," I yelled.

I was at the Mel High Lady Eagles' county basketball championship game to support my best friend, a starting Center and key player on the team. I admit I was never much of a basketball fan, which was heresy in Indiana, but it was mid-March and basketball was what the month was all about. We were ahead by four points over the Lady Titans, and it was a close game heading into halftime. Even though it was a Saturday night and it was women's basketball, not men's, the gym was packed with Mel High students there to cheer on the team. There was a trophy at stake, and since the guys' team failed to snag one in their tourney last weekend, it was up to the girls to save our athletic reputation.

Sitting behind me were James and Flip, cheering wildly. If I moved my feet too much in those tight bleachers, I'd kick Sara Davis and Jeff Atwell, who were sitting *this close* on the seat in front of me. Keeping her distracted with a boyfriend was working out well, because there hadn't been any recent snide remarks, blind gossip entries or outright articles about Mel High's Miss Match. Down a few rows were Jane and Agnes Bates, flanked by Darrin and Sam O'Brien. Faith Barlow was even there, sitting with her mother, Monica. On the other side of Monica and next to Faith was Hattie's mom Mrs. Smythe, dressed in a purple and gold Lady Eagles t-shirt, enthusiastically waving a banner, and occasionally springing to her feet to cheer her daughter on. She stood up and motioned me over, so I got up and lumbered down the bleachers.

"Emma, dear, I'm so glad you're here." Mrs. Smythe squeezed my hand. "We haven't seen you at the house much lately."

"I know, I've been crazy busy, but you know I wouldn't miss this game."

"You remember Ms. Barlow? She and Stella and I were all homeroom moms years ago, when you girls were in kindergarten." Mrs. Smythe stopped with a stricken look on her face. *Oh that was insensitive.* "I mean, uh, that is…"

I jumped in to let her off the hook. "Sure, I know Faith's mom. Nice to see you," I told Ms. Barlow.

"How's your father?" Monica asked, and then blushed in a way that reminded me of how her daughter blushed every time Miguel Castillo was mentioned. "I haven't seen him much at the bookstore since he got that new job."

It was clear that Monica had more than a passing interest in my dad. Now that he was back in therapy, had a full time job, an older but drivable car, and was on the hunt for better housing, maybe it was time for Dad to start a new social life. "Dad's doing well," I said.

"Please tell him I said 'hello,'" Monica said, the red in her cheeks deepening.

I nodded and pulled out my phone. I was almost on automatic pilot as I fired off a text. I stopped and thought about it after the fact and seriously questioned my sanity. "Enjoy the game," I told them, and returned to my seat.

I was sitting right between Hank and Nick, which

was awkward. Nick was following the game closely, pumping the air with his fists when our team scored, and occasionally yelling at the coach or the refs. You know, like a real fan. Hank on the other hand, was glued to his cell phone.

"What are you looking at?" I craned my neck to see what he found so fascinating.

Hank pointed to the screen. "It's baseball preseason," he told me, like it was something I should already know. *Baseball is a thinking man's game.* "The Cubs are ahead of St. Louis by one run."

Nick reached around behind me to playfully punch Hank in the shoulder. "Dude, you're at a basketball game. Turn off your thinking man's game and watch our Lady Eagles. And Hattie. Your girlfriend?"

Hank tossed Nick a look, blinked, and went back to his baseball game. *Girlfriend?* He rolled his eyes.

I found that reassuring. Hank was at a basketball game, which he obviously had no interest in, in order to support Hattie, but he wasn't watching the game and instead was sharing his passion for baseball with me. Me. Not Hattie. Not Rachel. Me.

"Hattie's doing great!" I pointed to the court just as she made a basket.

"Score," Nick shouted, standing up with the rest of the student body to holler and applaud.

"Hank, did you see that?" Nick pointed to the court and shouted over the crowd noise before sitting back down.

Hank put his phone away and stood up. "I'm going to the concession stand," he told me. "Want anything?" *Nick's about to*...that thought trailed off.

About to...what? I wondered.

Nick didn't take his eyes off the game. "I could use some popcorn."

"I'll bring you some," Hank said to me with a scowl at Nick. He climbed over both of us and made his way down the wooden steps, dodging empty cups, spilled popcorn and discarded trash along the way. Then he stopped and exchanged a few words with Mrs. Smythe. I tried listening to his words or "listening" to see what his thoughts were, but maybe I was too far away because I got nothing.

Nick followed my gaze. "You shouldn't be so nosy."

What? Nick didn't know what I could do, did he? Of course not. I glanced at him but he was once again engrossed in the game.

The halftime buzzer sounded and the teams left the court, headed to their respective locker rooms with their coaches. I stood up and stretched my arms and my back.

When Hank returned with the bags of popcorn, I immediately dove in. "Thanks. What do I owe you?"

Hank winked at me. "My treat."

He pulled his phone back out and I scooted over closer to watch the baseball game over his shoulder. It was a lot slower paced game than basketball, but if Hank liked it, I wanted to learn about it, too.

And then the recipient of my earlier and possibly ill-advised text showed up just before the start of the second half. He was standing at the bottom of the bleachers, searching the crowd. I got up and walked down to him. "Hi, Dad." I let him give me a quick hug.

"What was so urgent I had to rush over here?" He cast a glance at the scoreboard. "Close game, huh?"

"Follow me." I started climbing back up, but

stopped midway at Mrs. Smythe and Ms. Barlow's seats. "Dad, you remember Monica Barlow?"

Monica was blushing again, and Dad was looking a little uncomfortable himself, but then a smile crept onto his face. "Of course. From the bookstore." He clasped her hand as her cheeks reddened.

"Frank," Mrs. Smythe said, "please, join us." She scooted over a little and patted a small space between her and Monica.

"Dad, you go ahead and sit here with the ladies. It's pretty crowded up in the student section anyway." I didn't wait for an answer but bounded up the steps two at a time, took my seat, and waited to see what, if anything, happened.

Occasionally I looked out onto the basketball court during the second half, especially if Hattie had the ball or she was at the free-throw line, but I was a lot more interested in what was going on with my father and Monica Barlow. They were talking and seemingly enjoying the game, but I couldn't really tell much else.

The game continued to be close as the Lady Titans tied the score with only a few seconds left on the clock. Then Hattie laid up a shot and scored a two pointer, winning the game for us. Final score: Fifty-eight to fifty-six.

The fans were on their feet whooping it up, Kendall was leading the cheerleaders in enthusiastic flips, and then some of the seniors jumped out of the bleachers and rushed onto the court in their excitement to celebrate winning the trophy.

"Come on," Nick shouted over the noise. He took my hand and we joined the crowd.

Hank was down on the floor a few steps ahead of us,

high-fiving a very sweaty but exhilarated Hattie. *Way to go girlfriend!* I stopped dead in my tracks when I "heard" that, because I was just sure they were only friends. Did he mean girlfriend literally, or as slang? I didn't know, but on impulse I turned to Nick, threw my arms around him, and planted a big kiss on him.

"Wow," Nick said, coming up for air. "Cool." He kissed me back, and I could feel the heat coming off the laser-glares Hank and Hattie were shooting at us.

****

Hattie called me Sunday afternoon after her team's big win the night before. "Hey, bestie," she said. For a girl who just led her team to a championship, she didn't sound too perky. *Hank and I had a fight.*

Well, that explained her mood, but it didn't set my mind at ease about their relationship. And I still felt guilty for kissing Nick like that, which set it all in motion. Still, I hated to "hear" that my friends had a falling out. "What happened between you and Hank?"

Hattie exhaled a very loud, exaggerated sigh. "The upcoming Sweet Sixteen happened."

I sat down on the edge of my bed and crossed my legs. "I know Indiana University is in the playoffs, but what's that got to do with you and Hank?"

"Get this. He offered to take me to some dumb symphony concert on the same night as the Sweet Sixteen. Naturally I refused."

I rolled my eyes, glad this wasn't a video call. "Naturally."

"I told Hank that if he thought I'd give up watching that game on TV he was crazy."

"Hattie, were you and Hank…?"
Just friends.

183

Really? I perked up at that. "But if you're just friends, then how did this whatever it was get started between you two?"

There never was a "whatever." "Remember I told you Hank called me New Year's Day?"

I did remember and I also remembered I didn't like it.

"He seemed to want to talk about something, but he never got to the point. Finally I just said 'how 'bout those Pacers?' and the rest of the conversation was about sports – me talking strategies, him spouting statistics."

"So then why do you think Hank really called?"

"I don't know for sure, but I suspect it was you, and that kiss you two shared New Year's Eve. And then you turning around and kissing Nick. Anyway, he and I started hanging out as friends, but now it's clear that's all we'll ever be."

Suddenly I was in a pretty good mood. "Listen, Hattie, I can find any number of guys who'd be happy to hang out with the star of the Lady Eagles basketball team and watch the Sweet Sixteen playoffs. Just say the word."

"Emma, puhlease! Can't you be sympathetic for five minutes? I've liked Hank since seventh grade and this is the first time he's ever given me a second glance," she whined. "I thought.,."

"Did you really think it would turn into something more?"

Not really.

"I didn't think so."

"Just give me time to cool down before you start sending boyfriend candidates my way," Hattie said before hanging up.

Okay, truth time. I meant it when I said I didn't like my friends to fight, but I'll admit I was relieved to know there was nothing serious going on between Hank and Hattie. Now I just needed to know who his mind was really on, me or Rachel.

****

After talking to Hattie yesterday, I arrived at school early so I could find Hank. Not that I didn't commiserate with her, because I knew she'd gotten her feelings hurt and I hated that I'd contributed to that, even indirectly, but my heart was telling me this might be my chance with him, kisses with Nick notwithstanding. I spotted Hank in the hall with a group of senior guys, all of them laughing and joking.

"So, Friday night," announced Sam O'Brien. "Our house for the IU game."

"Yeah, big guy party," Darrin chimed in as he slapped Hank on the back.

Hank's face fell. *Isn't anyone interested in anything besides basketball?* "Um, well…"

Hank didn't even know I was standing right behind him, so he was startled when I piped up. "Sorry, guys, but Hank has a prior engagement. With me."

His shocked expression followed by his *thanks for the save* thoughts were totally worth it. "Oh, sure, that's right," he hemmed and hawed, "I, uh, forgot. We've got that…thing."

"Thing, huh?" Sam and Darrin exchanged dubious glances.

"Yeah, that Beethoven concert at the Performing Arts Theatre," I told them. That sounded so boring that the twins didn't even bother challenging us. In fact, they couldn't get away fast enough.

Once we were alone, I turned to Hank. "I know about the argument you and Hattie had."

Hank looked like he could do that thing where you stretch your collar away from your throat because things were getting way too uncomfortable. "Oh, well, yeah. I can explain."

I put up my hand to stop him. "No need. Hattie and I talked and she's okay with just being friends. And don't worry, the Friday night concert was just my way of giving you an out." Not that I wouldn't enjoy spending some quality time with him, but…

I don't want out popped into his head

My adrenaline kicked into high gear. "I didn't really expect you to buy expensive concert tickets, but," I smiled before turning and practically skipping down the hall, "I *am* free and wouldn't mind if we hung out. Text me and let's meet up somewhere." I was pretty sure Hank was staring after me, probably wondering what just happened.

Guess who I ran into next? Literally.

Nick put up his hands to keep me from mowing him down. "Hey, Emma, where you headed all happy?"

I stepped back and rearranged my book bag on my shoulder. "Family Relations."

If I could read Nick's mind, I'd guess he was thinking I wasn't this happy about class. But I couldn't, and he didn't say anything.

"You heard about Hattie and Hank, I guess." With me using my jealousy over Hank and Hattie as a couple as an excuse for the big kiss I laid on him after the basketball game, I could feel my face turning red with embarrassment. "There's nothing to hear. They were just friends who had a difference of opinion."

"Yeah, well, there's lots of buzz, since everyone knows they're in the friend zone," Nick said with an odd twinkle in his eye. "There's speculation on who you'll set Hattie up with next. Maybe that violin player from St. Malachi? What's his name? Robbie?"

The red in my cheeks just drained out.

"Was it something I said?" He grinned as he started walking backward. "Hey, there's a big project waiting for you in first period today."

Oh ugh. Some big homework project? Even if it was my favorite class, the end of the school year was less than three months away and teachers had been piling on the work. Like that was going to prevent senioritis.

The warning bell sounded and I ran to get to the classroom on time.

Miss Taylor had her hand resting on a stack of test papers that needed to be returned, but instead of distributing them, she kept staring at her cup of designer coffee. *He bought me a coffee. Did he know that was me in the car behind him?*

I've heard stories of people being in line at a drive-thru and when they got to the window, they were told the car ahead of them already paid for their purchase. It was one of those Pay it Forward moments. That must be what happened to Miss Taylor, but it sure did have her rattled.

I took my seat next to a scowling Hattie. "You okay?"

"Oh, sure," she snapped, "if you ignore the gossip mill running wild. My life is over." She slumped down in her chair, arms crossed over her chest. *Stupid high school grapevine.*

I almost laughed. Almost. I knew exactly how she felt, because I'd been the subject of plenty of gossip, especially this school year, and I knew it could sting. "You know how kids are. Just ignore it and pretty soon everyone will move on to the next big story." Hopefully it wasn't me.

Hattie sat up, a deep frown on her face. *You're probably right.*

"And like I told you on the phone, there are lots of guys…"

I wonder if Robbie…

"Not him," I said.

I glanced at the wall clock. We were ten minutes into the class period and the teacher was still sipping coffee, lost in her own world. All the kids were fidgeting in their seats, some breaking out their tablets or surfing their phones, so I got up and quietly walked to her desk. "Miss Taylor, do you want me to return those tests for you?"

And just like that she was back on Planet Earth. "Um, no, Emma, I'd better do that. But could you do me a favor?" She dug through her desk drawer for a notepad and pen. She scribbled something on the paper, folded it in half, and wrote a pass on the outside. "Please deliver this, and then come right back."

Seriously? A handwritten note? Why didn't she just text or email like normal people? I focused intently, hoping she was thinking about the contents of the note, but she was still ruminating about the coffee, so I headed off to make the delivery. *Mr. West, room 350B.* Hmmm.

I knocked on the door, and who should answer but Sara Davis. She lifted an eyebrow at me and called out, "Hey, Mr. West, it's Miss Match to see you."

I wanted to sink through the floor. If I hadn't promised Miss Taylor, I'd turn around and run. "Sara, I thought we'd called a truce."

"Think again," she said.

Mr. West was scurrying around his room, helping his journalism students who had a school newspaper to put out. "May I help you, Emma?"

I nodded and handed him the note. "From Miss Taylor."

He opened it and read silently. *"...for the kind gesture this morning..."* was all he mentally shared with me, but it was enough for me to finally have an Aha moment. Miss Taylor had a thing for Mr. West, and if he paid for her coffee, it was possible he felt the same.

"Why don't you email her a response," I suggested, "and meet for coffee in person this time." The moment that came out of my mouth, I saw Sara smirking at me. Did she hear what I said? Did Mr. West realize I said something I shouldn't have known?

I ducked my head and took off down the hall.

Then something stopped me cold. *There's a big project waiting for you in first period.* I thought Nick meant a homework project. Just how did he know?

****

At lunch, Hank was sitting at a different table on the other side of the senior section, far away from Hattie. As for Hattie, she had her headphones on and was totally ignoring everyone around her, including me. I still felt guilty about the part I played in their disagreement. Even though she didn't want me setting her up on a date, the least I could do was come up with someone for her to watch the basketball game with Friday night. Someone who wasn't Hank. Or Robbie Martin.

Nick walked up with his tray from the hot lunch line, sat down in the chair next to me and grinned as he popped open his chocolate milk. "How'd it go in Family

Relations?"

"How did you know about Miss Taylor and Mr. West?"

He winked at me and leaned over to whisper, "Guess who was in the drive-thru right behind them."

Lucky coincidence, I guess. I sighed and unwrapped my veggie roll. "I planted the seed in Mr. West's mind, but it's up to them."

Nick laughed while he smeared mashed potatoes and gravy all over the top of his meatloaf, and then tucked in. "Wanna watch the IU game with me Friday night?"

I stiffened. "I already made plans. With Hank."

Nick shrugged. "Well, Hank's clearly not a basketball fan."

Then an idea occurred to me. "I was hoping to find someone to distract Hattie from all this gossip, and no way she's gonna miss that game, so maybe the two of you could get together. Just to hang out."

Nick considered that. "I was invited to the O'Brien's, but I haven't given them an answer yet." He paused and then forked up a bite of his meatloaf concoction. "Their girlfriends aren't coming, but maybe they'd be okay with Hattie, since she knows the game so well."

I breathed a sigh of relief. "Great. Thanks, Nick."

"Sure," he said with his mouth full of mushed-together meat and potatoes. "Two friends just hanging out. Like you and Hank."

I quickly focused on my own lunch.

****

Hank and I agreed to meet Friday night on Main Street at The Mellow Coffee Bean, where they have live music playing on weekends. Not loud music, just a guy with an acoustic guitar. It was late March and the weather was getting warmer, so I didn't mind walking the mile or so from the condo to downtown Melville. When I stepped inside I saw Guitar Guy sitting on a stool, strumming and singing softly, but the place was empty except for a middle-aged couple having dessert. They must not be basketball fans either. I wondered how Hattie was getting along at Sam and Darrin's with Nick. She knew all the IU players and all the game strategy, so probably just fine.

I took a seat in the small, dimly lit café, next to a picture window that looked out onto the street so I could see when Hank arrived. I hoped he wasn't going to be too much later because I wanted as much of his time as possible.

My eyes glued to the window, I spotted four figures walking by, two by two, arms linked together. The girls were both wearing similar-looking stocking caps and lightweight jackets over their nearly identical jeans, and the two guys had on thick hooded sweatshirts. At first I just shrugged it off as date night, but when they stopped under the street light on the corner I got a glimpse of one girl's face. Jane Bates! So that had to be Agnes with her, but who were the two guys? Not Sam and Darrin, because they were hosting the guys-plus-Hattie basketball party. I craned my neck to see if I recognized either of them, but I didn't. College guys? St. Malachi students? I had no idea, but it looked like the Bates sisters were up to their old tricks, only this time they switched guys altogether. I groaned. When it crashed down on them, and it would, were they gonna expect me to fix it?

I was so busy staring out the window and feeling bad

for the O'Brien twins that I didn't see Hank walk up to the table.

"Hellooo," he said, waving his hand in front of my face to get my attention. "What are you looking at?"

"Hank." I gave him a warm smile, and then pointed out my problem. "Jane and Agnes, stepping out for the evening."

Hank followed my gaze. "Poor Sam and Darrin."

I nodded. "Never mind them. I want to know how you're doing."

Hank seemed to be in a good mood as he sat down, smiling, fairly bouncing in his seat, and to my surprise, he reached for my hand across the table. "Just happy to be here with you."

That gave me goosebumps, the good kind, so I tried to listen in and hoped for once I'd get a hint of what he was really thinking. But all I picked up was stuff about stopping for gas. After an awkward silence during which I studied his face and Hank blushed, I said the first thing that came to my mind. "So. Here we are on date night, just two old friends."

Hank released my hand. "Is that all we are?"

I blinked. It certainly wasn't all I wanted us to be, but since all I'd ever done was fix up other people with their crushes, I wasn't sure how to approach my own. "I don't know. I mean, after so many years…"

"Yeah, well, if you're thinking of fixing me up, Emma, I'm really too busy these days with school and debate team to think about dating." *And the only girl I want to date isn't interested.*

Stunned, I realized what had flashed across his mind. He was interested in someone? Definitely not Hattie, and I guess it wasn't me, either, judging by how fast he snatched his hand back. So the natural conclusion was Rachel Bomburg. My heart sank. "I guess being valedictorian is a lot of pressure," I replied, validating his academic concerns if not his romantic ones.

"Want some coffee?" Hank abruptly stood, his face unreadable and his thoughts closed off.

"Mocha latte," I told him, but I was talking to his back because he was already at the counter, intensely studying the overhead menu. I'd upset him and I felt awful. Part of me wanted to run over and throw my arms around him, tell him how much I cared about him, but the other part of me couldn't move.

So now besides dealing with the Bates sisters, again, I had Hank all miserable in love with... Rachel, I guess. I decided that I didn't like her one bit. I knew what he saw in her – she was beautiful, smart, sophisticated – but what I didn't get was why she didn't feel the same way. Or did she? I didn't want to know.

****

I got a flurry of texts over the weekend.

From Hattie: *IU won! Nick spent all night with Dr. O'Brien talking about hospital and medical stuff. BORING!*

From Sam O'Brien: *Can't reach Jane. Why the silent treatment?*

From Darrin O'Brien: *What's up with Agnes? Can you talk to her for me?*

From Sara Davis: *Saw Jeff at the mall with Katherine Howard. Seriously? This is all your fault.*

From Nick: *Spending the rest of the weekend shadowing Dr. O'Brien at St. Anthony's.*

Huh?

From Mary Bekins: *When I see Kendall I'm gonna*

smack her!

Whoa! I texted Mary back but she never answered.

The newest rumor around school was that Miss Taylor and Mr. West had been seen at various restaurants and coffee bars around town, which caused lots of giggles and whispering among students. I silently congratulated myself for facilitating that match, but judging by all the texts, some of my other fix-ups weren't working out so well.

I saw Nick at his locker and pounced before he headed off to wherever. I doubted he was going to class, or if he did, he probably wasn't going to listen to the lesson. I'd given up nudging him to keep up with his schoolwork. All he ever did was surf the 'net or volunteer work.

"How was your hospital thing last weekend?" I asked him as he shut his locker.

"Good. Really good," he said.

I started to ask him about his sudden interest in medical stuff, but chalked it up to his genius mind being bored. "Thanks for taking Hattie to the O'Brien's basketball party."

He shrugged. "No problem."

"What class do you have next?" Okay, so I was still nudging.

Nick didn't answer, but instead took my hand and walked me to my class.

"Why am I getting the royal treatment?" I asked as we stopped in front of the classroom door to Creative Writing.

He squeezed my hand and released it. "Your project last Friday worked out pretty well."

"So I hear."

"Well, now you've got a new assignment." Nick grinned and tilted his head toward the classroom.

I could think of a few "projects" I needed to work on, mostly related to fixups that had suddenly gone sour. But after my brief coffee date with Hank, one that ended with me walking home alone less than an hour after I arrived at the Mellow Bean, my most pressing issue was trying to accept that Hank had a crush on another girl and trying to understand why Rachel didn't reciprocate.

I turned my attention back to Nick. "What new assignment?"

Nick peeked into the classroom and I followed his gaze as he pointed right at Faith, who had her head buried in her notebook, writing furiously. I slapped my forehead. "Ohmigod." I didn't know if Nick was referring to my Creative Writing assignment or some other cryptic love match he thought I should make, but I knew I'd completely spaced that descriptive essay assignment, and even Faith couldn't bail me out this time.

Nick grinned as he headed off in the other direction. "Don't worry. I'm sure it'll all work out."

Don't worry, huh? Right. Only my life hung in the balance as I watched my chances of being accepted to my first choice school evaporate because of a failing Creative Writing grade. I took my seat and slumped down in misery just as the tardy bell rang.

"Ladies and gentlemen," Mr. West began, "your descriptive essays were due today…" *I was busy this weekend and got behind on my grading* was what he was thinking, and I immediately sat up and took notice. "…but because of IU's victory over the weekend, I'm sure you all had other things on your minds. Email me your papers by the end of school tomorrow, before we go on Spring Break."

A collective sigh of relief came from all the students, except Faith of course.

"Faith," I whispered, "can I read yours?" Maybe I'd get some inspiration.

She hesitated before handing me her notebook. I skimmed over it and saw that she'd gone beyond the teacher's simple instructions to describe a familiar person or place, and instead had written a character study.

He comes to mass every Sunday wearing a suit. Boys his age don't usually dress so formally, even for church, but his attire is a symbol of reverence. The boy is friendly with some of his peers but not intimate with any of them. After the service he nods and murmurs "Good morning" but will tarry for no one. He has many responsibilities: a job in the family business, schoolwork where he excels, and a strong passion for his artistry. His focus is...

"Ladies and gentlemen," Mr. West said, interrupting my reading, "I'm giving you this class period to work on your essays." He lowered his glasses and looked sternly at us. "Use your time wisely."

There was a little murmuring and whispering as kids got their notebooks or laptops out. I handed Faith's essay back to her, and even though I didn't get to finish reading it, I was sure the rest of it was just as amazing. "Miguel Castillo?" I whispered.

Faith blushed and didn't answer me, but of course it was him. They attended the same church and I already knew she admired his artwork. Admired *more* than just his artwork. Now I had to figure out how to get the two of them together, even though she didn't exactly ask for my help.

And then I recalled Nick's prediction about another project. He already knew about Faith's crush – we both did – so I guess he expected me to do something about it. But why didn't he just say so?

****

I texted Mrs. Evans that I'd be a little late to work, because I needed to go to the library after school and get some ideas for that Creative Writing essay. I'd tried to use my class time, but after reading the opening part of Faith's, I was pretty sure describing my bedroom wasn't going to cut it. I sat down at a quiet corner table and brainstormed some ideas. Downtown Indianapolis? The zoo? Isabelle's real estate office? Before I knew it, time had gotten away from me and I was more than just a little late for work.

Apparently I wasn't the only one still hanging around after school, though, because a few kids were milling around the locker bay like it was eight a.m. instead of four p.m. I passed Sara Davis and if looks could kill... *Jeff blew me off for holy-roller Katherine! Why did Emma even think...* "Emma," she hollered, and her voice seemed to reverberate along the near-empty hallways. "You set up my best friend with my boyfriend? Traitor!"

Where did Sara get the idea that Katherine and Jeff being together had anything to do with me? I ducked my head and kept walking.

But she followed me down the hall, still calling me out. "Or did you mind-read them? Either way, this is your fault."

I stopped to answer her, to try to defend myself, but then I noticed Sam and Darrin scowling at me while

197

similar thoughts ran through their heads. *Two- timing twins. Shouldn't ever have listened to Emma!* Why were they blaming me, when they knew exactly what sort of girls they were dating?

The O'Briens had their heads together with Greg Plowman, whose angry thoughts fired more ammo at me. *Mary won't go out with me now because she's too upset about her brother's failed romance.* Wait. What? I wanted to ask him what he meant, but that would mean responding to thoughts, not words. I kept moving.

Kendall was in a corner huddled with Hank. Hank? *Hey, Hank, how 'bout you and me…?* Why that fickle…I covered my ears, because I didn't want to know if Kendall had broken up with Todd to date Hank. My Hank.

Then I saw Hattie consoling a tearful Mary, who was shooting dirty looks at both me and Kendall. *Emma's the one who fixed them up and Kendall broke my brother's heart* kept flashing in and out of her thoughts. Even Hattie, who knew the truth about me, was looking at me with suspicion. I started to call out to her, but she was too focused on Mary.

They were all staring at me like they knew I could hear their thoughts. Sara planted that idea in their heads months ago and had continued to stoke the fire, so maybe they did believe it. I wanted to shout, "Yes, I can hear your thoughts. I admit it. I've been listening in on you all these years and you have every right to hate me."

Fraud!

You'll pay for this!

No one's gonna be friends with Emma anymore!

Emma ruined my life!

Thoughts were flying at me with increasing speed,

making it hard for me to decipher them, or even know whose thoughts they were. Suddenly I had a throbbing headache. I pressed my fingers against my forehead hoping it would subside. I felt confused and then woozy.

I clapped my hands over my ears in a futile attempt to block out the chaos. Why were they all mad at me? I tried so hard…

What was happening? It was like I was in a funhouse with all the distorted mirrors and everywhere I looked people were laughing and pointing at me. Why did I ever use mind-reading to make matches? Why did I play matchmaker at all? Did I want to help people find love or was it just a power trip?

I wished I'd never heard a single person's thoughts. I wished I'd never set up a single date. I wished…

Suddenly everything went black.

Chapter 13

"Emma, Emma! Can you hear me? Wake up!"

I tried to open my eyes but it felt like there was lead on my eyelids. I struggled and struggled, and finally one eye popped open, and then the other.

"Oh, thank goodness."

My vision was blurry as I stared up into Isabelle's frightened face. Despite my pounding head and sudden nausea, I managed to twist around to see Hank and Hattie. I felt around with my hands and realized I was lying on a bed somewhere.

"What happened?" I blinked a few times to get my eyes to refocus and rubbed my aching head. I felt like Dorothy in the *Wizard of Oz* when she woke up after getting hit by flying tornado debris.

"You fainted," said the school nurse, "and your friends brought you in to the clinic."

"The nurse called me," Isabelle said as she took my hand. "Hank said you hit your head pretty hard when you fell."

I reached behind my head and felt a lump forming. "Ouch." I tried to sit up but collapsed back on the pillow. "It hurts."

"You've been out for a while," the nurse told me. "You might have a concussion. You should go to the hospital ER and get checked out."

"I could call my mom…" Hank offered.

I shook my head, which was a bad idea, and then struggled to sit up. I was completely disoriented, and really embarrassed about the whole thing, because I wasn't some delicate flower who fainted all the time. And no way was I letting Hank bother his pediatrician mom. "Just take me home," I told my sister.

"Emma, what happened?" Isabelle asked.

I tried to answer, but my mouth felt like it was full of cotton and I couldn't focus.

"I think my bestie here got too stressed out by all those gossips in the hall," Hattie offered, "and of course she skipped lunch today."

"You skipped lunch?" Isabelle asked.

"Emma doesn't like the school's hot dogs," Hattie told her.

Okay, it was all coming back to me now. Too many thoughts that I shouldn't "hear," too much guilt about making a mess of my friends' love lives, and then the hot dog thing.

"Can you stand?" the nurse asked.

I slowly, very slowly, swung my feet to the side of the bed and even more slowly, stood up. But even that was too much exertion and I nearly collapsed again. Hank caught me, and then Hattie was on my other side, my two dearest friends propping me up.

All I wanted was to go home, away from all this negativity, and away from everything I wished I hadn't accidentally overheard today.

****

"You sure you don't want me to take you to the doctor?" Isabelle asked as she pulled the car into the garage.

With no medical insurance, the idea of a long wait

in some emergency room and the bill my sister would have to pay made me feel even worse. "I just need to rest."

Isabelle piloted me into the condo and carefully helped me up the stairs to my bedroom. She fluffed the pillow and helped me ease onto my bed. I closed my eyes to stop the room from spinning, but they popped open again. "I was supposed to be at work."

"I already called," Isabelle said, "and Mrs. Evans says to rest up, and not to worry about tomorrow either, since you won't be going to school." She brushed the hair off my forehead. "You want something to eat?"

I nodded. I drifted in and out of sleep for what seemed like hours but was really only a few minutes, because Isabelle was back with a bowl of chicken noodle soup and ginger ale on a tray. The soup smelled really good, so maybe hunger was part of my problem after all. I sat up slowly, very slowly, and took a spoonful of savory broth.

"You ready to tell me what happened?"

"Matchmaking gone bad," I said between slurps. "My friends think I made a mess of their lives."

Isabelle started to sit down on the bed next to me, thought better of it, and leaned against the doorway. "That's totally unfair. You can arrange the dates but it's up to them to build the relationships."

I set the spoon down. "You were right all along, Isabelle. I shouldn't have been fixing them up in the first place."

Isabelle opened her eyes wide in surprise. "What brought on that epiphany?"

I sighed as I felt for the bump on the back of my head. "Right before I hit the floor, I realized I'd been on a power trip, trying to control everyone's love lives." I eased back onto the pillow. "I feel like I let everyone down."

Isabelle brushed a stray hair off my throbbing forehead. "You had the best of intentions, Emma. Besides, kids have short attention spans. After everyone gets back from Spring Break, they'll have forgotten all about it and be hounding you for dates again."

Maybe. But I was glad to have a couple of weeks off to regroup. I set the half-empty soda can back on the tray and shoved it aside. "I think I'll take a nap."

"I wish you'd let me take you to the hospital," I heard her say just as I fell into a deep sleep.

"Emma?" My bedroom door opened and the light flipped on. "Are you up for company?"

I rolled over and peeked open one eye, blinked at the glare and glanced at the bedside clock. It was seven p.m. so I must have been asleep for a couple of hours. Company? "Can't it wait till tomorrow?"

"I called Dad." Isabelle stepped aside to let him enter my room.

"You shouldn't have…"

"He insisted on coming over, said he might be able to help you with some relaxation techniques." She quietly closed the door on her way out.

"Reiki treatments aren't going to fix what's wrong with me, Dad," I said as he came to my bedside.

"Reiki might be just the thing to heal the physical reaction to the emotional situation you're in."

I eased myself to a sitting position. "How do you know about my situation?"

He carefully sat down beside me and started massaging the back of my neck and spine, and it actually started relieving some of the pain. Maybe he was on to something, because his hands were working magic. "Your sister says you made some bad matches among your friends. I told you that you shouldn't be arranging dates."

I pulled away from him and then regretted the sudden movement, because it made me queasy. I had to wait a minute till the nausea passed before I could speak again. "When did you ever tell me any such thing?"

Dad went back to the neck massage for a bit. Finally he squeezed my shoulders, stood up and shoved his hands in the pockets of his trousers. "Four years ago, when you started high school and began fixing up your friends with dates. I told you not to meddle in your friends' love lives because you'd be the one who got hurt."

I wracked my poor, aching brain and vaguely remembered that conversation. "Okay, so this is 'I told you so'?"

Dad patted me on the shoulder and helped me lie back down on my pillow. "No. It's me reaffirming what we've always known about you."

I shaded my eyes to glance up at my father, but every movement hurt my throbbing head. "What you've always known?"

My father reached over and fluffed the pillows underneath my neck. "I knew about your grandmother's gifts, and she'd already seen the early signs in you."

I nodded. "I just thought everyone heard thoughts."

"Grandma talked to you, Isabelle talked to you, and even Stella reminded you that you have a gift that needs to be kept private. People just don't understand, especially kids. But when you started high school and heard your friends' crushes, I warned you…"

"Not to play matchmaker. Right."

"Get some rest." Dad opened the bedroom door to leave. "Say, while you're off school, why don't you come over and see the new house. That nice young man, Nick? Perhaps he could bring you."

Dad flipped off the bedroom light as I settled back down to sleep, our conversation rattling around in my brain. I drifted off and dreamed about matchmaking. Or was that a nightmare?

From far off in the distance I heard a cell phone ringing. I slowly opened my eyes and realized it was mine. Where was it? Oh, yeah, in my school bag, lying in a chair across the room. I stumbled over in the darkness, unzipped the bag and pulled the phone out just as it was about to go to voice mail. "Hello?" I croaked.

It was Hattie. "I got online and read up on concussions. It says someone should check on you every few hours for the first twenty-four hours. So I'm going to call you every two hours."

I sat down on my bed with my phone to my ear, thinking what a great friend she was. "You don't have to do that. Isabelle's here."

"Isabelle has a job to go to in the morning and needs to rest up after the scare you gave her."

"But you've got school tomorrow."

"You know nothing ever happens the last day before Spring Break, so it won't hurt if I'm a little sleepy."

"Thanks, Hattie. Talk to you in a bit." I disconnected and, just as I was about to fall back to sleep, the phone rang again. "Hattie, it hasn't been two hours yet."

"It's not Hattie."

"Hank?"

"I wanted to make sure you were okay," he said. "Are you?"

I was touched that he cared enough to call, even if it was late on a school night. "Still headachy, but I'll be fine."

"I talked to my mom, asked her about concussions, and she said…"

"Yeah, I know. Hattie's on it."

"Emma? You sure you're okay? You really scared me today."

If I didn't feel so crummy right now, I'd hope that this meant Hank cared about me instead of Rachel. But all this thinking was making my ears ring, so I eased back down onto the pillow. "What are you doing over Break?" I was fighting to keep myself awake.

"The debate team leaves right after school tomorrow for Cincinnati. After that, some sight-seeing around Ohio."

"Let's get together when you get back. Just text me." I disconnected the phone and set it next to my bed. This time I didn't fall back asleep so easily, because all I could think about was Hank.

In the morning, Nick called me on his way to school, and was surprised to hear about my concussion. He wanted to tell me that he and his parents were headed to San Francisco for Spring Break. He said his folks decided to combine a business meeting with a sightseeing tour and he was looking forward to the California weather. I guessed that missing a day of school wouldn't change Nick's academic outlook much.

Hank called again before school and repeated what he'd said about how I'd scared him. "I'll miss having lunch with you at school," he said. "Rest up, okay?"

I was going to rest much easier, that was for sure.

****

Hattie called me. "I'm bored out of my mind."

"Yeah, I hear you."

We were nearing the end of Spring Break. I wasn't working at the daycare either, since most of the kids were on vacation or doing stuff with family during the time off school. Once the headache let up and I got to feeling better, I realized I had a lot of free time on my hands, since I was also the school pariah. So I cleaned the condo from top to bottom, and then did all the laundry and straightened up Jonathan's third bedroom office area as best I could without disturbing any of his legal papers. I watched a bunch of stuff on the DVR followed by marathon episodes of House Hunters. I couldn't go jogging because of residual effects of my concussion, but now that it was April, I'd at least taken a few leisurely walks to enjoy the warmer breezes and smell the freshly-mowed grass and budding flowers. Still, I was ready to get out of the house.

"Wanna go to the mall?" Hattie asked. "I need a Prom dress."

I waited to see if her thoughts would reveal who she was hoping to go to Prom with, but I didn't pick up anything. "Do you have a date lined up?"

Hattie didn't respond, so I concentrated really hard. Nothing. Maybe I wasn't entirely recovered from the concussion. "Okay, the mall sounds good. What kind of dress are you looking for?"

"Well, what I'd like to look for is a little black dress, three inch runway-worthy shoes, all new makeup, sequin bag…"

I giggled at the thought of six-foot Hattie towering

over her date and every other guy in school. "Has Flip signed off on this? Because last year he told you…"

"He's meeting us there. And don't think this shopping trip is your chance to shop for a boyfriend for me. I'm saying yes to the dress, that's all."

"No problem. Anyway, I've sworn off matchmaking."

Big gasp on her end. "Did I hear you right? Did you say you aren't going to try to find me the Prom date of *your* dreams?"

I ignored her sarcasm. "Not just you. Not anybody."

"Good luck with that," she snorted.

"What time are you picking me up?"

****

The mall was a good place for teenagers to hang out during the long break if they weren't sitting on some beach in Florida, or touring museums in Cincinnati like Hank was doing. The shopping center was positively crawling with kids. Some were elementary-age kids with parents, but mostly it was teens. Hattie and I were enjoying our time gazing into store windows and admiring the spring fashions.

"Where did you say we were supposed to meet Flip?"

Hattie did a visual search of our immediate vicinity. "He said something about shoe shopping."

We kept our eyes peeled for men's shoe stores, and pretty soon we were rewarded when Flip emerged carrying multiple shopping bags.

He waved a bag in the air and hurried over. "Hey, girls. Let's get our shopping on."

I tried to peek into his bag. "New shoes, huh? Got a new suit to go with it for Prom?" I listened for his inevitable *none of your business* thoughts, but nothing was forthcoming.

"Hattie and I have to do some serious Prom dress shopping," Flip said. "And then we're hitting the makeup counter at Lacy's Department Store. Girlfriend's gonna look gorgeous if it kills me."

I looked from Flip to Hattie and back again and listened intently. They seemed to have some secret between them, but for the life of me I couldn't figure out what it was. I wondered if that bump on the head did more than give me a bad headache. What if...? No, I couldn't have lost my mind-reading abilities. Right? But now that I thought about it, I hadn't heard Isabelle's thoughts lately, or Jonathan's, or even Dad's when I talked to him on the phone, not since I hit my head on the floor. I sighed. "Who are you getting all gorgeous for, Hattie?"

Hattie looked at me and dared me to read her thoughts. I couldn't do it.

"Come with me, ladies." Flip wedged himself between Hattie and me, linked arms with both of us, shopping bags still in tow, and led us down the mall to a little boutique hidden in a corner next to a big anchor department store. "I just passed by here and saw some fabulous gowns through the window. Totally unique collection." He held the door for us.

Hattie and I walked in and I spotted... "Kendall?"

Did Flip set up this little prank or was it pure coincidence? I instinctively tried to eavesdrop on his thoughts and then got frustrated when I couldn't pick up anything.

Kendall frowned like we just ruined her day. "May I help you?" she asked in feigned business tone.

"I'm just browsing." Hattie commenced pawing through the racks.

"And she wouldn't dare choose a Prom dress unless I okay it." Flip gave Kendall an obvious once-over and then scouted out the shop. "I told her you've got an awesome selection in here." He pointed to a rack of evening dresses and took Hattie by the hand.

"Well, Hat, I don't know if we'd have what you're looking for in this *designer* boutique," Kendall said as she followed them, and I could almost see her nose rising in the air. "Not in your price range."

Hattie's name was already short for Harriet, so she bristled when Kendall shortened it even more. "Shut up Maneat…Manheim," Hattie said, making me snicker. Hattie made eye contact with me, probably thinking I was reading her thoughts. Little did she know.

"My dad the architect," Hattie said with a glare at Kendall, "gave me his credit card and told me to buy whatever I wanted." She pulled a poufy black tea-length dress off the rack, all lace and sequins and tulle, and held it up to her.

"Nope," Flip said with a shake of his head.

Kendall rolled her eyes. "We've got plenty of dresses suitable for a tall girl your size. Fourteen? Sixteen?" She tilted her head toward the Plus sizes. "Who's the lucky guy? He must be really tall."

"Size twelve," Hattie shot back, and then got a wicked look on her face. "And what about you, Kendall? Got a date to Prom? I heard you and Todd broke up, not that a grown man would attend a high school dance."

I backed away and pretended to be interested in a dress on a mannequin while I tried in vain to read anyone's mind. Still nothing. Kendall turned on her heel and walked away without any more fake attempts at pleasantries.

I sidled up to Hattie and Flip and whispered, "Mary Bekins was trying to tell me something that day I fainted at school. Well, okay, she was thinking it, but is that why she was so mad? Kendall's cheating heart?"

Hattie nodded. "'Fraid so."

I shook my head. "But why would Kendall break up with Todd? I figured once she had her claws into an eligible, not to mention hot, pro football player, she'd never let go."

"You and me both," Flip agreed.

"Come on, let's get out of here." For Kendall's benefit Hattie raised her voice. "These dresses are so last year," and marched out of the shop and back into the open mall, taking such long strides that Flip and I couldn't keep up. We exchanged glances and hurried after her.

"Hattie," I called out, but that was ridiculous because there were too many people and too much noise in the mall to get her attention.

She headed toward the food court, straight for the pizza booth. Come to think of it, that sounded pretty good. "Hungry?" I asked Flip.

"Always."

Once we had pizza and diet soda in hand, Flip and I joined Hattie who had already snagged a table and was chowing down on her pepperoni. "Okay, Hattie, don't tell me this dash through the mall was for the gourmet pizza." I tested the table with my finger for cleanliness before setting down my tray.

Hattie stuffed another big bite of greasy fast food into her mouth and pointed to it. With my current inability to get into people's heads, I assumed she meant she couldn't talk and eat at the same time. I took a sip of soda and hoped Hattie would open up when she was ready. Instead, Flip ratted her out.

"Harriet had a phone call…"

My head popped up just in time to see Hattie's eyes shoot daggers at him. He shrugged and busied himself picking onions off his veggie supreme. I glanced from one to the other, started to pick their brains and then reminded myself I couldn't.

"A phone call? When?"

Hattie had a wicked grin on her face. "Right before I talked to you this morning."

"She sent me a text," Flip said.

I hated being out of the loop. "Anyone mind telling me what we're talking about?"

Hattie took her time swallowing, followed by a few dainty sips of soda. She pointed her straw at me. "I'm surprised you haven't picked it out of my head yet."

Flip nodded. "Yeah, me, too. Or have you?"

I sighed and focused on my own mushroom pizza slice, which I had yet to bite into. Hmm, how to tell my friends I was talent-less. "Okay, truth?" They both nodded. "I must have bumped my head harder than I realized."

Hattie was sympathetic. "You still got that headache?"

"No, it's gone, but unfortunately so is my mind-reading ability."

Hattie and Flip both gasped and their eyes bugged out.

"Just before I lost consciousness, I wished I'd never been able to read minds because then I wouldn't have messed up so many people's lives." I shook my head. "Be careful what you wish for, I guess."

Flip reached over and patted my arm. "I'm sure this is just temporary."

"Yeah," Hattie said, "one of my teammates got a concussion and she wasn't back to normal for a month."

I smiled at both of them. "I hope you're right. I was gonna quit making matches anyway, so now's as good a time as any." I turned back to Hattie. "Since I can't read your mind, you'll have to tell me what you and Flip talked about."

Hattie visibly relaxed, knowing I couldn't go digging around in her brain. "Two months. That's all we've got left of high school," she said, "and then we're all going in different directions. I just want to have one night to remember."

I nodded. "Of course. Prom night. And your secret date…?"

"…shall remain nameless."

I tossed my remaining pizza on the plate and shoved it aside as I slumped into my white plastic food court chair and stared up at the institutional lights on the ceiling. "Yeah, okay, fine. Tell me when you're ready."

"You still don't have shoes or the right makeup," Flip reminded her, "and it's a good thing I'm here because you'd have bought that hideous dress from Kendall out of spite. We've still got power shopping to do." He turned to me. "And you, Miss Match, haven't even nailed down your own date, let alone a dress."

"I have a dress from last year and I'll have a date, too. Hank."

Flip lifted an eyebrow. "Are you sure?"

I cringed. "Well…" He was right. That was just

wishful thinking on my part. And I knew Hank was back in town, because he texted me the minute the tour bus hit Indianapolis a couple of days ago.

"Not to worry, Flip. Emma will find herself the perfect date."

I was glad Hattie was optimistic, because I wasn't. "It's possible I'll end up Prom dateless if Hank doesn't come through."

"What about Nick?" Flip asked.

"He hasn't asked me either."

Hattie and Flip exchanged knowing glances.

"What?"

Flip reached across the table and clasped my hand. "Remember last fall when I asked you why you never told Hank the truth about yourself?"

I shrugged. "What's that got to do with Prom?"

"I think you should come clean with Hank, then ask him to Prom instead of waiting till the last minute to see if he asks you," Flip said.

I withdrew my hand. "Come clean about what? That Sara Davis was right? That I was listening to everyone's thoughts but oh by the way, now I can't? What would that accomplish?"

"It would open up the lines of communication between you and Hank," Flip said. "Without trust, you two will never be more than convenience dates."

I blew out a puff of air, acknowledging the truth of Flip's words, but I needed to sit with it a while.

Hattie looked thoughtful. "Just ask him to the dance. If your mind-reading abilities come back, then you can tell him."

Thinking about Hank not asking me to Prom threw me into a funk. I truly wished we could go together, like last year at junior prom, but before I could answer her, someone tapped me on the shoulder. "Hi, Emma."

I snapped out of my pity party. "Hey, Faith. What's up? Wanna join us?" I indicated an empty chair at the table for four.

"I'm with my mom." Her eyes drifted to the Chinese buffet where Monica was placing an order. Monica looked nice today, wearing slimming jeans with a solid colored t-shirt and a shawl tossed over one shoulder. She was a plump fortysomething, but today, dressed more stylishly and with the wisps of gray hair framing her face instead of pulled back in a tight bun, she had a sort of mature attractiveness.

"We're out shopping. Today's my birthday," Faith said.

Hattie, Flip and I all wished Faith a happy birthday. "You got big plans tonight?" I asked her.

"Well, uh." Faith hesitated. "Mom and your dad are doing something this evening so she brought me here today…"

Oh, wow, that was interesting. Dad was dating Monica? I truly hadn't known if anything would come of re-introducing them, but I was happy to hear that he was getting out and socializing. "Then I guess that means you're free."

Faith shrugged. "Guess so."

I quickly came up with a plan. "The three of us are going for Mexican tonight." I threw Hattie and Flip a *don't you dare contradict me* look. "We'd love for you to join us. You know the place? Castillo…"

"Yes, I know it." Faith blushed, just like she did every time that name got mentioned.

"Seven o'clock okay?"

"Sounds good." Faith turned to leave, but stopped. "Thanks, Emma. This is really nice of you. I know you think Sara and I…" She shook her head and smiled at Hattie and Flip. "Well, thanks."

Although I wasn't a big fan of Mexican food, I was pretty sure I just did a good thing.

****

I put our name on the waiting list at Castillo Authentic Mexican Restaurant, and Hattie, Flip and I sat down on a bench near the front door. I'd been mulling over my conversation with my friends at the mall this afternoon. I wasn't happy about losing my ability to hear thoughts, but if it was gone for good, maybe I needed to accept it, focus on my own life and stop meddling in everyone else's. Because if I was being honest, the real reason I chose this restaurant for Faith's birthday party was because Miguel might be working tonight.

I checked my phone for the time. "Faith's late. Do you think she's bailing?"

"Maybe she didn't have a ride," Flip said.

Yikes! I didn't think of that. I started scrolling through my contacts, but I didn't have her number saved. "Do either of you know how to reach her?"

Both Hattie and Flip shook their heads. This was a disaster. All my good intentions and none of us thought to offer Faith a ride.

"You guys ready?" Miguel Castillo was working tonight, so I metaphorically crossed my fingers and hoped Faith showed. He picked up four menus and walked us to a booth at the back of the restaurant.

I lagged behind Flip and Hattie, craning my neck toward the door and looking out the picture window at the parking lot. I was hoping Faith would walk in any minute, but I had the sinking feeling we blew it. I blew it.

Miguel carefully placed the menus on the table and waited while the three of us slid into the booth. "Is there a fourth?" he asked, looking over his shoulder. "Nick Knight maybe?"

I shook my head. "Nick's probably not back from San Francisco."

"We're waiting for Faith Barlow." Hattie treated Miguel to a flirtatious smile.

Miguel blushed, which made him even more handsome. "I'll bring her over when she gets here."

"If she gets here," I muttered.

Hattie was already studying the menu. "Well, we tried. And I'm too hungry to wait."

I was feeling really guilty, but I reluctantly picked up my own menu. "This was all for her. I don't even like Mexican food."

"Try the tacos," Flip said.

I flashed back to my dinner with Nick a few months ago when he told me the same thing. "No, thanks. I'm gonna be adventurous tonight and try the quesadillas. How bad can melted cheese be?"

"Here's your fourth." I looked up from the menu to see Miguel standing there with Faith by his side. Very close by his side. She was smiling and blushing. And so was he. *AWWWW.*

Hattie stifled a giggle by burying her face in the menu. Flip also looked amused but he was better able to keep a straight face. Faith quietly scooted in next to Flip, across from Hattie and me. She looked really pretty tonight, and I doubted she'd worn that figure-flattering sundress for our benefit.

"This is a celebration," I told Miguel as I folded up my menu and handed it back. "It's Faith's eighteenth birthday, so could you bring us all some virgin margaritas? And we'd love to have you join us."

Miguel couldn't take his eyes off Faith, who played with her braided hair dangling over one shoulder and smiled up at him.

"I need to get back to work." And yet Miguel was still standing there, staring at her. Finally he recovered his professional objectivity, collected the other three menus, and took off with what some might call a spring in his step.

Once he was out of earshot, I turned to Faith. "I'm so sorry about not planning to pick you up." Hattie and Flip murmured apologies, too.

Faith shrugged. "It's okay. I called a ride share."

"Hope you're hungry. And dinner's on us." I followed Faith's gaze as she watched Miguel's every move, and oops, there I was sticking my nose in where it didn't belong again. Without my safety net.

Faith ordered the enchilada special she said was her favorite, I picked at my quesadillas which turned out to be pretty bland, while Flip and Hattie shared a steaming plate of chicken fajitas. We clinked our virgin margarita glasses in a toast and kept the conversation light, mostly about school. Just when I expected our waiter to bring our check and started mentally dividing the total by three, Miguel came back with a cupcake and a lit candle on top.

"Happy birthday." He set it in down gently in front of Faith. From the look on her face, this small gesture made her day.

"Make a wish," Hattie told her.

Faith closed her eyes a moment before blowing out the candle. I couldn't read her mind, but it was pretty obvious her wish had something to do with Miguel.

"I'm off to the ladies' room," I told them. I scooched out of the booth, actually intending to go the restroom after downing most of that thirty-two ounce virgin margarita, but it was like I was on automatic pilot. I ended up at the concierge stand. "Do you have a date to Prom?" I blurted out.

Miguel blinked. "Uh, which Prom? St. Malachi or Mel High?"

Oh yeah, there was that. "Either one. Both. Do you?"

He shook his head.

"Good. Because I happen to know Faith's available." There. I planted the idea, so I should just get the heck out of there and if he decided to ask her, he could. Their choice, not mine. Yet I couldn't force my feet to move until I got his answer.

Miguel hesitated, glancing first at the door where customers were coming in, and then over at our table where Faith had a mouthful of the cupcake he brought her. "Can I text you?" He pulled his phone out of his back pocket and handed it to me.

I punched in my contact information and made a mental note to input Faith's number in my phone when I got back to the table. Just as I handed his phone back to him, the restaurant door opened to admit two very beautiful people.

I was staring straight into Nick's face as he and Kendall walked in.

Chapter 14

Nick and Kendall? Seriously?

I turned my back to make a quick getaway before he spotted me.

"Emma," Nick called.

Too late. I hadn't seen the guy in a couple of weeks and then when I did, he was in the company of the Maneater. Oddly enough, she didn't really look like she was dressed for a date, but Kendall dressed down in jeans and white t-shirt was still a stunner. And I hadn't forgotten that I was still mad at her for the way she'd treated Hattie at the mall this afternoon.

Was I jealous? I remembered how mad I got when Nick kissed Kendall on New Year's Eve, but I had the same reaction when Hank kissed Hattie, so this big lump in my throat didn't prove a thing.

"Emma, wait," Nick called again. He followed me all the way across the restaurant to our table.

To cover my embarrassment, I snatched my purse off the seat and pretended to be preoccupied with going through my wallet for money to pay the check.

"Hi, Nick," Faith said. "I didn't know you'd be here."

"Spur of the moment decision," Nick told her with a sideways glance at me. "Oh, and happy birthday."

Faith giggled. "Thanks. How did you know?"

Nick pointed to her half-eaten cupcake, and then

turned his attention to me with that way he had, the sincere concern that always melted my resolve. "Didn't you hear me calling you, Emma? Why'd you run off like that?"

I glared at him. "Aren't you with her?"

Hattie, Faith and Flip all craned their necks for a good look at the "her" I was referring to. Kendall was standing with her back to all of us at the concierge stand talking to Miguel, and didn't seem to be the least bit interested in what Nick or any of us were doing. That was odd.

"Can we talk?" Nick didn't wait for an answer. He took my hand to help me out of the booth, and dodging waiters carrying loaded trays, piloted me through the back exit to the parking lot.

"You're being rude to my friends," I said, once we were out in the brightly lit parking lot. "And isn't Kendall waiting for you?" Adrenaline was coursing through my veins, causing my heart to beat really fast.

Nick rolled his eyes. "My parents and I just got off the plane an hour ago. We're all jet-lagged, and starved."

Suddenly I noticed how bone-weary Nick looked. He had day-old stubble on his usually clean-shaven face, and a rumpled Old Navy t-shirt paired with jeans and worn deck shoes. I looked down at my feet to avoid the pained expression on his face and scrambled for a logical explanation for my conclusion-jumping. "It's just that Mary Bekins told me Kendall and Todd broke up, so…"

"So you thought…?" Nick ran his fingers through his already unkempt hair. "Come on, Emma. I ran into Kendall in the parking lot and held the door open for her. That's it. She's picking up carryout, and so am I."

"Oh." All the righteous indignation drained out of

me. I was really ashamed of my behavior, because for once I was the one creating all the drama and Kendall was the innocent bystander.

Just then Nick's phone pinged and he glanced at the text. "Food's ready. I gotta go. Can I call you later, when you've calmed down and I'm not so fried?"

"Yeah, okay," I said. "Sorry."

Nick wrapped an arm around me and led me back into the restaurant. He squeezed my hand and released it before going to the counter to collect his takeout. I was on my way to rejoin my friends when I saw my worst nightmare. No, not Nick and Kendall. It was Hank with Rachel Bomburg.

They were following Miguel to a table on the other side of the restaurant. The dinner hour was in full swing and this place had gotten really crowded, so it was possible they didn't see me. I flopped down into my seat.

"They weren't together?" Flip asked me. "Nick and Kendall?"

I shook my head no. "But I've got a worse problem. Hank and Rachel."

Flip, Hattie and Faith all visually scouted the room for the next round of drama.

"Well, what d'ya know," Hattie said when she spotted them. "Hank's out with that gorgeous redhead from his Synagogue."

I shot her a dirty look.

"Go over and say hi." Flip gave me a little shove.

I groaned but got up and made my way across the room, where Hank and Rachel's heads were buried in their menus. "Hi, guys," I said.

Hank looked up, startled at first, but then he appeared pleased. "Hey, Emma. I didn't know you were here." He indicated his dinner companion. "You remember Rachel, right?"

I gritted my teeth. "Yes."

Rachel smiled up at me. "We just left Friday night services and I've never been here before. Hank says this place has great food. Want to join us?"

Rachel was asking me to join them on their date? But was it a date since they came here straight from church? Oh how I wish I could hear their thoughts so I'd know exactly what was going on with these two. But since I couldn't read them, I was going to have to rely on their body language and my instincts. So I did what normal people do. I fished for information. "No, thanks, I don't want to interrupt your date."

Rachel smiled, but didn't give any clues. "You're not interrupting, but you've probably already eaten. Another time?"

Why was she being so cordial? I'd be furious if some other woman tried to horn in on my date. "Sure. Another time."

"I'll see you at school on Monday," Hank said.

The two of them looked like friends out for a meal, but I was so used to relying on mind-reading that I didn't trust my own eyes. "Enjoy your dinner," I told them, and hurried off.

If my abilities didn't come back soon, I was going to have to learn a whole new way of relating to people. That idea really scared me.

****

"Isabelle," I said, "have you talked to Todd Bekins? How does he like the living room you designed for him?" I poured myself some orange juice and sat down at the kitchen table.

Isabelle poured freshly-brewed coffee into her travel mug. "Emma, I'm going to be late for work. What's this fishing expedition about?" Without realizing it, my sister had honed in on my new fact-finding technique.

I swallowed a big gulp of juice. "I thought Todd and Kendall Manheim were a couple, especially after she practically told him how to decorate his house, but they broke up."

"Why do you care? You don't even like Kendall."

Good point. "Yeah, but since I was the one who introduced them…" I shook my head and set the empty glass on the table. "Todd's sister Mary is my friend and she's concerned for her brother."

Isabelle gave me that "uh-huh" look. "I thought you'd sworn off matchmaking."

"I'm trying." I ignored the raised eyebrow.

Isabelle watched me like she expected me to react to whatever was on her mind, but of course I couldn't. My sister knew me too well, so she took a step back and scrutinized me. "By now you should've answered my thoughts. What gives?"

I sucked in my breath. "Truth?" She nodded. "Ever since I got that concussion I haven't been able to hear anyone's thoughts."

Isabelle looked thunderstruck. "What?"

"The last thing I…" using air quotes, "'heard' was Mary mad at Kendall for breaking up with Todd. Since then, nothing."

Isabelle walked around the kitchen table and peered into my face. "Oh, Emma, why didn't you tell me?"

"I kept thinking it would come back."

"Are you sure it won't?"

I shrugged. "It's been a few weeks, and people are

asking me for Prom dates and I don't know what to do."

"Let them find their own dates," she suggested.

My shoulders slumped. "I don't even have a date."

"Hank?" she asked. I shook my head.

Isabelle squeezed my arm reassuringly, then looked thoughtful. "What about Nick?"

Another shake of my head.

"Is Hank taking someone else this year?" Isabelle took a sip of coffee from her travel mug.

"I don't know. But he sure looked cozy with Rachel Bomburg the other night." In answer to my sister's puzzled expression, I said, "The girl from his Synagogue." Maybe I was getting better at this body language thing. "Any advice?"

Isabelle gathered her briefcase and purse while juggling the coffee in her other hand. "If you want to go with Hank, you could always ask him. Or ask Nick if he's the one you want. But please, Emma, worry about your own life, not everyone else's."

I nodded. She was right. After getting a concussion from stressing about my friends' love lives and promising to mind my own business, here I was again, wanting to fix things.

With Spring Break over and school starting on Monday, I'd have a lot to deal with.

****

Senior Prom was scheduled for next weekend. Like I promised both myself and Isabelle, I wasn't planning to fix people up. After the fiasco of "hearing" so much anger and discontent before Spring Break from kids I thought I was helping, and ending up with a concussion, I was almost sure no one would even speak to me, let alone ask me to get them a date. I was wrong.

Sara Davis cornered me in Creative Writing class. "So Jeff told me he and Katherine just bumped into each other at the mall during Spring Break. They aren't dating."

"Okaayy…" Why was she confiding in me?

"So Katherine and I patched up our friendship, and I want you to use your voodoo mind-reading to set me up with Jeff for Prom."

I blew out a puff of air. I was tired of having this same conversation with her. "For the last time, Sara, I can't read minds." And for once, I was telling the truth.

"Well, then use your," she used air quotes, "'instincts' and get me the date."

"I've sworn off matchmaking, Sara. You're a modern woman. Why don't you ask Jeff yourself?"

Her face registered surprise, maybe about the fact that I was retiring, but then she picked up her notebook and started scribbling notes with furtive glances my way. For all I knew it was the start of another news story about me.

"Fine," I told her. "I'll see what I can do. But I'm not making any promises."

I caught up with Jeff in the cafeteria lunch line and tapped him on the shoulder. "You got a Prom date? Katherine Howard?"

He blinked. "Why does everyone think I'm dating her? Have you talked to Sara?"

"Well…"

He shrugged. "I called Sara over Break and she about took my head off for having a coffee with her best friend."

This is where in the past I would have listened for Jeff's thoughts, but now I watched closely as his face contorted into a mishmash of anger, frustration, and disappointment. "Sara told me she and Katherine talked," I said, "and it's all good now. So Prom with Sara?"

He hesitated a minute, then nodded.

"Good. Great. Call her and set up the details." Since that was as far as I was willing to go, I ignored Jeff's surprised look, and hurried off with my lunch tray before he could ask me to make the arrangements for him.

I hadn't talked to Faith Barlow since her birthday, so I didn't know if Miguel had asked her to Prom. His or hers. After I finished that abbreviated date setup between Jeff and Sara, I put my lunch tray down next to Faith at the senior table where she'd taken to eating lunch lately. "Have you seen Miguel?"

She blushed, nodded, and showed me a text he'd sent. *Hope you'll go with me to my Prom. Got a date for yours?*

"And?"

"I said 'yes' to his and asked him to ours." Faith was beaming. And blushing.

Score another one for the retired matchmaker.

Hattie continued to be elusive about her plans, but Flip said she was going to look gorgeous on the arm of her mystery man because he'd personally seen to it. I supposed I'd have to wait and see who he was, assuming I got a date myself.

Marshall Everett pleaded with me to help him find a Prom date, even though I tried to convince him that I was out of the matchmaking business. He recently won the county Mathlete competition, bringing home a huge trophy that was now displayed in the main school entrance alongside the athletic trophies. That meant girls were seeing him as something of a school hero and less of a nerd. I told him Hattie already had a date, if that's what he was hoping for, but then I remembered that Katherine Howard wasn't actually dating Jeff Atwell, so I cornered her in Family Relations and asked her about Marshall. To my great surprise, after all the grief she'd given me this year, she said "yes."

I looked for Hank all day at school and never saw him. I even sent him a text, thinking maybe he was sick and had stayed home.

In the speech classroom practicing for debate tournament this week was his reply.

Good luck! I sent that text, thought about it a minute, and sent another one. *You going to Prom?*

After a long wait, the only reply I got was *Thanks.* It appeared I wasn't going to Senior Prom with Hank, the guy I'd gone to every other high school dance with. I was so disappointed I felt like crying.

At work after school, I tried to concentrate on the kids, but my heart just wasn't in it. As I was about to ask Mrs. Evans if I could go home early, my phone pinged with a text. I hoped it was Hank, but it was Nick.

You got a date to Prom?

No. You asking?

Yes! ☺

Nick was a nice guy, a perfect gentleman, someone I could at least have fun with. But he wasn't Hank.

It's a date.

Chapter 15

Nick arrived to pick me up for Prom at seven p.m.
He looked very handsome in his black tux with black
satin tie, and he complimented me on my pink chiffon
dress as he inched the corsage onto my wrist. We posed
while Isabelle snapped dozens of photos, took a few
selfies, and then Nick drove us to downtown
Indianapolis for dinner at a private club with a skyline
view of the city. The food was fantastic and the service
exquisite, including the finesse with which the waiter
served our sparkling cider as if it were champagne.

"Did I tell you my parents are members here?" Nick
handed the waiter his credit card without so much as
glancing at the bill.

Of course they are.

Nick was the perfect date, all impeccable manners
and attentiveness, and the twinkling lights of the city
from the top floor of that building should have been quite
romantic, but for some reason my mind was on Hank. I
wondered what he was wearing, what kind of corsage he
got for his date, if it was nicer than the one he bought me
last year, and I even wondered if he'd ask me to dance.

I could feel the electricity in the air when Nick and
I walked into the Shamrock Hotel. The Prom committee
had been putting out the word for weeks that it was sure
to be the best one ever, probably to justify the increase
in ticket prices, and claiming the live band's versatility

as one of the reasons. No one except the juniors on the Prom Committee and the chaperones knew the theme, and they were the only ones allowed past the hotel lobby until precisely nine p.m. However, before anybody got into the ballroom they first had to stop at the check-in desk.

"Hey, Miss Taylor," I said as Nick handed her our tickets and we both flashed our student IDs.

"Good evening, Emma, Nick." She checked us in on her tablet. "You two make a handsome couple." Miss Taylor looked pretty tonight, too, not in formal wear, but a lovely tea-length floral sundress with spaghetti straps that showed off surprisingly well-toned arms. "You kids have fun."

I started to ask what was up with her and Mr. West, but it wasn't any of my business so I zipped my lip. "Thanks."

"She's right you know," Nick said, squeezing my hand. "We're a hot-looking couple."

Did Nick think of us as a couple? I didn't know how I felt about that.

The moment we'd all been waiting for finally arrived. The doors to the ballroom opened and the guests of honor, the Senior Class, were invited in first. I took Nick's arm and we entered amid a crush of students, while everyone oohed and ahhed at the gorgeous decorations transforming the ballroom into A Starry Night. We were greeted with twinkling ceiling lights and a hand-painted backdrop over the stage depicting a night scene in blues and yellows, reminiscent of Van Gogh's famous painting. Tables were arranged around the perimeter of the dance floor and covered with pale blue cloths and tiny glittered stars, sporting centerpieces of school-colored blue and yellow flowers in cut glass vases.

There was a lot of excitement in the air, with the guys in tuxes and the girls in every imaginable style of cocktail or evening dress, and most of them on the arm of a special person. I glanced at Nick to see him smiling at me, and maybe I was just used to his gorgeous eyes, because instead of feeling all tingly, I started scouting around for my friends. For Hank.

I spotted him, walking in with his date on his arm. But wait. That wasn't Rachel. Hank was escorting Kendall. Kendall? I sucked in my breath and gaped at the two of them. Hank was here with the Maneater, a girl he could barely tolerate, instead of gorgeous, sophisticated Rachel Bomburg. I had no idea how that had happened, but I was too relieved to care. And already he didn't appear to be having fun. He was wearing the kind of tux I'd pictured him in, and Kendall was in a too-tight, too-short and too revealing cocktail dress.

To my professional eye, some of the couples were completely mismatched, but I decided to stay detached. Like the fact that Greg Plowman was with Amanda Baker instead of Mary Bekins, making me wonder what happened. Greg was talking to Marshall Everett who was indeed with Katherine Howard, but she was yawning and had her back turned to him, chatting with Jane Bates. Poor Marshall. I did notice that the Bates sisters were with Darrin and Sam O'Brien, so two of my previous fix-ups were back together without any help from me. At least for tonight.

And then Mary Bekins strolled in with some guy I didn't know, and the two of them walked right by Greg and Amanda without a word. Mary's date was definitely not in high school and he was about half a head shorter than she was, or maybe it just appeared that way because Mary was wearing three-inch strappy heels. If she had asked Flip for a wardrobe critique, he probably would have advised against that footwear.

"Hey Mary," Kendall said, looking down her nose at Mary's date, "who's this?"

"Friend of Todd's," Mary replied, letting her nose tip slightly in the air in counterpoint.

There was an awkward pause before Kendall snorted. "You mean you couldn't find a date, or even let Emma try, and your big brother had to fix you up? That's as bad as if you'd come with Todd."

Mary glared at Kendall. But instead of shooting back a snarky retort, she slowly smiled and said loud enough for anyone to hear, "Todd has better things to do than go to a high school dance. He's on a date with one of the Colts' cheerleaders."

The color drained from Kendall's face. She jerked Hank's arm and dragged him away, but her dramatic exit was marred when she wobbled on her stilts, grabbed onto Hank's arm as she nearly lost her balance, and had to tug at the dress to keep it from falling down, or up. I stifled a snicker.

I hadn't seen Hattie yet. I suddenly felt really guilty, because as her best friend, I should have been there offering moral support for this important date, if not fashion advice. Luckily Flip stepped up and did what he does best.

"Hey girlfriend." Flip slipped an arm around my shoulder and gave me a squeeze. He looked sharp in a traditional black tux with a white tie instead of a bow tie. James was wearing an all-white tux with the same style of tie as Flip's, only his was black.

"Hey, Flip, James," I said, nodding approval at their coordinating outfits. "Have you seen Hattie?"

Instead of replying, Flip grinned like a Cheshire cat and gave James a little elbow nudge. "I'm dying of thirst. Let's get some punch." And they took off.

Faith Barlow and Miguel Castillo slipped in quietly. Her usual bohemian style of dress had given way to a more fashionable look, a slinky grey gown with a flowing skirt and curved neckline. Miguel looked hot tonight in his tux, his black hair slicked back into a stylish ponytail, and one silver diamond earring catching the light. No one would dare try to cut in on them because they only had eyes for each other.

Miss Taylor and Mr. West were both there as chaperones, assigned to opposite ends of the room with totally different duties, but that wasn't stopping them from eyeing each other across the ballroom. He was hanging out with some of the male teachers over by the punch bowl, to prevent spiking no doubt. I glanced over at Miss Taylor, who was standing near the ballroom entrance chatting with PE teacher Mrs. Hawthorne, when in walked Sara Davis on Jeff Atwell's arm.

Sara appeared taller in a long black jersey gown, her flaming red hair in a curly bob. Jeff wasn't what you'd call handsome, but with his long hair cut short for a change, they made an eye-catching couple. I just didn't want her to catch my eye.

"Nick," I said with a nudge, "let's go talk to Mr. West."

"You wanna go talk to a teacher?" Nick at first seemed puzzled, but then he followed my gaze to Sara and Jeff, and grinned. "Sure." He offered his arm and we strolled to the other side of the room.

"Good to see you here, Mr. West." Nick offered his hand to shake.

"Are you planning to dance tonight?" I asked the teacher.

Mr. West hesitated, then shook his head. "I'm not much of a dancer. I'm just here to keep an eye on you kids." His eyes wandered the room.

I followed his gaze. "Miss Taylor looks pretty tonight." Mr. West shifted his stance and stared down at his feet.

"Go for it, Mr. West!" Nick gave him two thumbs up and then put his hand on my back to inch me toward the dance floor, because the band leader had just stepped up to the mic. Actually, they looked more like an orchestra than a band. In addition to the lead and bass guitars and drummer, they had a keyboardist, violinist, and percussionist. Maybe they'd be worth the extra cost after all.

"Ladies and gentlemen," the band leader said, "we're the VersaTones, and we hope to make this evening a night to remember." He signaled his fellow musicians to start playing, and when he opened his mouth it was obvious he wasn't just the band leader, he was an amazing singer. They led off with a romantic song that incorporated all the pieces of the band.

Nick escorted me out onto the dance floor and stopped right next to Hank and Kendall, which made me jittery. He wrapped his arms lightly around my waist and we started to dance. I looked over and saw Hank with a pained look on his face, but Nick twirled me around and I didn't have time to say anything because I nearly bumped into Hattie – and Robbie Martin.

I blinked and my jaw dropped.

She looked gorgeous tonight in the dress that Flip hand-picked for her, a seafoam-green chiffon strapless with a high waist to help feminize her boxy figure. Robbie was his usual sophisticated-artsy self in a multi-colored jacket with black tuxedo pants. He was grinning at Hattie, holding her close and swaying to the music, and Hattie had a faraway, dreamy look on her face.

"Um, hi, Emma," she said, chagrined. Before I could voice any kind of disapproval, she took Robbie's arm and hauled him off to the refreshment table.

"Was that the guy from New Year's Eve?" Nick asked me.

I nodded. "Yeah, Robbie Martin, violinist extraordinaire." I wasn't surprised that Hattie didn't think she could confide in me. I hadn't been very supportive of her, and I'd known for years how she felt about him.

"They look happy." Nick watched them feed each other petit fours.

I had to agree, judging by the expressions on their faces and the way Robbie was holding tightly onto Hattie's hand. I hoped I was wrong that he would hurt her again. Maybe he had matured.

The dance floor was getting crowded. Before I knew it, the push and shove of kids jockeying for space had jostled Nick and me right next to Hank and Kendall again.

"Emma, you look amazing." Hank gave me an affectionate smile and a lingering glance.

"Ooh, Emma, you sure do know how to rock that dress a second time," Kendall snarked as she gave me the once over. Yes, I was wearing the same dress from last year. It was expensive, a gift from my sister to help compensate for our father's absence at the time.

I could strangle Kendall.

"And I saw Hattie." Kendall's eyes floated around the room. "She looks so…interesting." She said that part really loud.

Flip's head jerked around and he looked like he was ready to throttle her. James took Flip by the arm and led him to a spot on the dance floor right in front of the band.

Pretty soon Kendall went from fashion to her other favorite topic, good-looking guys. "Robbie Martin sure looks hot!"

Hattie rolled her eyes.

The VersaTones were trying to appeal to a wide range of tastes and living up to their name by mixing it up musically, playing heavy metal, some clean rap songs, R&B, a country line dance, movie scores, and even some swing.

Nick tapped me on the shoulder and pointed to the chaperone table. Mr. West and Miss Taylor were chatting, and then he offered her his arm and led her out onto the dance floor, just as the band started playing a sort of nostalgic piece about days gone by. It couldn't have been a more romantic moment.

The evening was slipping away, and Kendall had kept Hank so busy that he hadn't had time to glance my way. At least I didn't think so, but with the lights dimmed it was a little hard to tell. Nick and I took a break to go to the refreshment table, just before the grand finale.

"Ladies and gentlemen, we're going to end the Prom tonight with 'All We Are,' celebrating your time in high school as you look toward the future. So grab your significant other, step out onto the dance floor and hold on tight."

Nick and I had lost our space, but we hurried back to the floor and pushed our way in. He put his arms around me and we started swaying to the music. I searched around till I found Hank, who looked pained. He was desperately trying to keep from smashing Kendall's corsage pinned to her waist, or looking down her cleavage, a challenge for any teenage boy. My heart ached for him.

Nick danced me around Jane and Darrin, and Hattie and Robbie, till we were standing next to Hank and Kendall. "Hey, Hank, mind if I cut in?"

I pulled back and looked at Nick in surprise, but I could have kissed him, and not in a romantic way. Did he really want to dance with Kendall? Or was he doing his body language thing and knew how much I wanted to dance with Hank? I didn't know and I didn't care.

"Thanks, Nick." Hank quickly relinquished Kendall and took me in his arms.

That song was a great way to end the evening. Hank pulled me close and whirled me around just in time to see Kendall draped all over Nick. That sight almost caused me to lose my gourmet Chicken Marsala. Then I saw Hank beaming at me, and I finally felt like I was where I belonged.

Chapter 16

The Prom itself, so long anticipated by all us seniors, was over too soon. After the last song finished and the lights in the ballroom were turned up, everyone immediately started talking about after-parties. Hank and I didn't go to an after-party last year because Isabelle wouldn't hear of a sixteen year old staying out past one a.m., and Hank's parents weren't in favor of it either. Knowing that seniors would be set on going somewhere after Prom this year, the Doctors Zimmerman came up with a creative solution. Hank asked me if Nick and I were coming to the after-party at his house.

"Nick," I said as we walked to his car, "did you have a particular after-party in mind?"

He shrugged. "I just figured we'd try to hit most of them."

"That's like fifteen parties. You didn't narrow it down any?"

He winked at me. "No, but you did, right?"

Nick dropped me at home so I could change clothes and update Isabelle on my plans. I carefully hung up the evening gown that had served me well two years in a row and would come in handy again someday, pulled my now-limp hair into a ponytail, and changed into jeans. I also put on my jean jacket, since it was only the first weekend in May and still chilly at night.

Isabelle was doing something on her laptop in the

living room in front of the TV, where a late night talk show was on that she wasn't paying attention to. I was too old for my sister to be waiting up for me, if that was what she was doing.

"Why aren't you in bed?" I asked her.

She looked up from her computer. "I couldn't sleep so I got up to do some work. I must've eaten something that didn't agree with me."

She did look a little pale. "There's an after-party at Hank's."

"I assume the party's going to be well-chaperoned," she said as she continued pounding the keyboard.

"Of course. Hank's parents have always been the hands-on kind."

I didn't know what just flashed across Isabelle's mind, but her brow was furrowed as she glanced up at me. "So that's the only place you're going?"

"Yeah. I'll be home in the morning."

She nodded and picked up the remote to flip the channel on the TV, landing on an old black and white, sappy romantic movie. She yanked up a handful of tissues and dabbed at her eyes. "I love this one."

"*Casablanca* makes you cry?" My sister had seen that film a million times. Whatever she ate not only disrupted her digestion but her emotions as well. I stared at her for a minute, shrugged, and went outside to wait on the front porch for Nick.

****

Nick and I arrived a few minutes before two a.m. and the party was already gearing up. From the looks of the growing crowd, this promised to be one of the more popular after-parties. It was being held outside by the heated pool, even though no one was dumb enough to try to swim. The air temperature was hovering around sixty degrees.

The backyard lights were creating a rainbow of colors bouncing off the pool and illuminating all but just a small section of the adjacent rose garden. There was plenty of deck seating arranged tastefully around the pool, and lots of extra chairs on the patio. But with about twenty kids there already and more arriving, some of us might end up sitting on the dew covered grass.

I waved at Hattie and Robbie who were lounging in lawn chairs near the pool, but they were totally focused on each other and didn't even notice me. Although Jane Bates had her back to me, I could see that she was now talking with Sam O'Brien instead of Darrin. I looked around for Agnes and saw her chatting with Allison Baker and Katherine Howard, with no sign of Darrin. Flip and James walked in right behind Nick and me and snagged chairs on the deck. A bunch of other kids had removed their sandals and were dangling their toes in the water. Watching them made me shiver and hug my jean jacket around me a little tighter.

The Zimmerman house sported an outdoor kitchen, equipped with a stainless steel gas stove attached to a state-of-the-art grill, which Dr. Zimmerman had fired up.

"Should we go say 'hi' to our host?" Without waiting for Nick's response, I took off toward the grill, where Hank was nibbling on some savory barbecued meat-on-a-stick. His dad was grilling several other items that all smelled divine.

"Hi, Hank." I wasn't able to control the blush creeping across my cheeks.

Hank had dressed way casual for the party, but I thought he looked adorable. He had on an old pair of khakis with a frayed hem that he'd worn every summer since seventh grade, a Ball State sweatshirt, and flip flops which might be a little chilly for early May.

His eyes lit up. "Hi," he replied, his mouth full. He swallowed the food, but the smile disappeared. "Nick."

"Hey, Hank," Nick said. "Food smells good."

"Emma, what a pleasure." Hank's dad, wearing his Kiss the Cook apron, turned from the grill, spatula in hand, to greet me. "And who's this young man?"

I averted my eyes from Hank to avoid his frown. "Nick Knight," and to Nick I said, "This is Dr. Henry Zimmerman Sr."

"Oh, you're the guy who enrolled at Melville High last fall. From Chicago?" Dr. Zimmerman wiped his hand on his apron and extended it to Nick.

"Yes, sir." Nick shook hands with him. "Nice to meet you. I've read some of your research. I particularly enjoyed the paper in which you described how Type Two diabetes and cardiovascular disease have a lot in common."

Hank's eyes bugged out and Dr. Zimmerman appeared surprised as well. I already knew about Nick's high IQ, so I wasn't too surprised that he read medical journals. I decided to change the subject. "Can't wait to taste whatever you're cooking, Dr. Zimmerman."

Hank's dad pointed to items on the grill. "Little of everything: hot dogs, burgers, chicken, veggie burgers. And of course we're serving a full breakfast at sunrise." He winked at me as he flipped over the marinated chicken-on-sticks, which sizzled and caused big flames to shoot up into the air.

Someone tapped me on the shoulder. I turned around to see Sara Davis, eyeing Nick like he was the meat on the grill. He smiled politely at her, probably because he could read her body language.

"Hey, Sara," I said. "Where's Jeff?"

"Oh, he's…"

Whatever she mumbled, I didn't catch it. I glanced around the backyard and saw Jeff sitting by the pool with Katherine Howard. That guy needed to make up his mind which girl he was interested in.

"Emma, you've hogged this handsome guy way too long, so I'm stealing him." Sara didn't even wait for my response before linking her arm in Nick's and dragging him over to join Agnes and Allison.

"Where's Kendall?" I asked Hank. Not that I cared.

Hank rolled his eyes. "She went home to change."

I tried to stifle the snicker that was escaping, but I couldn't control myself. Before I knew it I was laughing. Out loud.

"What?" Hank asked.

"The look on your face," I said between guffaws, "like you didn't really appreciate the full effect of Kendall's Prom dress."

"Yeah, that's it. I didn't 'appreciate' it." He snickered, and pretty soon he was laughing, too.

Once we'd both settled down, Hank asked, "You hungry?" He reached around his dad and skewered a sizzling burger with a fork and plopped it onto a bun on a paper plate. "Mustard or ketchup?"

Condiments were the last thing on my mind. All I could think about was the Prom that Hank and I didn't attend together, absentee Kendall, and Rachel, who mysteriously wasn't even at the after-party. Maybe she turned down his offer of a Prom date and really hurt his feelings, and that was why he'd settled for Kendall.

Thinking Hank had been hurt like that choked me up for a minute, and I couldn't seem to find my voice, so I helped myself to the mustard and bit into the burger.

"Emma, dear, how nice to see you." Mrs. Zimmerman stepped out of the kitchen with a plate of veggies and fruit and placed it on the picnic table. Leave it to the pediatrician to make sure kids ate healthy. "I was disappointed when Hank told me the two of you weren't going to Prom together. I was going to place this year's pictures next to the ones from last year."

Hank groaned. "Mom…"

If I didn't feel guilty before, I really did now. So much so that my palms were starting to sweat. Maybe I was standing too close to the grill.

"We can take some pictures after graduation," I offered, as if that was going to make up for breaking our years-long tradition. "I'm sure you got some great shots of Hank and Kendall."

Do adults roll their eyes? Because I'd swear Mrs. Zimmerman did just that before turning back to finish arranging the healthy food on the table.

Hank looked as uncomfortable as I felt, so without another word I decided to beat a hasty retreat. "Emma, wait," he called after me.

I turned around, but Hank looked so sad. If only he'd tell me what happened between him and Rachel, I'd come out of retirement and try to fix it, just to see him happy again. Or maybe I'd smack her for being so stupid that she didn't see what was right in front of her. "Yeah?" I asked, walking backwards.

"Hey, watch it, bestie." Hattie put up a hand to keep me from backing into her.

I turned. "Hi, Hattie. Where's your date?"

She ignored me as she went to Hank and draped an arm casually around his shoulder. "I'm starved!"

Hank let her drag him off to the grill, where Dr. Zimmerman was removing some sizzling hotdogs. "Maybe we can talk later," Hank called over his shoulder.

"Sure," I said as breezy as I could manage.

What got into Hattie anyway? A minute ago she and Robbie were staring lovingly into each other's eyes, and now he was gone and she was all over Hank. I mean, really, how many guys could one girl crush on in a year? Nick, Hank, Robbie, and then Hank again? I promised myself to have a long talk with my best friend. Later.

Last I saw of Nick he was being dragged off by Sara toward a group of girls who probably swooned at the sight of him. Before I could decide if I wanted to do anything about it, I heard a murmuring spread through the growing crowd and turned to see that Kendall had finally arrived, smiling and waving as if she was the guest of honor. She now had on hot pink Capri jeans with a thin white blouse showing off a very visible black lace bra. Without bothering to even wave at her date, she made a beeline for mine. I walked over to the pool where she had a death grip on Nick's arm.

"Hey, Emma," Kendall purred while batting her eyes at Nick.

"Kendall," I muttered, "shouldn't you go say hello to your date?"

"I was just on my way." Kendall flipped her long brown mane and slowly unwrapped her arms from Nick. She was about to walk over to the outdoor kitchen when there was yet another buzzing among the guests, and all eyes turned to see the new arrivals.

"Hey gang!" Mary Bekins' voice rang out from across the yard as she waved at everyone. And she was no longer with her Prom date, but instead was standing side-by-side with her brother Todd. Naturally some of the girls squealed and giggled. Greg Plowman and James Harrison rushed over to shake his hand.

Up till then, Sara had been flirting outrageously with Nick, but she seemed as star-struck as everyone else when a handsome pro football player waltzed in. Sara dashed over to join the crowd gathering around Todd, and because she was so tiny she easily squeezed in right next to him.

From over by the outdoor kitchen, Kendall stared at Todd and the kids around him, shot dirty looks at Sara, and hurried across the yard. Maybe she wasn't used to being on the receiving end of a boyfriend-grab, but she really had no territorial rights because she broke up with Todd weeks ago. Still, it looked like Kendall was gearing up for a fight. She elbowed her way in to plant herself firmly next to Todd, grabbed Sara by the collar, and was preparing to yank her away from her man. Who knew Kendall Manheim could get jealous?

Sara pushed Kendall's hands off her and the two of them, hands on hips, curled lips and narrowed eyes, glared at each other. Todd got between them, his arms outstretched, attempting to keep them from going full-on girl fight.

"Back off, Davis," Kendall said through clenched teeth as she side-stepped Todd.

Sara pulled herself up to her full height, all five-feet nothing of her, and got in Kendall's face, figuratively speaking, because Kendall towered over her. "You're always going after everybody else's boyfriends, so your ex is fair game." Sara stomped her foot and stood her ground.

Todd threw up his hands and backed away, his face a bright red from embarrassment or anger, I couldn't tell which.

Jeff Atwell appeared at just the right moment and put an arm around Sara. "Come on, let's go talk."

"Get off me," Sara growled as she shrugged his arm away and kept glaring at Kendall.

I expected Todd to be totally disgusted with his ex and all her drama, but to my surprise, he was looking at Kendall sort of like he did when they first met on New Year's Eve. Huh.

I wanted to fix this, or at least keep a fight from ending this nice evening the Zimmermans planned for us. But without my mind-reading ability, I wasn't sure if I could be of any help. I decided to trust my instincts.

"Kendall, let's take a walk." I gave her a little shove, and even though she tossed a backward glance at Todd and a snarl at Sara, she allowed me to lead her away.

"What?" Kendall snapped when we reached the opposite side of the pool.

"Kendall, dial it down." I stepped back to give her some breathing room. "If you want to get back with Todd, I can help. He's not over you either."

Her eyes widened. "How do you know?"

Not my usual way, that was for sure. "Well, it was the look on his face, kinda like the night I first introduced you two."

Kendall must have seen the expression on Todd's face, just like I did. Her whole body slumped. "It's all my fault. I couldn't resist…"

"Yeah, I heard the rumors."

She shook her head and to my utter amazement, tears started falling down her cheeks. "I love him. I just wanted to see if he felt the same."

I blew out an exasperated puff of air. "Kendall, you can't play games with grown men." I reached over to a nearby table, picked up an unused napkin and handed it to her. "How 'bout I try to smooth things over?"

She sniffled, dabbed at her eyes, and nodded, so I pointed to a lounge chair next to the pool. "Stay put, and don't even think about flirting with any other guys."

True, I'd sworn off matchmaking, but since I'd been the one to get Todd and Kendall together, I felt like it was up to me to straighten out this misunderstanding between two people who obviously cared about each another. I could feel everyone's eyes following me, especially Nick, Hank, and Sara, as I hurried over to Todd, who had a grim set to his jaw as he piled food onto a paper plate.

"Todd," I said, "I know you still care about Kendall, and she feels the same. Is there any chance…?"

He set his plate down. His body language said "yes," but he shook his head and said, "I don't think so, Emma. I'm pretty sure we're done."

I smiled to myself, knowing that was just his pride talking. This would be easy. "I've known Kendall a long time," I told him, "and even with her looks, she's really insecure. She needs constant reassurance, which is why she plays games. But if you two could just talk…"

Todd glanced over at a very forlorn Kendall, sitting all by herself for once. He sighed, picked up his plate of food, two forks, and headed over. Before long, they were smiling and sharing bites of the chicken and fruit.

Sara Davis tapped me on the shoulder, smirking.

"Hey, Miss Match."

I rolled my eyes. "That nickname was your idea."

She folded her arms and tapped her foot. "How did you know Todd and Kendall wanted to get back together?"

"I just...knew."

"I saw you watching them. You were reading their minds, weren't you? I was right!"

I did a slow burn. "I. Can't. Read. Minds." *At the moment*. "I just saw how they looked at each other, the same way they'd eyed each other the first night they met, and I could tell how miserable they both were. Same way I can tell Jeff's mad at you right now and you need to do damage control."

Stunned, Sara glanced over at Jeff. Sure enough, he had his head together with Greg and James, occasionally casting angry looks at Sara. She couldn't get away from me and over to him fast enough.

Hank appeared by my side and offered up a high five. "Way to go, Emma."

We high-fived each other, but then Nick was on my other side. I looked wistfully over my shoulder at Hank as Nick took my hand and walked me to a secluded and poorly lit spot by the rose garden.

"That was nice what you did for Todd and Kendall," Nick said.

I shrugged. "It's kind of what I do. Now I just hope all this," I waved a hand in the direction of all the happy couples, "holds till we get through graduation."

He turned to face me, taking both my hands in his. "Speaking of graduation..." Nick looked really serious.

"What?"

"I want to tell you how much fun I've had this year,

getting to know you, your friends." He shifted his stance uncomfortably. "All this high school stuff."

All this high school stuff?

Nick released my hands and took a step back. "But I won't be at graduation."

I blinked, shocked to my core. "What are you talking about? Of course you'll be there. You have to graduate. Colleges expect…" Then I stopped, remembering all the times Nick wasn't studying. "Did you fail a class? Is that why you're not graduating? Do you have to go to summer school?"

For some reason Nick burst into uncontrollable laughter. I just stood there, stunned, because not graduating high school wasn't funny. After a couple of minutes and one final guffaw, he got control of himself. "I haven't been completely honest with you, Emma." He paused while he stared up at the sky, still grinning, searching for the words. "Okay, here's the thing. I already graduated from high school."

Say what? "How? Did you take online courses or something?"

Nick shook his head. "Remember I told you I came to Mel High from Colson Academy?" I nodded. "That was true, but I graduated when I was twelve. I've got a bachelor's degree and a master's in pre-med from Northwestern University in Chicago. I leave this summer for medical school in San Francisco."

My jaw dropped and I felt like I couldn't catch my breath. "Is this some kind of joke?"

"No, I'm serious." He looked it, too. "I've never been around kids my own age. When Mom and Dad decided to move to Indiana, they wanted me to stay at Northwestern and get my Ph.D., but I was burned out on school and needed a break. Medical school wouldn't admit me till I was seventeen, so I had some time to kill. I convinced my parents to let me have one last chance at normalcy."

I narrowed my eyes at him. "And just how old are you?"

Nick looked down at the ground and mumbled, "Seventeen. In June."

I swallowed hard and slumped down onto the dewy grass. Oh. My. God. I've been dating the equivalent of a high school sophomore, which explained his immaturity, but this guy had the education of a twenty-three year old. No wonder I never saw him do any homework. "So all that volunteer work, all that tutoring…"

"Stuff I wanted to try, stuff I never had time for before." He smiled that gorgeous smile and sat down on the grass next to me. "I've had an awesome time, Emma. Going back to high school was the best decision I ever made."

I frowned. "So all of us average kids were just a science experiment?"

"Of course not. You and your friends, it was so…normal. I even loved all the gossip."

"What?"

"You know. Hattie and Hank and Robbie. Miss Taylor and Mr. West. Faith and Miguel. Even all that stuff Sara Davis stirred up. Graduate students don't have time for any of that. It's been a great seven months, four days…"

I put up my hand. "I get it."

Nick gave me a kiss on the forehead. "Come on, we're missing the party." He helped me to my feet.

Todd and Kendall were in the middle of what

appeared to be a very serious discussion, but he had his arms wrapped around her and it looked like it was going okay. Hank was sitting at the patio table chatting with James, Flip, and Mary, who had her hand on Greg's knee. Hattie was over there, too. Jane and Agnes were dangerously close to the edge of the swimming pool, dancing with Sam and Darrin, respectively, to crooner music blasting through the outdoor speakers. And Sara, with Jeff at her side, was nibbling from the veggie tray. She must have gotten Jeff to forgive her for the chaos she caused, because he had his arm protectively around her.

"I'll get you a plate." Nick sat me down next to Hank and went for food.

"What's up with Nick?" Hank asked.

"You'll never believe," I said.

Chapter17

After Sara's near girl fight at Hank's house, and her scrutiny of my matchmaking methods that night, she surprised me and everyone else with one last editorial.

Dear Readers,

This is my last entry before retiring (aka graduating) as your Melville High School Weekly Herald *editor. I've wrapped up my ongoing investigation of fellow classmate Emma Austin, which first appeared in the Senior Feature section last October. Yes, I dubbed her Miss Match and questioned her methods, even speculating that she was either psychic or a mind-reader. But last weekend at one of our many After Prom parties, my eyes were opened as I was made painfully and personally aware of how Emma makes those matches. I won't go into the details, but suffice it to say that Emma proved to me beyond a shadow of a doubt that she enjoys no such supernatural abilities. She's simply an astute judge of character.*

And that in itself is a gift.

If she decides to pursue matchmaking at college, students there will be fortunate to have her.

I was both surprised, relieved, and yes, flattered, when I read Sara's editorial. I still struggled emotionally and physically with the loss of my ability to hear thoughts, but I was coming to accept that they may be gone for good. And in the meantime, my classmates have stopped staring at me like I was some sort of freak of nature. I got acceptance letters to Ball State University and Community College, but since I no longer needed to escape further gossip, I felt confident about returning the admissions packet to my mother's alma mater, Ball State.

****

I didn't have a roommate for the dorm at Ball State. I could either choose a roommate or take whoever they randomly assigned me, but I'd prefer to room with someone I already knew so I'd have an idea what I was getting into. Problem was, I had no one in mind.

I couldn't be roomies with Hattie because she was going to Indiana University. I wracked my brain trying to think who to ask at this late date, but I came up blank. I even thought about Kendall, but I heard she was taking a gap year, and anyway I wasn't that desperate. If I couldn't find a roommate, I might be forced to take potluck.

It was the final week for seniors, followed by a flurry of activities before graduation. We also needed time to clean out lockers, turn in books, settle any unpaid accounts, and write our class's official Senior Memoirs, a tradition that dated back to the 1950s. The old ones from decades past were in big scrapbooks stored in the school's basement. In the twenty-first century, the seniors' farewell messages were posted on a social media page where they could be viewed forever.

Nick officially withdrew from school. I guess his mom told the shocked principal the truth about him, but the student gossip mill was at work again. Kids were saying he got kicked out, or he flunked out, or he got in trouble with the law and was on home detention. I knew the truth, but it wasn't my story to tell.

Nick texted me this morning and asked if he could come over to the condo tonight, supposedly to help me study for final exams. I was pretty sure that was just an excuse, but I was curious to know what he really wanted to talk about.

Isabelle was sitting on the sofa again, the place where she seemed to spend a lot of time lately, looking green. That flu bug she came down with Prom night had hung on for weeks. She left work early again today, and Jonathan promised to stop by her favorite deli on his way home from the office to pick up some homemade chicken noodle soup. Lately that was all she'd been able to keep down.

"Here, drink this." I handed her some freshly-brewed herbal tea. "I put a little honey in it to give you some energy."

"Thanks." She took a sip from the steaming mug, sucked in her breath as she waved her hand across the hot beverage, and set it down on the coffee table to cool. "Shouldn't you be studying?"

"Shouldn't you see a doctor?" All I got from Isabelle was a dirty look. I plopped down across from her in Jonathan's recliner. "My Creative Writing final is tomorrow and I'm nervous. If it weren't for Faith's help…"

"Monica's daughter?"

"Yeah." Which reminded me that there hadn't been any word from Dad about Monica, so maybe it didn't work out. "Faith's an amazing writer. But Nick's coming over to help me study."

Isabelle eyed me suspiciously. "Why Nick and not Faith?" She sipped some of the cooled tea but she still looked pretty nauseous.

I shrugged. "Nick offered." Just then the doorbell rang and I hopped out of the chair to answer it.

"Hi, Emma," Nick said with a grin. "Hey, Mrs. Calloway." He poked his head into the living room. "You don't look so hot."

"Gee thanks," Isabelle muttered.

"Flu," I told him.

That smirk on his face told me something was buzzing around in his head, but of course I didn't know what. "Emma and I are meeting a friend at the library," he told my sister, "so enjoy the peace and quiet."

"Since when are we going to the library?" When he didn't answer I reluctantly picked up my book bag next to the front door and stepped out on the porch. "Hey, where's your car?"

Nick closed the front door behind me. "Already parked at the library. It's such a nice evening, I thought we could walk." We strolled down the sidewalk and covered the short distance in silence. It was late May, lots of sunshine even though it was early evening, and the smell of fresh flowers wafted toward us on a light, gentle breeze.

"So did you get a roommate?" Nick asked as I simultaneously said "so did you decide to stay for graduation after all?"

We both laughed. "You first," Nick said.

"I was just wondering what your plans are."

Nick shrugged. "All the kids at school think I've been expelled." He stopped walking and turned to face me. "But I may have a solution to both of your problems - Creative Writing exam and roommate."

I cocked my head to one side. "Okay…"

"Faith," Nick said.

I scrunched my brow. "Faith? Do you mean religion or Barlow?"

Nick grinned. "Barlow. She's meeting us at the library."

Sure enough, there was Faith at a study table in a back corner near the stacks, notebooks and papers spread out in front of her, and hard at work writing in her notebook. I dropped my overstuffed book bag on the table, startling her.

"This is a library," Faith warned in a whisper.

"Hey, Faith," Nick said.

"Hi." Faith motioned to two empty chairs. "Nick says you need my help studying. I don't mind, but you could text Mr. West…"

"I trust you," I told her. If it hadn't been for her help this semester, I wouldn't have made that C+ that Mr. West gifted me with on the last assignment. And I sure didn't want to blow the final exam.

Nick took a seat in the old-school-style wooden chair. "Hey, Emma, did you know Faith got accepted into Ball State's Creative Writing program?"

I glanced at her in surprise and admiration. "No. That's great."

"And," Nick said, glancing from me to Faith, "you both need a dorm roommate and neither of you has one yet, so…"

So Nick thought we'd be compatible roomies? I didn't know anything about Faith's living habits. Was she a night owl or morning person, a neat-freak or a slob? All I knew for sure was she had a single mom who may or may not be dating my dad, a boyfriend I helped her get, and she was a serious student.

"Faith wouldn't be out dating every weekend because she's serious about her education." Nick winked at me. He was infuriating.

"I don't know," Faith hedged. "Emma and I…"

"No, you two would be the perfect match," Nick said.

It was an odd kind of match if you asked me, but not a bad idea really. Why didn't I think of her before? "That might work. Faith?"

She shrugged. "I guess we can try."

I appreciated Nick looking out for me like that. Maybe he was never cut out to be boyfriend material, at least not for me, but you could never have too many friends.

Mr. West had given us a take-home essay as a final exam assignment and the prompt had left me shaken: *You walk into your house and it's completely different — furniture, decor, all changed. And nobody's home.* Talk about life imitating art. Maybe that was why I was having such a hard time getting started on it. I told Faith about all the emotions from Valentine's Day a year ago, and that I didn't want to relive it. She was thoughtful for a moment, and then suggested I focus more on what I saw rather than how I was feeling.

I took her advice and just started writing. I did an okay job, too, because when I got my paper back a few days later, Mr. West had circled the B+ in red. He commented that, although my mechanics could still use some work, it was the best writing I'd done all semester. I was so proud of myself that I took it home and stuck it on the fridge like I was twelve.

****

I fidgeted with my cap and gown, and tapped my

foot impatiently as I watched the clock on the fireplace mantel tick off the minutes. Isabelle was taking her sweet time checking herself from every angle in the entry hall mirror, and Jonathan wasn't even downstairs yet. My sister frowned at her reflection as she adjusted her skirt, which didn't seem to fit very well. Maybe the cleaners shrunk it. Too bad, because it was her favorite black pencil skirt that she'd paired with a flowy lime green blouse, which tonight she didn't tuck in.

"I have to be there at six o'clock," I reminded her.

"But graduation isn't until seven." Isabelle turned to look at her backside and tugged at her blouse again.

I groaned, a big, long exaggerated sigh as if I were still a preteen. "There are three hundred and eighteen of us. Just how fast do you think we can all line up?"

Jonathan finally came down the stairs, dressed in a business suit, white shirt and no tie, and hopefully ready to roll. He gave Isabelle an approving once over. "You look beautiful, hon," he said.

Isabelle caught Jonathan's eye in the mirror and they exchanged meaningful smiles.

Great. What a time for me to not have my mind-reading abilities, because I was dying to know what was going on between them. "You two look like you have something on your minds."

Isabelle's eyes twinkled with whatever her secret was, but all she said was, "I spoke to Dad and he's coming tonight. With Monica."

Isabelle and I fist-bumped.

"I wish Mom could see you right now." Isabelle gave me a quick hug. "And Grandma."

Graduation was being held in the basketball gym to accommodate so many people, but all of us seniors were in the auditorium for the purpose of lining up. Not only was it crowded in there, it was also getting really hot, what with everyone wearing non-breathable polyester gowns and no windows to open. Lots of faculty members were there to make sure there was no stepping out of formation, and no contraband food or drinks. Despite the seriousness of the occasion, some kids were ignoring the rules and talking loudly to each other, or slipping out of line to check their text messages.

Mr. West was on the auditorium stage with a microphone. "Ladies and gentlemen, we practiced this afternoon for a reason. Consult the number on your placement card and find your spot."

There was some booing and laughing, and then Greg Plowman yelled, "Hey, West, who died and left you principal?"

I guess being in the last moments of high school made some students gutsy. I didn't think Greg was funny, but apparently lots of other kids did, because there was a huge roar of laughter followed by more loud voices and more chaos.

"As you know," Mr. West replied back with what I thought was admirable restraint, "Principal Longstreet, his wife the Mayor, and Superintendent Calvin Bekins are already on the stage, *waiting for us.*"

Okay, that last part sounded a little less patient, but Mr. West was right. If kids didn't start cooperating, we were about to be late to our own ceremony. I pulled my card from my pocket to see number ten, up near the front behind Jeff Atwell. If Hank Zimmerman weren't valedictorian, he'd be the last one in line, but instead he was at the front, followed by salutatorian Mary Bekins, and then all the fifty or so honor students, including

James Harrison and Marshall Everett, who got to wear white sashes draped around their shoulders to denote their academic standing.

I was finding my place in line when I heard, "Psst, Emma." I turned to see Jane Bates standing in front of Agnes. A new twist on the old Bates and switch?

"Miss Bates, kindly trade places with your sister."

"Aw, geez, Miss Taylor, how did you..." Jane whined. Then she shrugged and switched places with Agnes.

"You look nice this evening, Miss Taylor," I said. She didn't reply, just blushed and smiled as her hands self-consciously smoothed down her white linen pants and pink silk blouse. That was when I spotted it, a big diamond ring on her left hand.

"Miss Taylor!" I grabbed her hand for a closer look. "Wow. Congratulations!"

Agnes peered over my shoulder and Jane stepped out of line to see what the fuss was. "Oooo, nice," Agnes said as her sister nodded in agreement.

"Well, I have you to thank, Emma. If you hadn't helped Mr. West and me realize we have a mutual love of ...coffee..." Miss Taylor flashed a grin and then hurried off down the line to make sure other students were in their proper places.

Good job, Emma, I told myself. At least I got that match right.

My mind flashed back to all the kids I thought I was helping this year with my mind-reading-matchmaking abilities, but things never quite turned out as I planned them, especially with my close friends. And myself.

"Yo, bestie!"

I spotted Hattie waving at me from way down the

line, and I waved back. Something told me she was still pining for Robbie Martin, even though he left her in the lurch during the Prom after-party. Although I never thought he was good enough for her, I should've kept my opinions to myself.

I couldn't see Flip Richardson so far behind me, but James Harrison was lined up with all the other honor students. That was one match that worked out, but it was possible those two would have gotten together without my help. Jane and Agnes were making eyes at the O'Brien twins who were standing in front of Greg Plowman, but with those girls' track record, who knew how that would end? And worst of all, I'd never been able to find out what happened between Hank and Rachel. Okay, I hadn't tried very hard.

"I think we're all lined up correctly now," Mr. West said a little too loudly into the mic, causing a squelch. "It's time to begin our processional." There was a long pause. "Miss Austin," he shouted.

I got out of my head, realized I'd lagged behind and ran to catch up to Jeff Atwell. He was already almost out the door while I was holding up the line behind me, kids scrunched up body to body all the way to the edge of the auditorium stage.

I had butterflies in my stomach as we marched down the halls so familiar to all of us, but it was a good kind of excited.

There was a dais set up on the gym floor under the scoreboard with chairs for the principal, superintendent, mayor, Hank and Mary. Next to them was a huge table, or actually several shoved together, under a large purple tablecloth with a gold underskirt, stacked high with diplomas ready to be handed out. The bleachers were filled with people who applauded as Hank and company led us to the section that was roped off for graduates on the home side center court. Without losing pace with my classmates again but still trying to maintain a dignified walk, I did a visual search to locate Jonathan and Isabelle. I spotted them up near the top of the bleachers where they had a good view. Isabelle stood up and waved her arms overhead, and then I noticed Dad and Monica sitting next to Jonathan. Another success story? It was too soon to tell, but I had high hopes.

"Ladies and gentlemen," Principal Longstreet said in a loud voice that commanded attention, "please welcome Melville High School's Graduating Class."

Thunderous applause broke out. And then in one choreographed moment, all three hundred and eighteen of us took our seats. The dignitaries took turns addressing us, but thankfully kept it short, because we were all eager to get to the main event.

Hank's speech was amazing. His message was to never settle for less than our most cherished dreams, no matter the obstacles. I was in awe and bursting with pride as I watched him graciously acknowledge a standing ovation.

Next was Mary's speech. She made an analogy between being active in sports and being active in life, good advice and pretty clever, too. Then it was time for us to do the actual walk, standing up one row at a time, walking to the bottom of the steps, and then up onstage. I received my diploma and paused for a photo opp, shook hands with the principal, and returned to my seat. Since I was near the beginning of the alphabet, there was a long wait till Principal Longstreet at last called Henry Zimmerman, Jr., who only had to walk a few steps. Then at Superintendent Bekin's signal, we all stood up in unison and turned our tassels. Tears were flowing everywhere at the milestone we just passed.

Newly-minted graduates poured out of the gym onto the school's front lawn, and everyone was kissing parents, hugging each other, laughing, crying, or high-fiving. I spotted Hattie with her parents, and was heading her way when Robbie Martin beat me to it. They hugged, she waved at me, and hand-in-hand, the two of them walked away. I had no idea what had gone on between them, but I silently wished them well. Off in the distance, I saw Kendall Manheim leaning her head on Todd's shoulder, and Todd's sister Mary was standing next to Greg Plowman, who would be accepting a football scholarship to The University of Oklahoma. With Mary planning to attend Notre Dame, I expected there would be a lot of texts and phone calls going back and forth.

I located my sister in the crowd and pushed my way over.

Isabelle gave me a warm hug and held me at arm's length. "Let me look at you, baby sister. A high school graduate and off to college in a few months. I can't believe it."

"Congratulations, Emma." Jonathan patted me on the back.

I smiled, blushed, and felt pretty proud of myself. "Where's Dad?"

"Right here." Dad was behind me, beaming as he gave me a big hug and a quick peck on my forehead. "I'm so proud of you."

"Thanks, Dad." I watched as Monica Barlow took my father's arm. "Off to find Faith?" I asked them.

"Do you mind?" Dad asked.

I smiled as they strolled off together. I was thrilled that he had seemingly gotten his life back on track, with a new job, Reiki that he enjoyed as a hobby, and even a cute little rent house. I wanted so much for my dad to be happy, and from the easy way he draped his arm over Monica's shoulder, it seemed like it was all within his grasp.

Isabelle put her hands on her hips and seemed a little put out by Dad's abrupt departure. "And we were about to give him the big family news," she said with a wink at her husband.

I looked from Isabelle to Jonathan. "What news?"

"You mean you don't know?" Isabelle asked.

I shook my head. "I haven't been myself ever since I got that bump on the head," I reminded her with a sideways glance at Jonathan. They were both grinning like they had some huge secret and for once I was totally out of the loop. "What?"

Isabelle smiled as she tapped her belly. "Our family's growing. We're pregnant!"

I stared at her in shock. I took in her rosy cheeks and the too-tight skirt, and slapped my forehead. "Ohmigod, I'm such an idiot. You didn't have the flu, did you?" I hugged my sister and then impulsively threw my arms around Jonathan. "When's the baby due?"

"Not till next winter, so we've got plenty of time to fix up a nursery." She elbowed Jonathan playfully. "Aren't you glad I talked you into the three bedroom condo?"

Uh-oh. This presented a whole new set of problems. "You're probably gonna want my room back, huh?"

"Don't worry," Isabelle said, "we'll figure something out."

I hoped so, because I was just giddy with the news and didn't want to focus on anything else. I was going to be an aunt. Would I be good at it? Although I've helped care for tons of children, I've never been around newborns. And I wanted to be there for my little niece or nephew from the beginning, just like Isabelle had always been for me.

There was a tap on my shoulder and I turned around. "Nick, you came."

Isabelle seemed puzzled. "I didn't see you up on the stage, Nick. Did you graduate?"

"Mind if I steal her away?" Nick asked, deflecting her question.

"She's all yours." Isabelle waved me off and wrapped her arms around Jonathan.

"So when's the baby coming?" Nick asked me as we walked away, side by side.

I should be surprised, but I wasn't. "Winter."

"So, Emma, what would you think if for once I played matchmaker?"

I wrinkled my nose. "I don't think you'd be very good at it," I told him. "Go back to your brainiac work and leave fix-ups to the pros."

"Just bear with me a minute, okay?" Nick pointed to the other side of the school's front lawn. "Hank's over there, with his parents. Remember that girl he's been crushing on?"

I stopped in my tracks. "Yeah, I remember."

He winked. "Come on."

Sort of a buzz kill after this fantastic day, because I was seriously not interested in polite conversation with Rachel Bomburg. But Nick wasn't taking no for an answer. He took me by the hand and practically dragged me over to where Hank was deep in conversation with his parents.

"Oh, Emma!" Mrs. Zimmerman waved when she saw me approaching. "Congratulations, dear."

"Thank you."

"Zimmerman, we've got business," Nick said with a jerk of his head. "Excuse us," he told Hank's parents as he gave Hank a shove.

I was baffled, Hank looked offended, but we both followed Nick to a relatively unpopulated area under the flagpole. "That was rude, man," Hank said. "Talk fast because my parents have guests coming over."

Nick had a delicious grin on his face. "Emma tells me you've had a crush on a special girl for a while and," he gave me a quick wink, "I'd like to introduce you to the woman of your dreams."

Hank looked like the proverbial deer in the headlights. I jerked my head around searching for Rachel, but there was no one there but the three of us.

"Hank, I'd like you to meet Emma Austin. Emma, this is Hank Zimmerman."

I groaned. "Not funny, Nick."

Nick put one hand on my back, the other on Hank's, and shoved the two of us together. Then he smiled, waved, and walked off, leaving us alone.

I visually scouted out the surrounding area. "Where's Rachel? Or did you two call it off?"

"Rachel Bomburg?" Hank blinked. "We never called it *on.*" *Surely you didn't think I was interested in her.*

I sucked in my breath. Was that what I thought it was? Could it be that after all these weeks, my ability to hear thoughts had returned? *I've missed the two of us,*

Emma.

There it was again, this time confirming my hopes. All of them. I cleared my throat. "Well, I always thought you and Rachel…"

Hank laughed. "Emma, where did you get an idea like that? Rachel's got a boyfriend from school."

"But…New Year's?"

Hank rolled his eyes. "He was out of town. Emma, she's like my sister, if I had one. It's you I'm interested in. Always been you."

"Me?" My hands flew to my reddening face. "But what about Prom?"

Hank blushed and looked down at his feet. "I heard that Nick had already asked you, so when Kendall cornered me…" He broke off, shrugged and stared up at the first few evening stars coming out. "I didn't want to interfere if you really cared about Nick."

I reached over and turned Hank's face so I could look him in the eye. "Nick and I didn't have that kind of relationship."

"You didn't?" His face relaxed into a smile. He put his forehead next to mine and whispered back, "I can't believe I never spoke up."

"Me, too." But then flashes of the conversations I'd had with Flip, about telling Hank the truth about me, popped into my head. Flip was right, I needed to come clean. If the man I loved didn't want to be with me because of my unique abilities, I wanted to know now rather than later. "Hank, there's something you need to know."

I don't want to talk about Nick or Rachel.

I smiled. "No, it's not about Nick. Or Rachel."

Hank's eyes widened as he dropped his arms to his

sides and breathed. "Did you just…?"

I nodded. "Sara Davis was right about me. Outside of my family, only Flip and Hattie know, but yes, I can hear people's thoughts. It's just that, whenever I tried to focus in on your thoughts, we got interrupted, or you were thinking about school, or…" I tilted my head to study his face. "I was never sure how you really felt about me."

I am so in love with you, Emma Austin.

"I love you, too, Henry Zimmerman Jr."

After a quick glance around to see who might be watching, Hank leaned down and gave me a long, sweet romantic kiss. It reminded me of that New Year's kiss when I felt chills all the way down my spine to the tips of my toes.

I sighed, totally happy with the only guy I've ever cared about.

Epilogue

I took one last look around my bedroom. Boxes were packed, bedding had been stripped and tossed in the wash, and all that was left to do was close my suitcase. I was ready to move on.

It was the third week of August and this was the day I'd been looking forward to all summer, the day I'd be moving into my college dorm room. I was thrilled that it was finally here, but I was also feeling nostalgic about leaving Melville. I'd be back for school holidays, but it wouldn't really be the same.

"Emma?" Isabelle called up the stairs.

"Yeah, I'm about ready," I called back. I zipped up the soft-sided duffel bag and slung the strap over my shoulder. I looked around the room at my life in boxes, packed and ready to load into the cars. I opened the bedroom door and headed for the stairs.

"Surprise!"

I stopped in mid-stride and gaped. Isabelle, Jonathan, and Hank were all at the bottom of the stairs, wearing party hats and blowing paper horns. Isabelle was holding a cake glowing with lit candles, and they were all grinning at me.

"Happy birthday," they yelled in unison.

"You didn't think we'd forgotten, did you?" Isabelle said. "This is a momentous occasion. Eighteenth birthday *and* the start of college."

With all the excitement of moving, I'd completely forgotten about my birthday. And Hank was there, even though he was moving into his dorm today, too. I smiled, blushed, dropped my bag on the stairs and hurried down to join them. I took a deep breath and blew out all eighteen candles, followed by cheers and tooting of paper horns. We then went into the kitchen to eat birthday cake for breakfast.

Isabelle said she and Jonathan had a birthday surprise for me, but it would have to wait till we got to the dorm. I tried to pick it out of her brain but all I was getting was *make sure everything's packed, load the cars, stop for gas, stall Emma...* I shot her a look and she had a wicked grin on her face.

Hank handed me a small wrapped box and insisted I open it. I carefully removed the paper and tiny bow, and lifted the lid. Inside was a beautiful heart-shaped necklace with a small diamond at its center, dangling from a silver chain. Tears came to my eyes as he fastened it around my neck. "You have my heart," he whispered, and I choked back tears of joy as I gave him an affectionate hug.

I got control of my emotions and raised my glass of orange juice for a toast. "Okay, let's get this party started," I said. "I mean, let's go to Muncie."

To which the three of them added, "Hear hear!"

****

The place was total chaos. People were elbowing past each other in the crowded hallways and through the many open dorm room doors, everyone loaded down with suitcases, boxes, bags, sleeping gear, electronics, small pieces of accent furniture, and wall posters. There was a long wait for the elevator and when it did arrive, it was crammed full of people, and then made a stop on every floor to and from the lobby.

Faith and Monica were already in our dorm room and had her stuff unpacked and neatly arranged, leaving the other half of our shared room a blank canvas.

"Coming through," said a voice in the hall. I turned around, and was totally blown away when I saw my dad with a bouquet of Happy Birthday balloons in his hand.

I picked my way over the boxes and let Dad give me a big hug. "I can't stay long." He thrust the balloons in my hand. "I have to get to work back in Melville, but I wanted to wish my little girl a happy birthday and happy college move-in day." He released me and stepped over to hug first Isabelle, and then Monica and Faith. *All my favorite girls here today,* he thought. Seemed like he was finally happy, and that made me happy.

In this crowded space, I didn't know where the balloons were going to go, so I let loose of them and they hit the ceiling. Dad glanced around the dorm room and then out the window which overlooked a courtyard leading to classroom buildings, and a thought flashed into his head. *How are we paying for all this?*

"Don't worry, Dad," I said with a wink. "I've got my scholarship money, the 529 plan Jonathan set up, and a job at the on-campus day care." I owed Mrs. Evans a lot for recommending me, so in return I'd promised to work for her during Christmas break and summer holidays.

Always practical, just like your mom. Dad gave my shoulders one last squeeze. "Monica, you ready?"

Naturally she blushed, nodded her head, and they waved goodbye.

"I'll walk you out," Faith said. *Give Emma a chance*

to get her stuff unpacked.

"Thanks, Faith." The idea of me and Faith as roommates, let alone friends, would have been impossible a few short months ago, especially when I thought she shared all of Sara Davis's opinions about me. But once I helped her get together with Miguel, and reconnected our parents, it seemed our lives were destined to be intertwined.

I turned around to see Isabelle about to pick up a box. I snatched it from her and shook my head. "So do you think it's serious between those two?"

"Dad and Monica?" Isabelle asked. "Who knows?" *Babies tend to unite families.* She smiled and patted her baby bump. "But my mind is on the nursery I need to decorate."

I frowned at that thought. Even though I couldn't wait to meet my new little niece or nephew, I was still worried about our tight living quarters. "Speaking of the baby, where is he…"

"She…" Isabelle interjected.

"Whatever," I said, throwing up my hands. "Where's the baby going to sleep? My room?"

Instead of the admonishments I'd been getting all summer every time I brought up this subject, Isabelle smiled. *That's the big secret.*

"*What's* the big secret?"

She lifted an eyebrow at me. "That's your birthday surprise, but you'll have to wait a few months. Jonathan and I have decided a small condo is not the place to raise a family, so we're putting it on the market and buying a house. We made an offer on a four bedroom, three bath with a huge fenced backyard. Maybe we'll even get a dog. From that shelter where Nick volunteered."

"Ohmigod where? When do we…you…move?"

Isabelle put her hands on what was left of her hips. "Emma, we're all four of us going to live there, at least when you're not in school. As for when, as soon as the paperwork goes through."

I exhaled because I felt like another weight had been lifted off me.

Jonathan had carted another couple of boxes up from his car and into my dorm room, and he dropped them with a thud and a groan just inside the door. Isabelle was busy arranging my personal items on shelves over my twin bed and in the bathroom that I'll share with Faith. But this was Isabelle, my sister who flourished when she was working on interior design, so my side of the room already looked like the cover of a magazine.

Too hot, too crowded Jonathan was thinking as he leaned against the open door and took off his baseball cap to fan himself. "I don't remember freshman move-in day being this crazy."

"Maybe Harvard students were more organized than Hoosiers," Isabelle said. She put the finishing touches on the artfully made bed, complete with designer quilt and colorful throw pillows.

I glanced at the thermostat on the wall. "It's eighty degrees in here, so I guess with all the people in and out, the AC isn't keeping up." I did a visual search of the room and found my desk fan on the floor, hunted for a plug, and turned it on full blast.

Jonathan stepped over some boxes to stand right in front of it, lifting his sweaty t-shirt to catch the breeze. Isabelle reached into the mini-fridge under my built-in desk for a bottle of water and handed it to him. "Stay hydrated 'cause there's still more stuff in the car."

"Need any help in here?"

"Hank." I'd like to run and throw myself into his arms, but there were too many boxes on the floor between him and me, so I had to navigate around and over the obstacles to reach him.

"Don't you have your own room to move into?" Jonathan asked.

"I'm all settled." Hank will be living in a dorm across campus that was for honor students only, while I was in this one mostly filled with social science and education majors. "Mom and Dad had this move planned down to the minute," Hank assured him.

"There's one last load downstairs," Jonathan said, "and I'm double parked, so if I don't move the car soon…"

"Emma and I can go get the stuff." Hank accepted Jonathan's car keys and reached for my arm to steady me as I climbed over the rest of the boxes. We dodged trash and debris thrown in the hall by people who would soon be my neighbors, on our way to the elevator.

When the door opened in the lobby, we squeezed past the crowd and out to the street in front of the overflowing parking lot. "There's Jonathan's car," I said, one hand shielding the sun from my eyes. We unloaded the last of the boxes and bags, beeped the car locked and headed back inside the supposedly air-conditioned lobby.

I balanced the box on my hip and rang for the elevator. It was almost supper time, but even at this late hour, people were still moving in. The elevator doors opened to reveal a dad hugging his son, a mom wiping tears from her daughters' eyes, and then hugs all around before saying goodbye. It reminded me of the traditional family I'd briefly had, then lost when my mother died.

Hank saw me watching them and put an arm around me. "You have me, you know."

I nodded, but I felt the loss all the same, especially here where my mom had gone to school. Maybe even walked the same halls.

Isabelle scrutinized my face as we walked back into my dorm room. "What's up?"

"Crowded elevator," Hank said.

And you saw all those other parents... Isabelle was thinking. I made eye contact with her and nodded.

Hank put his arm around my shoulder, making me feel safe and secure. Then Isabelle joined in the hug, and not to be left out, Jonathan made it a group hug. We were all laughing and jumping up and down, enjoying the moment, when suddenly Isabelle pulled back with a startled look on her face. Her hand flew to her belly and she gasped, eyes wide.

"What's wrong?" I asked.

Jonathan reached for her. "Is everything okay, hon?"

Her look of shock slowly gave way to a smile, a nod, and glistening tears. "The baby just moved."

Amazing. New life, new beginnings for all of us. I couldn't stop the tears flowing down my cheeks as I put my hand on her baby bump. "He's kicking!"

She I got from both Isabelle and Jonathan. "Stella," Isabelle said.

I got a warm, fuzzy feeling from the idea that my niece would be named after our mom.

Like we talked about in Family Relations, families get made in a lot of different ways. That included parents, step-parents, grandparents, older siblings, and close friends. And I knew all those people made up my family.

"Let's unpack some boxes," I said. "I'm ready for my new adventure."

We got back to it, all four of us working together as a unit.

"Heeeyyy Emma!"

I recognized those two voices in unison and turned to see Jane and Agnes standing in my doorway. "Hi...?"

"Emma," Jane said, "there's a girl on our floor who thinks this guy on the third is just the cutest. Can you fix them up? I told her you're a pro."

I groaned. Isabelle rolled her eyes, Jonathan blinked, and Hank shook his head.

"Jane, please tell your new friend that she'll have to meet that guy the old-fashioned way – on an app."

Isabelle looked relieved. Hank and I locked eyes, both of us knowing I was done with all that.

I was Emma Austin, college student, future aunt, girlfriend of Hank Zimmerman, but I was no longer Miss Match.

www.ingramcontent.com/pod-product-compliance
Lightning Source LLC
Chambersburg PA
CBHW070100030726
47506CB00002B/535